MW01233276

WELCOME TO STORYVILLE

WELCOME TO STORYVILLE

TOMMY HOUSWORTH

Copyright © 2005 by Tommy Housworth.

ISBN: Softcover   1-59926-683-0

All rights reserved. No part of this book may be reproduced or transmitted in any
form or by any means, electronic or mechanical, including photocopying, recording,
or by any information storage and retrieval system, without permission in writing
from the copyright owner.

This is a work of fiction. Names, characters, places and incidents either are the
product of the author's imagination or are used fictitiously, and any resemblance to
any actual persons, living or dead, events, or locales is entirely coincidental.

This book was printed in the United States of America.

To order additional copies of this book, contact:
Xlibris Corporation
1-888-795-4274
www.Xlibris.com
Orders@Xlibris.com
30765

CONTENTS

DEDICATION

For Warren Zevon and Hunter S. Thompson, whom I miss.
For Wendy, Grady, and Maggie, whom I love

WELCOME TO STORYVILLE
(AN INTRODUCTION)

S o, here's how the legend goes: Bird used to hang at this place
called Charlie's Tavern in midtown New York. All his disciples
were there, watching his every move, trying to soak in an ounce or two of
his soulfulness by proximity, believing osmosis and shared oxygen could
provide the grit to make a pearl. Bird would go to the jukebox, drop in his
spare change and play nothing but country songs. Here was a man who
had created a new sonic architecture, Kerouac with a sax, the musical
equivalent of Picasso, and he was queuing up "Your Cheating Heart".

Picture it: A roomful of hepcats, black men raised on blues and gospel,
suddenly being forced to endure the torch and twang, high lonesome, the
ache of the western winds; watching their Coolsville god weep to the
sounds of a hillbilly band.

One day, they could take it no more. They elected a sideman to
approach Bird, find out why the hell, with Duke on the juke, he kept
dropping nickels for Hank.

When asked why he chose such elegies, Bird smiled. "Listen. Listen
to the stories."

Who could argue with that? Stories remind us of our humanity, and
give us a glimpse of our shot at divinity.

So, welcome to Storyville, a place where characters live and breathe
in 4/4 time. A lot of these stories were inspired by music: a line, a phrasing,
or a mood set by Miles, Trane, Springsteen, Robert Johnson, Tom Waits,

Emmylou, Mingus . . . and yeah, Bird. Suffice to say, if ASCAP weren't an issue, this collection could come with its own soundtrack.

As he did for so many, Johnny Cash summed it up for me: "I love songs about horses, railroads, land, judgment day, family, hard times, whiskey, courtship, marriage, adultery, separation, murder, war, prison, rambling, damnation, home, salvation, death, pride, humor, piety, rebellion, patriotism, larceny, determination, tragedy, rowdiness, heartbreak, and love. And Mother. And God."

Amen.

AUTHOR'S NOTE

September 1, 2005

*A*s this book goes to press, the title has taken on a bittersweet irony. For me, the idea of 'Storyville' worked on two levels for this book; the first obviously being that this is a collection of tales, a place where stories live. The name also harkens images of the Red Light District in the French Quarter. New Orleans is hailed as the cradle of jazz, and Storyville was a central figure in jazz's evolution and its migration to the rest of the country. Jazz infuses many of these tales, and even where it is not subject matter, you can be assured that it was a sonic presence as almost every story was written. Coffee and Coltrane, my vices of choice.

Today, New Orleans struggles for her mere existence in the wake of Hurricane Katrina and its aftermath. But I know of no one more tenacious than those who call the Delta and Pontchartrain their home, and I know of no more soothing proof of God's reassuring voice than the sound of jazz emanating from the hot confines of Preservation Hall, from Snug Harbor, from the sidewalk outside the Café du Monde. Even when the police shut down Storyville, the music lived on.

1

Deep Six Holiday

Stargazing. An August sky peppered with luminous pinholes. I was on my back, suckling the sweetness of a cigarillo. Donny sat Indian-style on a blanket, fiddling with a transistor radio. He found "Me and Bobby McGee" and we listened to Janis sing about having nothing left to lose.

"That's it, man," said Donny.

"What's it?"

"That's what I want played when I die."

"Where'd that come from?"

"I'm just saying," Donny said, "when the day comes, know this is the song. Next week or fifty years, you tell 'em to play 'Bobby McGee'."

"Alright. Kristofferson or Joplin?"

"You pick."

"No. No. Don't lay that shit on me. It's your funeral."

"Right, so I won't be there. You pick."

"Fine. Kristofferson."

We stared at Orion a while. I brushed the end of my cigarillo, sending a cluster of ashes into the air, a hundred black fairies parachuting to earth.

Donny broke our silence. "Why Kristofferson?"

"Because that song's all about the story. Janis sings it. Kris tells it."

"Fair enough," said Donny. "How 'bout you?"

I perched on my elbows and looked at Donny.

"What song do you want at your funeral?"

I laughed. "You aren't planning some kind of ritualistic suicide pact tonight are you?"

"Ya gotta think about these things. Otherwise, a stranger decides some doddering organist should play 'How Great Thou Art' on a Casio."

I told Donny I hadn't thought much about death, particularly not about my funeral. We were young—early 20's—with our whole lives ahead of us. I didn't see any reason to start planning something that was likely decades away, but he persisted, so I played along—our own macabre version of twenty questions.

"O.K. then, Cremation or burial?" I asked.

"Cremation. Definitely."

"Put you in an urn or scatter you to the wind?"

He thought a moment. "The ocean. Rent a boat, go out a few miles, and let me go."

"Poetic, Donny. You'll be eaten by minnows."

"Who'll then be eaten by bigger fish, and bigger ones. I could end up in the belly of a whale."

"It's your funeral, Ismael."

"I don't want anyone calling it a funeral," continued Donny.

"No? What then?"

"I dunno." He thought a minute, staring at a patch of crabgrass growing wild around its stunted fescue neighbors. "A deep-six holiday."

I smiled. Donny was a sucker for film noir.

"Yeah," he said. "Sounds more hopeful that way."

*   *   *

The phone rang around 10:45 p.m., and I let the machine pick up. Julie and I were already in bed, and figured it could only be another wrong number. Our phone number once belonged to a pharmacy that used to be on the city square, and from time to time, we'd get late night calls from old people, trying to get a prescription refilled or rambling about overdoses and childproof caps.

This time, though, it was Beth Harbrew, Donny's younger sister. I hadn't talked to her in years, so I knew something was wrong. By the time I got to the phone, she had already hung up. The words 'accident' and 'Tuesday' were all I really deciphered as she left her message. That, and Beth was crying. She was definitely crying. Rather than listen to the machine, I got Beth's number off the caller ID, and she answered on the first ring.

She got straight to it. Donny was gone. Barely 30 years old. He was waiting to cross a busy intersection and slipped on the curb. He fell forwards, right into the grill of a van toting a half-dozen seniors back to the local assisted living center. No way to hit the brakes in time, the driver said. An Arby's bag clutched in his left hand, Donny died on his lunch break, second day of his new job painting houses.

Donny was dead because he didn't use the drive-thru. He was gone because the tread on his boots had worn to a smooth sheen. Because the driver of the van thought he had to get a bunch of gray hairs back to their makeshift prison before the goddamn "Price is Right" was over.

The full impact of losing a childhood friend can't be fully absorbed. Especially when it's not some lingering cancer or illness. This was just right out of left field. Years had passed—Donny and I had drifted, kept in touch by email mostly. Random notes about concerts, or job changes. We got together a couple of times a year—for a ball game or a beer. It was nothing like we thought we'd be. After being inseparable for so many years through high school and college, you just figure you're together for life. But, I got married. I went into advertising. Donny stayed single, jumped from town to town . . . never settled; finally ended up in Boston in a small apartment, with a pug named Cassady and no evident source of perpetual income.

We had remarked once that we envied each other's lives, but wouldn't trade places. I needed the security Donny so willfully dodged. Donny wished he could live behind a white picket fence, but where I saw comfort, he saw jailer's bars.

I told Beth I'd see her tomorrow morning, meet her at the funeral home to be with her family before the viewing that afternoon. Turns out Donny didn't have a lot of close friends, at least none that his family knew of, so they wanted me around to . . . well, I don't know what exactly, but Beth wanted me there, and I was fine with that.

I didn't sleep much that night. Julie made coffee, we sat up, and I told her all I could remember about Donny. She'd met him a few times, but always wanted to give us our 'guy time', as she called it.

I told her about meeting Carl Yaztremski on a day trip to Boston when we were in college; about the all-night study sessions that resulted in sophomoric dares, philosophical rants, and merely adequate GPA's. And, I told her about Donny's parents: two uptight suburbanites whom Donny resembled only facially. Lance Harbrew was in insurance—life and disability—played 9 holes every Wednesday and Saturday. Donny's Mom,

Norma, was textbook paranoid, with a fundamentalist zeal that only aggravated her disorder. Donny, on the other hand, was as free-spirited as a beat writer, with a mind so open to people and possibilities that he sometimes got taken. Hoodwinked, as his dad would call it.

Donny's parents never had figured him out. They confused his wanderlust for instability, and worse, his sensitivity for weakness. Rather than beat their heads against the wall that was Donny's future, Norma and Lance reinvested that energy into making sure his kid sister, Beth, survived her adolescence in mint condition.

I caught myself before my reminiscence turned malicious. These were grieving parents after all, and I can't imagine anything more gut wrenching than laying your own son in the cold ground. "I'm sure they did their best," said Julie before I could expend too much energy nursing my bitterness. My better angels concurred. "Yeah. I'm sure they did," I said.

Julie rested my head in her lap, gently brushing my hair while I stifled my sobs. Eventually, I succumbed to the exhaustion. I dreamed I was sailing with Donny somewhere off Bar Harbor in Maine. Pilot whales spy-hopped by our boat, while seabirds circled us like some kind of aerial Navaho ritual. The sun kindly bathed our bare backs.

I'd lived my whole life in New England. Never been sailing. Not once.

* * *

Funeral homes smell different than I remembered. I hadn't been in one in years, and I guess I was expecting the waft of embalming fluid to greet me, but it was nice—at least this one was. Lilacs, wildflowers. Of course, with all the goddamn floral arrangements that pile up at funeral homes, I guess the formaldehyde doesn't stand a chance.

That was when it struck me. The conversation that Donny and I had on that summer night: cremation, the ocean, Bobby McGee. I remembered Donny had said that he didn't want flowers at his funeral. He thought all that money should go to someone who needed it. "I can forgive putting a suit on a corpse," he said, "but the flowers . . . who's that for, anyway?"

"The family, I guess," I said.

"Yeah? They got enough on their minds. Now, they gotta write thank you notes for flowers. How hard is that when you're blind with grief?"

Donny thought of those things. He spent so much time in other people's shoes; he could've been a novelist. He wanted to be Kerouac, or one of those beat guys, never settling down, always trying new things. But, instead, he just kept all that empathy to himself.

Beth's touch brought me out of the haze. She clasped the cuff of my shirt, and then just pressed herself against me. It was one of those hugs that come from deep anguish, like a lost child squeezing her Dad after he finds her wandering the shopping mall in tears. She latched on and just sobbed.

I wished I could've been more of a comfort to her. All I could come up with was, "I know, I know," while stroking her long brown hair with my free hand. I was a full head taller than Beth, so I had a clear view of the vestibule, and saw Donny's folks coming to greet me. I took Beth's shoulders and gave them a gentle wring. She gathered herself and stepped back, as if sensing her parents' approach.

"Mom, Dad," she said as she sniffed. "You remember Marc Kenton? He grew up with, um . . . Donald."

I didn't give them a chance to answer. "I'm so sorry for your loss, Mr. and Mrs. Harbrew. I really am."

Mr. Harbrew extended his hand for a businesslike shake. "Marc. Thanks for coming. We thought you might be able to help us with the arrangements."

"Well, I'll be happy to try. What, exactly . . ."

Mrs. Harbrew trembled. "We didn't ever really know Donald. We tried, but he had his ways about him. We don't even know what kinds of friends he was consorting with these last few years, or what he's really been doing."

"Well, I wasn't in close contact with Donny . . ." I started. Mr. Harbrew gave me a cutting glance. "Uh . . . Donald. But we did stay in touch. I'll do my best."

That his parents insisted he be called Donald brought back a flood of images from our younger days, when Donny spent much of his time under that same harsh stare his father had just given me. How could you get to know your kid when you couldn't even see him as the rest of the world did? To everyone, he was Donny. Everyone, save two.

The funeral director approached us with the temerity of a beaten dog. His inability to make eye contact and his hushed delivery revealed a total lack of understanding for what a grieving family needs. Where were the firm hands? The certain, gentle eyes? The voice as warm and encompassing as a hand-stitched quilt? I wondered if funeral homes hired temps.

"We're, uh . . . we're ready to sit down with you now, sir," said the little man. "To finish reviewing the arrangements, I mean." He pointed feebly to a room next to his office—a little waiting area that appeared equipped to seat four or five mourners. We all went in as he lagged behind to shut the two large, stained glass doors behind us.

"Again, on behalf of Patterson's, I'm so sorry for your loss, Mr. and Mrs. Harbrew." He waited for a response, but none came. He turned his attention to Beth. "You as well, young lady. And you . . . you must be the husband." He reached his hand out to me.

"Oh, no." I chuckled. Then, sensing no one else was going to step in, "I'm Marc. I was . . . I am a friend of Don . . . Donald's."

"Pleasure, sir." The man continued with no introduction of himself. "So, we have a few details to finalize, and I realize this isn't easy, so I'll try and make it as comfortable as possible for you all. Now, where did we leave off?" He pulled out his crib notes. "Oh yes, the preacher."

"We'd like our minister to do the service," said Mr. Harbrew. "Pastor Brooks."

"Oh, from Morningview Baptist, of course," replied the man, as he wrote down the information on his pre-printed form.

It made perfect sense to have a form to gather his information, but it still struck me as disconcerting, like some sort of ghoulish census taker.

"We took the liberty of contacting him. He'll be here shortly," said Mr. Harbrew. Mrs. Harbrew's lower lip began to quiver, as if the ice around her pinched mouth was finally beginning to thaw.

"He's a man of God," she said.

"Of course," said the director. "And is there something we should put in the program—a favorite passage from the Bible Donald might've wanted shared at this time?"

"Doubtful," said Mr. Harbrew, staring hard at the gray linoleum flooring.

I wanted to remind him that Donny had won more than one Bible "sword drill" in church as a youth. The sword drill—Protestant America's answer to the quick draw—was designed to teach children the chronology of the books of the Bible by shrouding their learning curve in a format that was two parts game show, one part Josey Wales.

Donny had been a master. I'd visited his church with him numerous times as a kid and when he was in those Sunday evening competitions, his nimble fingers could find 1 Thessalonians like a safecracker feeling out tumblers.

Obviously, Mr. Harbrew believed Donny's skills had waned since he left the church.

"I'll find something suitable," said Beth. "I mean, if that's o.k."

"Sure, honey," said Mrs. Harbrew. "Just run it by your father first."

The tension in the room was thicker than cream, and it wasn't borne of grief. Remorse? No . . . resentment. Like Donny died before he could get his life on the track preordained for him, and his parents held him responsible for it.

The director stood. "I think that about covers it. Donny will be in
state from four 'til eight tonight, then again tomorrow at ten. The funeral
is set for two o'clock. I've notified the newspaper and the county office.
A certificate and transit permit are being sent here, and a proof of the
obituary will be emailed over—I'll share it with you when it arrives."

None of this felt right. So many decisions already made and I was
pretty sure, based on all accounts, that none of Donny's wishes were being
taken into account, if they were even known in the first place. Maybe this
is why Beth wanted me here, but how do you even approach these things?
I felt weak, impotent. How was I supposed to persuade these people to
undo everything they had already set in motion? To undo everything they
believed?

Beth took my hand. "You want to see him?" I looked at her parents,
who seemed to be separated by a dense layer of metaphysical fog. They
didn't even acknowledge us, so we slipped out and walked down the hall.

I'd always held a fondness for Beth, like the kid sister I'd never had,
but with the added affection that came with knowing she'd had a tiny
crush on me when we were in high school. I'd always made an effort to
look out for her, ask how her grades were, who she was seeing, that kind
of stuff—like an actual friend, rather than just big bro's frat buddy.

Today, Beth—so resilient while we were growing up, the cute tomboy
with perpetually skinned knees—was pure gossamer, a mere shallow breath
away from collapse.

I wasn't doing much better once we crossed the threshold into the
viewing room. There was a scattering of folding metal chairs, some
peppermints on a table, pristine floral arrangements. Everything Donny
hated about life, he hated about death—structure, formality, the
acceptance of all things antiseptic. Donny would've despised this room.
And, yet, there he was, floating in the midst of it like a boat lashed to a
dock.

Beth gave me the gentlest of nudges, coaxing me to get close enough
to see Donny. I peered down and was suddenly face to face with my
childhood friend. The embalmers had done their job well—no sign of
Donny's injuries. In fact, no sign of the real Donny at all. In the casket
laid the Harbrew's perfect son: his ever-present goatee shaved off to reveal
a boyish countenance, his hair trimmed to military length. Donny's silver
stud earring had been removed, and he was fitted in an off-the-rack gray
suit that he wouldn't have been caught dead wearing. But there he was,
an unconscious prisoner of conformity.

"This just doesn't seem real," I said. "He never . . ." My words trailed
off before I could figure out what I wanted to say.

"I know. Never got to finish," said Beth.

"Finish what?"

"Anything." Beth almost laughed, then began to tear up. "Donny was always starting things . . . he just never finished them." Her tears flowed freely now, perhaps for the first time since Donny died. The Harbrews weren't ones for showing emotion and Beth probably had all the suppression she could take. I put my arm on Beth's shoulder and she sagged into my chest. "Donny never figured out what he wanted to be. Or do. I hated that for him," she said.

"I don't think he was unhappy, Beth. He never seemed to care what he was doing for a living, just so he was making one."

"It just breaks my heart. He never really found himself."

I didn't have any answers for Beth. Donny really did seem happy. Every time I saw him, even at his most pensive, he exuded an appreciation for life. He drank iced tea like some sort of Zen ritual, commenting on how savoring cold, sweet tea was one of life's greatest pleasures. He listened to songs on the radio with an intensity that would baffle most people. He refused CDs and tapes, not because he couldn't afford the investment, but because the radio was better, he said. He loved the anticipation of wondering what song would be next.

Donny didn't wait for Christmas or birthdays to celebrate. Each day was just a small tangible gift. Funny looking dogs in the park. A 6-4-3 double play to end an inning. Anything Tom Robbins ever wrote. Donny didn't have to look far for life's full and quirky beauty.

I assured Beth that the Donny I knew was happy and at peace with his life. It was a pat response, and I guess she sensed that I was struggling with what to say. She touched my arm and walked out of the room, her eyes hidden under her open hand. I looked back at Donny. I tried to picture his goatee and earring still intact, and realized that I might have gotten Donny better than anyone he ever knew. Not that he was an enigma, just a rarity. In a world of cell phones and 401K's, Donny lived a seemingly disconnected and unprotected life. His dad would've called him 'bare', as he carried no health insurance. To Mr. Harbrew, this was like wearing the Mark of the Beast. He might as well have had a scarlet "B" for 'bum' on his denim shirt. Donny once told me his mom suspected him of being involved with a cult—'you know, one of those that refuses medical help when they're sick'. His reason for being 'bare' was much simpler than that—"I hate getting friggin' bills, man'.

I smiled at Donny. Maybe he'd gotten the last laugh. He went out without needing the health insurance. Beth told me that Donny was dead before the driver could get out of the van. He would've loved the notion that he at least dodged the collector, if not the reaper.

I gave Donny a brush on the forehead, and stepped back into the hallway. Beth was nowhere in sight. Instead, there stood Mr. Harbrew, staring right through me. The chill of his gaze made me even more apprehensive about what to say. I'd always had a great rapport with my friends' parents as a kid. But Mr. Harbrew always gave me pause. Every exchange felt like it had to go through an extra censor. The usual Eddie Haskell routine didn't play at the Harbrew home.

"Marc. Can we talk?"

"Sure," I said. He placed an unsteady hand on my shoulder and led me down the hall and back outside.

He reached inside his jacket and produced a roll of Tums. "Want one?"

"Uh. No. Thanks."

"This goddamn funeral is gonna aggravate my ulcer. I can feel it." Harbrew rubbed his gut and winced like he'd just had a labor pain.

"I can't imagine how hard it is on you. Is there something I can do?"

"Yes, Marc. Actually there is. That's what I wanted to chat with you about." Harbrew walked me a few feet further toward the parking lot. "Now I know that in the coming days my family will be asked to get Donald's belongings out of his apartment. His mother's just not going to be up to it, and I hate to ask Beth to do it alone. Would you be willing to help pack things up?"

"Sure, Mr. Harbrew." Why the hell not, I figured. Donny would sure as hell prefer me going through his stuff over his parents.

"Call me Lance, Marc. You're a man now, you should call me Lance."

"Alright, Lance."

"Oh, and Marc. I know you're aware that Donald and I weren't close. We just never could see eye to eye on most things . . ."

"But you know he . . ."

"Let me finish." My new friend, Lance, made sure he cut me off before the word 'loved' could pass my lips. "The one thing Donald and I shared an affinity for was good books. We both loved Hemingway. In fact, one of my greatest treasures is a copy of 'The Snows of Kilimanjaro'. It's the original story in a 1936 Esquire magazine. Very rare."

"Wow."

"Ever read it?"

"Uh, in school maybe. I dunno. I'm more of a Steinbeck man."

"Kilimanjaro. It's the highest mountain in Africa. Know that?"

"No."

"20,000 feet or so," he continued. "Anyway, the story's a classic."

"What's it about?"

"Tell you what, you can read it when you find that magazine. Donald borrowed it a couple of Christmases ago and I haven't seen it since. You understand, right?"

So that's what this was about. I've been elected to head up a scavenger hunt through Donny's belongings for any purported stolen goods.

Harbrew reached in his pocket and pulled out a checkbook. He started scribbling. "I'd make it worth your trouble. Just clear out his stuff, and anything you and Beth think might be important to the family, just have her bring it over. The other stuff can go to Goodwill. Or you, if you need it." His nerve stunned me; using Beth and me to appropriate his dirty work, paying me off like some small time hood, then offering me the pennies off my dead friend's eyes.

I reigned in my anger and mustered a merely irked response. "I don't want your money," I said, pushing his hand away as he tore the check from the register. I didn't feel like he deserved an explanation of why I was willing to do this.

"I'm not trying to insult you, Marc. I just don't expect you to do this without some compensation."

"Well, that's how it has to be. You have a key?" My patience was at an end.

"The landlord will let you in. He's expecting Beth, so you two work out the details."

"I'll do that. See you tomorrow."

I didn't even go back inside to speak with Beth or her mom. I went straight for my car. My face was flushed with indignation for my dead friend. For dear Lance's dead son. The magazine thief.

I drove home and called the office. I would be taking the rest of the day. Then, I left a message on Beth's voicemail, telling her I wanted to meet her over at Donny's that night, whenever she was done with the evening viewing. I wouldn't be going back to the funeral home. Now more than ever I couldn't imagine standing around watching the Harbrew's friends fawning over them, all the while oblivious to the only ray of light in the room.

Besides, I was exhausted. It was the kind of tired you feel after a long run, or maybe a car wreck. My body ached and my head felt like a stone spiked onto my shoulders. I wanted to lie down. Despite the emotional toll of the morning, I felt I could be asleep in moments. I lied down with the cordless beside me. My eyelids sank under the weight of the day, and I was gone.

Sailing again. Maine? Or maybe the Gulf Stream. It was warmer this time. That was certain. The sun had turned my skin a cocoa brown that my pasty likes had never known. Donny was there. Shirtless, barefoot. Staring at the sea like he was in the midst of some telepathic exchange. The wind nudged the boat further out to sea, pushing us toward a sky smudged with orange and autumn brown—a lipstick sunset on an elusive horizon.

"It's always been like this," Donny said suddenly.

"What?" I asked.

"This," he said, moving his hand east to west, as if to take in the whole of it: God's overflowing canvas.

Donny noticed my white-knuckled grip on the railing. "Let go, Marc," he said.

"What?"

"Just let go." He extended his arms wide and placed all his weight against the railing. He didn't care if he fell or flew. He was alive.

A harsh ring yanked me off of my nautical ride. Beth, no doubt. It took a second and third ring for me to get my bearings, being catapulted out of a dead sleep into a groggy stupor.

"'lo?"

"Marc? Is that you?"

"Beth. Hi."

"I woke you up, didn't I?"

"That's o.k."

"I got your message. Marc, this isn't really a good time for me. I'd like a few days after the funeral before I start sorting through Donny's stuff. I'm just . . . I'm toast."

"I know. I'm sorry for asking."

I wanted to tell her why I had to go. I wanted her to know her father was a mendacious suckfish, and that I wanted to find something, anything in Donny's apartment that would set the record straight about Donny. I wanted to ruin their funeral. I wanted to run fucking "Kilimanjaro" through a paper shredder when I found it.

"Your dad was hoping I would at least stop by there tonight," I lied.

"Oh, did he need something out of . . ."

"He just wanted me to check on the place. Not the best part of town, you know. I guess it's a peace of mind kind of thing." I could feel the lie starting to slip out of control.

Beth offered up the help I needed. "The address is 414 Lancaster. Apartment 34B."

"I have the address, I just . . ."

"I'll call the landlord and tell him to let you in. I already talked to him once today so it shouldn't be a problem."

"Thanks, Beth. I appreciate it. Get some rest."

"See you tomorrow," she said, her voice heavy with resignation about the prospect of what tomorrow would bring. The day you say goodbye to your big brother. Hell of a thing.

I had never been to Donny's. The few times we saw each other the past few years, we met at my place. He never minded getting out of the city and up toward the Cape. Besides, I had owned one home since getting married. This was Donny's fourth apartment.

I knew the neighborhood, though. It wasn't the type of quaint subdivision that I'm sure the Harbrews had hoped Donny would find himself nestled in someday. It was a stretch of town that was an anomaly with much of New England—slummy, crime-ridden, with an edgy stench. Lance Harbrew wouldn't even go there to meet with a prospective client, much less his deadbeat son for some take-out.

I left Julie a note and headed out. The drive over was a plodding journey through economic de-evolution. Each block, the real estate signs were pricing houses a little less than the last. Every half mile or so, there were a few more Rotweillers behind fences and a few less security company signs by mailboxes. In fact, even the number of standing mailboxes was starting to dwindle.

I found Donny's complex and pulled in. A man—Cambodian, perhaps—was picking up trash in the parking lot. He gave me a cheery wave as I pulled in a nearby spot. I asked him where I could find the landlord's office and his answer—in English so broken it bordered on untranslatable—directed me in the vague direction of a row of apartments adjacent to Donny's complex. I thanked him and headed that way.

Once in the vicinity, I saw a sign, made up of store bought adhesive letters—the kind you use on mailboxes—that pointed me to "MAIN OFFICE". There was a large black man behind the desk, hunkered down over a stack of paperwork and having at it with someone on the phone.

"I'll take the boot off of your car when you come back and pay me fifty-five bucks for illegal overnight parking. Because you don't live here, that's why! I don't care who you used to go out with, you ain't a resident, and we ain't a parking garage." He winked at me as he hung up the phone. "You gotta play hardball sometimes, or people'll run roughshod right over you," he said. "How can I help you?"

"Oh, my name's Marc Kenton. Did Beth Harbrew call?"

"You're Donny's friend. Yeah. Yeah, she did. You need to get something out of his apartment?"

"Yeah. It may take awhile. I don't even know where to start."

The man led me out of his office and down the sidewalk as he shared his condolences. "Damn shame. Man like that. Young. Really nice. Always paid his rent on time, never a complaint. And believe me, there was some shit he could've complained about up in here."

"Oh?" To look at the place, it was evident. I feigned shock to curry favor with him, but you'd have to be blind in at least one eye not to notice that Donny, bohemian that he was, had been living at the corner of Bedlam and Squalor.

"Loud parties going on. Plumbing problems you don't wanna know about, and a couple of certified loons across the hall for neighbors," continued the landlord.

"Well, Donny had a way of looking on the bright side," I assured.

"That he did. Shame what happened." We climbed a flight of stairs, and he put a key in the door of apartment 34B. "This is it." Donny's mailbox was stuffed. I relieved it of its fill. Behind us I could here the guttural thud of industrial music seeping through the neighbor's wall. The landlord pushed the door open, and let me step inside.

The room was pristine—an aesthetic oasis amid a complex of graffiti and fear. Donny had rigged a small indoor fountain that circulated water from a tiny pool, through a tube, and up over some small stones that held a statuette of an Asian fisherman, sitting in perfect zazen with his fragile pole. The trickle of liquid was soothing, reassuring—a pacifistic response to the traffic and Chemical Brothers remixes.

The wall featured a framed copy of Picasso's "Don Quixote"—a charcoal stick figure, seated sunken on a horse, trying to get a read on the next windmill. And the books. Christ, the books covered an entire wall. Some running alphabetically across the four overflowing shelves, and others stacked knee-high on the floor. Next to that, a tiny desk with a laptop, and another stack of skinny blue books—part of a series, perhaps.

"You gonna be o.k. in here?" asked the landlord.

"Yes, yes. I'll lock up, and I'll stop by on my way out."

"Good enough." He closed the door, and left me to reckon with Donny's world.

My mouth was all dried out, and my head felt light. I went to the fridge and grabbed a pitcher of sweet tea Donny had brewed . . . geez, probably the night before he died. Shit. I poured a glass, and sipped. It was sweeter than marzipan. Donny always liked that Down South tea. I could see why—what a sugar rush. It was like shooting pixie sticks right into your veins.

I gazed around the place, trying to get my bearings on where to start, and what I might be looking for. I wanted something that would trump old

Lance Harbrew. A hidden computer file with Donny's expansive stock market records on it, or maybe some paperwork that proved Donny's lifestyle was a front for his real life as a CIA agent.

But I kept feeling the tug of the bookshelf. I went to it and started scanning: Ambrose, William Burroughs, Doctorow, Emerson, Faulkner, Graham Greene, Hammett, Hemingway, Joyce, Kerouac, Elmore Leonard, Flannery O' Connor, Philip Roth, Salinger, Twain, Updike. Mixed amid this alphabetical who's who were editions of lyrics and poetry by Leonard Cohen, Bob Dylan, and Lou Reed. Could Donny have really read all these? I was lucky to get through one Stephen King book before he had published his next.

Then, I remembered "Kilimanjaro". I went back up to Hemingway and found it nestled between "Death in the Afternoon" and "The Nick Adams Stories", turned sideways to fit on the shelf. The magazine was about as close to mint as 70 year old paper could be. I thumbed to the index: "August 1936". "Kilimanjaro" started on page 27.

I sat down at Donny's desk, and decided to give the story a read. How long could it be, anyway—it's in a magazine for Christ's sakes. The drawing above Hemingway's by-line featured a thin man stretched out on a makeshift gurney. He was bare-chested, and his green pants stopped just below the knee to accommodate a bandage that came to just above his ankle. His draping bare feet and arms hinted that this story, like most of Hemingway's, would end in death. And why not? I was waist high in it this week.

I sat down at Donny's desk and heard the distant jingle of dog tags. Cassady the pug waddled in from another room and sat down next to me, panting like he'd just completed a track and field event. I looked at his ugly orphaned mug. "You miss your daddy, Cas?" He reared his head and grunted. "Yeah . . . me too."

He curled up by my feet and I began reading. Papa cut right to it—a writer in Africa, faithful wife by his side, waiting for the infectious gangrene devouring his right leg to swallow him whole. His lone lament was that there were so many stories he hadn't written, so many tales never captured for antiquity. A hundred stories of love and adventure, never told . . . never finished. Kilimanjaro is where his last thoughts take him—a summit he never scaled, a mountain of regret. Then, the whimpering of a hyena, breathlessness, and death. That Donny and his Dad both loved this story was understandable. Hemingway's terse brilliance glared off the page like a rare stone. But where Lance saw a gruff hunter facing his pre-mature death amid the jungles of Africa, I imagine Donny saw the pain of a life unlived—"and the odd thing of it was a hyena slipped along the edge of it."

I closed the magazine and rested my arm on the collection of books Donny had on his desk. I asked Cassady if he was hungry and got up to look for his bowl. When I stood, I took the stack of books with me, tumbling off the desk, narrowly missing the squat pug.

A couple of the books fell open to reveal longhand writing. A journal perhaps?

Maybe I'd found pay dirt—something from Donny's life to fly from a flagpole tomorrow. Something, dare I say, respectable?

Instead of a collection of first person musings and intimacies, however, I found that I was thumbing through what appeared to be a novel—and from what I could glean, a pretty damn good one. I mean, what the hell do I know, but the first page I read grabbed me, and not out of morbid curiosity.

Something about a Cuban refugee—he and his son are on a ramshackle raft, I figured heading for Florida. The couple of pages I first read placed the two in shark-infested waters with little food and little hope left. I had my night cut out for me. I called Julie and told her I was staying at Donny's until I finished the book—don't wait up. Of course she thought I was crazy, but seemed to understand. I also asked her if she was o.k. foster-parenting an ugly little pug until we could find him a home. "Bring him on over," she sighed, as if she knew I had little intention of finding someone else to take care of him. "Just be sure you get home in time to get some rest. Tomorrow's going to be a long day."

"I know, hon. The funeral's not until two . . . we'll be fine. I'm sure you'll hear me come to bed." We exchanged "I love you's" and hung up. I poured some more of that saccharine laced iced tea, found a bag of tostada chips and hunkered down for the long read.

Donny's writing was fluid. These five blue notebooks were full of some of the most stunning prose I'd ever read. Rodger and Osjami— father and son—were fully alive on these pages, battling God's torrent— heat, violent wind, sharks, riptides, dehydration, hunger. And each other. The stubborn Osjami and the proud Rodger were iconic. A deep love, masked by constant quarrelling and resentment. Osjami's sister dies on the raft early on in the book. Osjami wants to give her a proper burial in the U.S., but Rodger insists she be buried at sea to lighten the raft and give them a better chance at survival. When Osjami sees his sister sink beneath the waves, the tension between him and his father is savage. That Donny had a frame of reference for such emotion didn't surprise me, but how well he told this story certainly did. All that empathy I'd said he had been harboring was actually being funneled into this book. This breathtaking book.

The ending of the book brought freedom to only one of the raft's passengers. Osjami guides the vessel to shore with his father's corpse lying beside him. With Rodger's leg devoured by a shark, Osjami is able to get him back on the raft and divert the fish away with frequent punches to the nose, using the pole that had once been the mast. He steers the fragile craft another twenty-five miles on his own to the shoreline of the Keys. The Coast Guard catches up to him only after he lands. He is ritualistically pouring sand over his father's body, trying to give him the burial his sister had deserved when Tony Sanchez, a rookie Coast Guard officer, comes up and takes Osjami's hand. He tells him everything is going to be alright. After all, he's in America now.

The final tableau is of Osjami walking from the coastline, facing the city, periodically turning back to look at his father's body, now being unearthed by officers. Then, a parting glance to his raft, all tatters and kindling on the white sand. He smiles. He doesn't need the raft anymore.

It was four in the morning when I closed the final blue book. I was unable to shake the majesty of Donny's work. It was raw, honest. Every detail painstaking, as if Donny had been on that raft himself. I wanted to rush it home to Julie, wake her up and read it to her, page by page. I wanted to knock down Lance Harbrew's door and show him who his son was. I wanted to get on the phone to some New York publisher and get this book to them pronto.

If the book had a title, it wasn't evident. I flipped through each volume again, searching for some background on the book itself, but nothing surfaced. I even went so far as to boot up Donny's laptop to see if he had it transcribed and saved on his hard drive or a disk, perhaps to send to agents. Nothing. These handwritten documents were the only apparent evidence of Donny's authorship.

The funeral was now less than ten hours away. I needed some sleep, and some time to process all this. I took Donny's writings and the Esquire magazine to the car, then came back for Cassady and his menagerie of toys and treats. He seemed agreeable enough to leave the empty apartment. I wondered if he knew that Donny was gone; they say that animals sense these things. I dunno, but he was certainly happy to go where his water bowl and bag of kibbles were going.

Rather than disturb Julie, I curled up on the couch with Cassady lying on the floor beside me. I didn't even bother taking my shoes off; I just collapsed and melted into the sofa like butter oozing onto hotcakes.

Not four hours later, that was the very smell that awakened me. Julie was making pancakes—an occurrence so rare I wondered if I'd forgotten our anniversary amid all this. But, no, she thought a hot breakfast would carry us both a little further down the difficult road ahead.

Cassady scarfed down two strips of bacon like a canine possessed. I was keeping pace with him, devouring a five-high stack of buttermilk cakes, bacon, and the strongest cup of coffee Julie had ever brewed. After my high octane breakfast and a long, hot shower, I was a man renewed.

Beth called from her cell phone, en route to the funeral home, to see how the previous night had gone. "Everything o.k. at the apartment?"

"Yes. I brought Cassady home with me. I thought it'd be easier this way 'til we find him a home."

"Yeah. You find my dad's Hemingway story?"

"I . . . how'd you know?"

"What, you think he didn't try to send me to get it first? It's like he's afraid someone's gonna break in and steal it, or Cassady was going to pee on it. I knew he must've asked you to find it, I just couldn't believe he didn't wait until after the service."

"Yeah, well . . . it wasn't there. I mean, as far as I could tell." Where did that come from? Why was I suddenly lying to Beth? She was my ally, after all. And yet, I didn't feel like I should level with her. Not now.

"Oh. Well, maybe he had it tucked away somewhere. We'll have to find it later."

"Yeah." Moving on. "So, what time should I be there this morning?"

"Well, there's a viewing this morning, and the family has a prayer at 1:15. If you want to join us . . ." The lilt in her voice inferred she hoped I would.

"Yes, of course. I'll be there before 1:00. Uh, see you then."

I wanted off the phone. I was never good at lying, and I felt like a particularly shameful bastard this time, because I wasn't even sure what my untruth was in aid of.

When I hung up, I busied myself with pressing my suit, choosing a tie—mental busy work. But something nagged at me, and it wasn't just lying to Beth. Midway through ironing my dress shirt, it became real. At that moment, I hated myself. I hated that I hadn't told Donny what he meant to me, I hated that we had fallen so far out of touch and, mostly, I hated that I didn't speak up about how he should be honored today. I was the worst kind of coward, because I pretended none of it mattered. Ever the milquetoast diplomat, I had betrayed a friend who could no longer speak for himself. I let a father lighten the raft of one child's spirit, and was watching that spirit sink among the deluge. My hands weren't tied. They were just passively clasped behind me. I, too, was sinking.

Here I stood, at the crossroad of one of life's defining moments—a test of loyalty over propriety, the right thing staring in the face of the proper thing. I couldn't blink. I quickly concocted a plan that would reverse this dreadful tide of cowardice.

Two and a half hours later, I was at Patterson Funeral Home, ready to honor my friend. He was in state in the viewing room, where a few mourners still lingered. Beth was at the doorway, thanking people as they signed the guest book. The minister was there, consoling Mrs. Harbrew, who had seemingly gone from purse-lipped prude to anguished mother overnight. Somewhere in the night, the tempest of grief finally came ashore. She seemed to be feeling the biological tug now, the cruel irony of a mother seeing her child stilled for eternity. Even Lance Harbrew, so distracted the day before, seemed quieted by sorrow.

The funeral director announced that it was time for the family to have a final prayer and goodbyes with Donny, and the guests were asked to step into the chapel to wait for the service, which would start in fifteen or twenty minutes. As the cliques began to funnel through the threshold, I walked over to the casket. The family was busy with the preacher and the director. I was alone with Donny.

I walked to Donny's side and took in his gentility for the last time. The wholeness of him. The sparks in his eyes were extinguished, but the peace on his face in death was not unlike the peace on his face while alive, and that was reassuring. He had lived a life in full, regardless of his familial critics.

I thanked my friend for what he meant to me. I kissed him on his forehead, and vowed to be a little more like him from now on. I told him I loved him. I took the rolled up copy of Esquire, containing the elusive "Snows of Kilimanjaro", and placed it inside Donny's jacket, pressing it down gently to assure it wouldn't be spotted. I told him I'd take good care of Cassady, and said goodbye.

The preacher called us together to pray—me and the Harbrews, and an assemblage of cousins, aunts, and the like. Kind as he was, the minister knew nothing of Donny, so to my ears the prayer was rote—page 119 of "Lamentations for the Unsaved"; a plea for mercy that Jesus might leave the door cracked and look the other way for this one well-meaning pagan to slip past.

After the casket was closed and wheeled from the room, the family followed in procession to the chapel. As they filed into reserved seats in the front of the hall, I found the technician—a wiry wisp of a man, a comb over in shirtsleeves—sitting in the back corner of the chapel. He had both hands nervously on the controls of the sound system, as if he were awaiting a spate of complex cues to be called. "Excuse me, are you the audio guy?"

"Hi. Yes. Kent Whipple." He shook my hand. I had caught him so completely off guard that he went into meet-and-greet mode. When he stuck out his hand to shake mine, I filled it with a newly purchased CD.

"Well, the family asked me to give you this. They want it played at the end of the service, when the deceased is carried out."

He looked at the CD cover. "You sure you cleared it with them?"

I pointed to Mr. Harbrew. "You see that man? He's Donny's dad, Lance Harbrew. Very important man. He wanted Donny's favorite song played, but couldn't find it in time. You understand. I was able to scrounge it up, and . . . it's track one. Alright?"

My answer seemed to assuage him. I gave him a slight smile—one of those funeral smirks that express appreciation being wedged through a grate of stifled pain. His pleasant return was reassuring. I knew Donny's ceremonial dirge was now in safe hands. I took odd solace in picturing Donny coasting out of that anodyne hall to the raw gravel of Kristofferson's voice warbling about the purity of freedom. How this atonal folk philosopher could so capture Donny's essence was a marvel to me; the rambler, adrift on a gypsy wind, never giving a tinker's damn about landing, and loving the hell out of the ride.

I raced out to my car and sped away, never looking back toward Donny's hollow shell, Beth's quaking shoulders, or the parents whose facade may have, at last glimpse, begun to crumble. I couldn't look back. I had a funeral to get to.

Twenty-seven miles east of Patterson's was the expansive coast of Massachusetts—the choppy down-easter waters at war with stone-lined shores. Julie was waiting for me there, at a dock in Cape Ann. She had chartered a twenty-four foot fishing boat called "The Ospry". Julie knew how to manage a small craft from her childhood, out on the water with her dad, a deep-sea fisherman. She took us out a few miles from shore until we were far enough to have a sense of sanctuary from all the whale watching tours and schooners that populated the waters during the afternoon.

Our boat was a wee drop of white paint, bobbing on an endless blue canvas. Overhead, two birds played kamikaze with the sea's surface. This was the place.

Reaching into a picnic basket Julie had packed, I pulled out a copper double-handled urn. I stood over the bow, holding the truest part of who

Donny was—the ashy remains of the one thing he most assuredly had finished. I closed my eyes and tasted the salty air. I removed the lid and, tilting the urn into the westward breeze, I let go. I just let go.

Rodger and Osjami were at sea again. So, at last, was Donny.

2

ALL THIS USELESS BEAUTY

The sheets felt like tar on her legs, weighted layers of warmth causing her calves to sweat, so heavy she couldn't roll on her side without first giving the bedspread a calculated push with her toes. But he liked it that way; a half dozen sheets and blankets creeping up to his neck gave him a certain security.

She, on the other hand, longed to toss and turn to find some measure of comfort. Instead, the best she could do was wedge a foot out from under the morass of linens and let the cool air seep in around her ankle. He seemed aware of her slightest motion. The morning always began with a list of complaints about how she slept, or kept him from sleeping, with her grinding teeth, her anguished little sighs, and her attempts to escape from the smothering covers.

He had no time in the morning for pleasantries. He was out the door by six thirty, and expected a hot breakfast awaiting him when he was done showering. He sold pre-owned vehicles and needed to be on the lot by seven if he was going to stay near the top of the board. But the grievances always managed to break the morning silence. Those he had time for.

Getting up this morning was no problem for her, given her restless sleep. At 5:45, she peeled herself from the mummy wrap of sheets and walked to the kitchen. The sausage, the biscuits, the coffee were all underway. She'd cracked the second of three eggs when he stepped into the kitchen, something he never did before his shower.

"What the hell was that last night? The Mexican Cot Dance?"

"I've told you, all those sheets. It's only September. I get hot."

"Stick a foot out."

"I did. That's not a catch all, John. I still get hot."

"I'm just saying, when you can't sleep, I can't sleep, and I gotta be sharp." He walked up behind her, wrapping his arms around her waist. It seemed an act of gentility, rather than belligerence. Still, she clinched, tightening her arms to her sides. "What now?"

"I just . . . I need to get your breakfast ready. I'm sorry about keeping you up."

"Jesus, Susan, you act like I'm a leper." He slouched his shoulders, making his already husky physique seem wider, flatter. She walked around him to the refrigerator, grabbing a package of bacon and tossing four strips onto the frying pan next to the sausage.

"Sausage *and* bacon? You trying to kill me or something?"

"Oh hell. Well, you got me all flustered."

He tried to approach her again. "That's what I mean, why are you like a cat around me?"

"Can we not talk about this now?" She dodged him again, grabbing a fork and stirring the egg yolks in a bowl.

"Fine. Jesus." John shuffled out of the kitchen to take a shower.

Her breathing was accelerated, but when she was certain he had gone down the hall, she got her bearings and finished her work: three scrambled eggs, four strips of center cut bacon, two sage sausage patties, a fat buttermilk biscuit, and a cup of coffee as black and strong as Cassius Clay.

His showers were customarily short, but this morning he must've been stewing over her duck-and-cover routine in the kitchen, because breakfast had been on the table for over ten minutes when he came back in, pulling his collar down around his tie.

"Looks good. Thanks." He sat down to eat, and she fully expected a barrage of bitching about how cold the food had gotten. But, he ate much of it as if it were still fresh from the stove, not a word of condescension; that, coupled with the compliment on her presentation really made Susan wonder. If anything he was consistent: a grumpy bear of a man in the morning, a tired, passive creature in the evening. Today, he seemed to be making some feeble attempt at retribution for his curtness. She'd rather he didn't bother.

As he left, he gave her a brush on the forearm, an act of uninhibited passion to his stoic mind, and though he'd never struck her, she pulled away as if it were a tightened fist angling toward her chest. He shook his head, grabbed his briefcase, and walked out the door.

Once she heard him pull away, she turned on her Billie Holliday CD, twelve cuts of raw, unadorned anguish in which she reveled almost every morning, her daily bloodletting ritual. She swayed gently as she gathered up the dishes and filled the sink with soapy water, her bare heels tapping the linoleum as she scrubbed the grease from every crevice of each pan.

She lied down on the sofa and closed her eyes, hoping to get in a bit of a nap before a shower and some errands. Her mind wandered back to a time when John could touch her and she'd feel something other than dread, a time when she could pretend she found some comfort in his arms. She wondered where the imperceptible drift began, and when it became chiasmic. She wondered if she ever really loved him, or if they'd both just fallen for the myth, the societal monolith of security that turns to dust when touched by human hands. But she couldn't hold a thought for long. Soon, she was in a slumberous haze. She'd drifted deep into limbo when there was a loud knock at the door. She gathered herself, peered through the spy hole and saw a small, older man in a burgundy Oxford, a stack of pale blue papers in his hand.

The idea of answering the door in her nightgown would've been out of the question, but today, she wanted to let another man see her like this, just to pervade the numbness. She was a woman most would call attractive, and this gown was modest enough that it wouldn't seem altogether improper. Only she would know the game she was playing.

She cracked the door. "Yes?"

"Hi. My name's Walt Dreisser. I'm new to the condos and am having a little get together this Friday, sort of an open house. May I give you one of these?"

He seemed a man she could trust, so she opened the door in full.

"Oh, I'm sorry. I guess I stopped by too early. I wanted to hand these out before I left for work. Did I wake you?" He steadied his eyes away from her spaghetti straps and bare shoulders, panning her like a camera for a place to cast his gaze so as not to offend, but even fixating on her toes made him feel self-conscious.

"Don't worry about it. I had to get my husband off to work; I just haven't gotten myself ready yet. Don't be embarrassed. You'd see less on many women at the mall these days."

He laughed, and raised his eyes to meet hers. "Yeah, that's the truth. So, I hope you and your husband can come. Just a small gathering, h'or dourves, wine, music. I hear you like Billie Holliday." He pointed toward the ceiling, as if the music were tangible, floating above them.

"God, yes." She giggled, sounding much younger than her thirty-three years.

"You'll feel right at home. I don't think I own anything that's come out after 1960."

They stood in silence for a stretch of five seconds or so that felt millennial. He looked in her eyes and caught her staring back hard. His eyes drifted down, past the hint of her cleavage, and the gown clinging around her midriff, stopping with the gown's hem at her knee, an innocent enough haven, he hoped. "So, please bring your husband, and call me if you have any questions. My number is on the flyer. Nice to meet you . . ."

" . . . Susan. Susan Chamberlain. Nice to meet you . . . Will, was it?"

"Walt. Walter. Well, Walt. So, see you Friday, I hope. Sorry to disturb you." He started to offer his hand, but thought better of it. Susan gave a tiny wave and a goodbye as she closed the door.

This unimposing man, an impish wallflower who was approaching fifty if he hadn't already passed the mark, didn't infatuate her in the least. But the feeling that he saw her in some sort of sexual context, whether aroused or merely embarrassed, gave her a tinge she hadn't felt in too many months.

Sex with John had become a formal dance, an automated, restrained romp. Once, she could've sworn she saw him glance over at the Wall Street Journal on the nightstand right before he climaxed. But she'd never cheated, and she never had a reason to believe he had either. By now, he was this asexual cohabitant, sharing the cave and the kill with her. He hunted and gathered, and she was to do the rest. So this Walt, unimpressive as he was, had at least provided her a cheap thrill, and that carried her through the rest of her day. She showered, applied more makeup than usual, played with her hair longer than she had in weeks, and put on a pair of sleek black boots and matching skirt she had previously only worn to John's company Christmas party.

Her errands were mundane: Wal-Mart, the grocery store, the card shop to buy a birthday card for her Aunt Rene. She felt pretty walking down the aisles, though, and became aware of every head that seemed to tilt her direction, man or woman. When she came home, she kept her shopping clothes on, instead of resorting back to the sweat pants and slouch socks that had become her at-home staple.

By six, she had a pork roast, roasted red potatoes, and crescent rolls on the table, along with John's nightly screwdriver. At 6:45, she put everything back in the oven on the lowest setting to reheat. At 7:30, she turned off the oven, and went to change into her sweat pants and slouch socks.

John came in at 7:40. Without so much as an 'I'm home', he found his highball glass, poured out the watery remains of his screwdriver, and replaced it with straight bourbon. He stood in the kitchen and finished off his drink, then began searching for Susan.

"Hey! Hey, where are you?" He let out a shrill whistle. He found her in the bed, a mystery novel holding her gaze. Never looking up, she said, "Your dinner is in the oven. You'll have to reheat it."

His sigh was seismic. "Look, I couldn't call, o.k.? There was this couple, and they were gonna buy. I was ready to close on these two, had 'em in the office doing the paperwork, then after all the credit checks and everything, the wife starts crying. They get in this huge fight about some loan, and I had to play marriage counselor right there in the back office. If I had left them alone for one minute, they'd have been out the door. You understand, right?"

"Sure," she said, still staring at her book.

"They closed. I did get the sale."

"Good. That's good, John." She kept her eyes fixed on page sixty-two, though she'd not absorbed a word since he came home. She could feel him staring at her, but she refused to return the look.

"The hell I bother anyway?" He walked back in the kitchen and started pulling the food out of the oven. Putting together a serving, he threw a plateful into the Microwave and poured another drink. The slamming of Corningware and oven doors pulled Susan out of the bedroom. She stood in the doorway, watching him fume. How pathetic, she thought, a little boy having to make his own PBJ. She watched him for what must've been two full minutes, as he wandered about the kitchen, a stranger in a foreign land, digging for a long-handled spoon, scanning the refrigerator shelves for butter, making sure every item hit the counter with an insipid thud. She was silent. He could sense her. Only when he turned around to take his food to his den chair did he give her a glance.

That night, as she slept, he threw an extra quilt over the bed.

She awoke around 2:30, a trickle of sweat in the crook of her left knee. She tried to scoot her foot out from under the covers, but the sheets wouldn't budge. She finally wriggled herself out of the cocoon of layered cotton, one awkward limb at a time, and ripping her pillow from the headboard, went out to the sofa to spend the rest of the night.

John knew better than to expect breakfast when he awoke. Instead, he went straight from the shower to his closet, then out the front door, but gently pulling it to, so as not to disturb Susan, who was sound asleep, sprawled like an alley cat on the couch.

Susan awoke to the sound of a garbage truck's brakes. The clock read 7:52. "Shit," she said, jumping up to awaken John. Then, she remembered last night and figured he had crept out long ago. She looked around at the empty room, lit only by a ray of sun shooting through the blinds, illuminating a legion of dust, rising up and falling again in a dance between the walls. She fell onto the couch and lied there for what seemed hours. She looked at the clock. 8:31. Maybe she'd call the temp agency and see if anything promising was on the horizon. Or Pilates . . . she took a Pilates class at the YWCA last month and really liked it, but felt guilty for going very often. John liked her to look fit, but moaned about her paying to work out when she had an Ab-inator, her only e-bay impulse, in the bedroom gathering dust.

She glimpsed out the window to gauge the weather, and spotted Mr. Dreisser. Walt. He was sitting by the pool reading a hardback, shirt half-unbuttoned to reveal a tangled matte of gray hair. He was no one, a hobgoblin whose only attractive feature was his love of Billie Holliday; that, and maybe his bashful stammer. But he did seem alive, hopeful, even as he was reading his book; there was vitality there.

The open house was tomorrow and she wanted to go, wanted to make another impression on him. She'd never so much as flirted with another man while married to John, and though she had no intention of this going further than raised hemlines and eyebrows, to her it felt like the plotting of a surreptitious tryst. She went to her underwear drawer, and dug beneath the neat stack of folded silk, curling her fingers around a roll of bills she kept as her 'mad money', extra cash she stored from temp jobs and clandestine 'cash back' withdrawals off their debit card when buying groceries. She thumbed through the phone book and found the name of a spa down the street, where she scheduled a Friday afternoon appointment—facial, manicure, pedicure, the works. Setting all this in motion put a hum in her head, a jet idling on the runway. She glanced back out at Walt while making her appointment. He had set his book down, and was sitting with his feet in the shallow end, staring at the blue morning sky with a piercing gaze and an odd little smirk on his face. She smiled.

The phone call to the spa gave her momentum, and within half an hour, she had a temp job lined up for at least part of the next week, a by-the-day data entry project, and she was dressed and headed to the Y. She passed the pool en route to her car, but Walt was gone.

John was home from work at his usual time, and behaved as if there had been nary a scuffle the night before. As for Susan, she was separated from him by a dense fog, his small talk reaching her ears through a mesh silencer, the meal itself an automated exercise of hands, forks, spoons, lips. She was elsewhere, but John didn't dare mention it. It was enough that they sat, that they ate.

After dinner, John worked to aid the thaw by helping with the dishes, an honor he'd not bestowed on her since her birthday, when he managed to scrape most of the food off the plates and prop them in the dishwasher. This time, though, he stood shoulder to shoulder with her silently scrubbing, scouring, rinsing. They sat on the couch, watching old sitcoms on the rerun channel. He got her a beer. He rubbed her socked feet for a moment, smiling each time he earned the slightest glance. Then, as if clocking out, he gnawed on his upper lip, and left to get ready for bed. Susan was unsure if he was performing penance or ill at ease with her. After Susan remained prone through another sitcom, John reemerged, wearing only his boxers. "As you're seemingly not coming to bed, just know I'll grab breakfast at the bagel place tomorrow again. I got this Greek coming in early to buy cars for his twin teenagers." She gave a barely perceptible nod. "You hear me? You hear any damn thing I said tonight, Susan?" She turned and closed her eyes, holding them shut and then opening them, a defiant blink that said more than she had all night.

"Something wrong with you, Susan? Because I thought we had this little tiff behind us. I told myself I wasn't gonna make a deal out of it, bringing flowers, sweeping you off your feet, 'cause it wasn't all that big a thing. But you've been acting like a fish all night. I dunno what to make of you. Been lying back there for half an hour waiting for you so we . . . aw, fuck it. I'm just sayin', don't make me breakfast. And don't sleep out here either. I hate having to be so fucking quiet when I'm getting out the door."

Before she could gather herself to speak, John was gone. The bedroom door caught the latch with a hard slap. There was a part of her that wanted to get up, go in there and, if not apologize, at least explain. He was trying his best she thought. But she hated his best. And so, she sank deeper into the couch, nuzzled her beer bottle, and found an old Liz Taylor movie on the Classics channel.

She didn't mean to fall asleep on the sofa, but there she was at 5:30 in the morning, face down in a burgundy throw pillow, a calcium deficiency infomercial blaring at an unholy level. John made a point of creating noise as he passed through the den, shuffling papers, brewing an unnecessary cup of coffee, and swearing at Jesus when he couldn't find his keys. Susan was still half-asleep when John gave his parting shot, a sneering 'have a nice day' punctuated by a much louder 'Shit!' when he sloshed the coffee from his mug onto his hand as he attempted to give the door a slam. Susan waited for the sound of his car starting, this morning a jolting revving of the engine, and then transported herself to the bedroom for a more comfortable morning nap. She managed to stretch that nap until almost noon, and woke with a start. She'd have to hurry. Aside from her spa visit and pressing her clothes, she fully intended to have supper on the table for John when he got home. Even though she planned to be at Walt's open house by then, she found more vindication in knowing John was eating her home cooked meal alone while she was a few hundred yards away, enclosed in another man's rented walls.

Her Crock Pot spaghetti was the perfect offering: brown some beef, toss the canned ingredients in and set it on low until around five, then leave it simmering next to a colander of freshly cooked noodles. All he'd have to do is ladle it onto his plate.

With the slow cooker gently warming his dinner, Susan showered, and headed to her spa appointment, where she was lavished with the kind of care she'd only afforded herself twice since getting married. She soaked in a hydro-mineral tub, and then snuggled into a robe so soft it tickled her back. Then, three women led her to a reclining chair, where her face was coated with a soothing mask of aloe and ginger, her ruddy fingernails turned into smooth ruby jewels. The tough layer of skin built up on her soles and heels from too much time wandering barefoot was stripped away by warm oils to reveal a pair of delicate feet, beautified further by the matching polish applied to each evened nail. Eunuchs and peeled grapes, she thought, were all that were missing.

She left the patchouli-scented spa to return to a house stifled by oregano and stewed tomatoes, dust still dancing amid the fading sunbeams. But she felt none of it. She was ironing, applying liner and lipstick, flossing. Her breasts sheathed in a chic red blouse, her favorite black skirt hovering around her thighs, she slid her newly adorned feet into her black boots. Standing in the full-length mirror, she saw the person she at times allowed herself to imagine she was. She penned John a note: "Dinner is on the stove. I've gone to a friend's open house. Last minute. Sorry." The message was cursory and vague—he'd think she was at a girlfriend's most likely, and that was fine. What John thought, at least tonight, was the slightest of her concerns. She set the makings for John's nightly screwdriver on the kitchen counter and left the overhead light on for him.

She drove to Walt Dreisser's apartment, if only to eliminate the questions John would have about why she was gone but her car wasn't. Having a secret, even one so guiltless, made her smile. She'd just as well be tangled in a stranger's satin sheets.

The door opened wide at 23A, Walt Dreisser's pug-like mug widening to a smile when he saw Susan. "Susan! So glad you could make it!" He took her hand and guided her past the threshold. "Thank you. Good to see you again, Walt." She listened for the chatter of guests, but only heard the faint musings of Dave Brubeck's piano. In her eagerness to get out of the apartment before John got home, she put herself in the awkward position of being the first to arrive, showing up at 5:58. "I'm sorry, Walt, am I too early?" He smiled. "Oh God, no. It's an open house; someone's got to be the first to show up. I'm glad it's you." His kindness was a wave of warmth in an apartment that seemed designed to amplify such gestures. It was a home of antiques and art, soft lighting overhead and soft carpet underfoot. Family photos adorned every flat surface, telling the stories of generations back to the Civil War. All this flared in contrast to Susan's existence, the bare floor, sensible lighting fixtures and beige walls that John insisted remain unadorned, save a photo of him shaking hands with former Reds catcher Johnny Bench at a car lot promotional event.

Walt offered her a drink from his portable mahogany bar. She asked for a Cuba Libre, a drink she loved but hadn't tasted in over a year. Walt was generous with the rum, miserly with the Coke and ice. She sipped and let out a cough. "Too strong?" he asked. She assured him she could handle it.

For nearly thirty minutes, she toured Walt's apartment, learning firsthand about his favorite relics: his great-grandfather's writing quill, a signed first edition of Updike's "Rabbit, Run", and a shadow box with shot glasses from twenty of the world's finest watering holes. Susan told him about an Irish pub called James Joyce's that she used to frequent when she was single. He knew of it, had been there more than once, in fact. She talked about her evenings at the pub and the faces and voices that still rushed back to her when she smelled just the right potion in the air. She talked. He listened. She drank. He poured. It all felt so delicate, as lithe as the rug beneath her boots. She was two-thirds through her refilled highball glass of Cuba Libre when she saw her hand, as if detached from the rest of her, reaching for the back of Walt's furry nape, the initiation of a kiss, an embrace; of what she wasn't sure, but her head, too full of liquor and aloneness, couldn't stop her errant fingers from seizing their mark. As her body moved toward his, she felt a gentle nudge at her abdomen, Walt's fingers pressing her, giving her retreat. His kind prod felt like brick and mortar hitting her belly, the shame of rejection bleeding into her like a growing wave. Adrenaline blended with alcohol, her head swum and she grabbed the door jam to steady her. "I'm sorry . . . I don't know what . . . I . . ."

Before she could stammer out her apology, and before Walt gave any indication as to why he'd stopped her, there was a pounding at the door, syncopated by the repeated ringing of the doorbell. Walt left Susan in the hallway and answered the door. She heard loud voices—a strident couple that Walt obviously knew well. Walt eased into the role of gracious host and escorted the couple in to introduce them to Susan. "Uh, Susan, this is Tom and Ginny Seacourt. They publish Good Health magazine. I write for them." Susan shook their hands, but their chatter about Walt's talents as a writer and the regional demand for such periodicals floated by her like distant yelps, warped snippets of tape humming from a faraway recorder.

The moment Walt disappeared to the bar to pour the pair their drinks Susan hurried for the door. Her feet now felt as separated from her body as her hand did moments ago. She was racing to the car, a legless spirit floating to safety. Once there, she fumbled with her keys, started the engine and drove out of the apartment complex.

She knew she couldn't stay on the road. She was a lightweight drinker and the chance of getting pulled over and Breathalyzed was too great a risk, even if she passed the damn thing. She only needed to find a drug store so she could get some mouthwash. She wanted the taste of that murky rum gone. The closest drug store was a mere half-mile, and when she parked, it all came up on her—the guilt of what she'd done, the confusion over what it meant, the mystery of what might've happened had the doorbell not rung. For all she knew, Walt was only pushing her away because he knew guests would be arriving. Had she been the last at the party, he might've escorted her to a quiet room. He might've just held her hand and talked. He might've unbuttoned her blouse and unzipped her boots. He might've shared the darkness with her.

Reassurances did little to change the fact that Susan was now a refugee from the party. She could go back, sure, but what if there would've been no quiet room, no soft lighting and laughter over a nightcap? What if he pushed her away because he found her brash and uninviting? What if that Grecian urn he had on his mantle was half-filled with the ashes of his deceased wife and he was still grieving? She hated the ambiguity, and hated the thought of resolving it, be it with a humble apology or a convivial hug. She bought her Listerine, and a pack of Dentyne for good measure. She sat in the driver's seat, swigging and spitting three times from her open window, then she shoved two pieces of gum in her mouth and drove home.

When she pulled into her parking space, she saw that John was not home. Once inside, she went straight to the phone. One message: Walt, maybe? Had he called to see what had happened to her? She looked around to make sure John wasn't coming through the door and she hit 'play'. "You there? Hey! You there? Listen . . . I dunno when I'm getting home tonight. I got a bunch of paperwork to do, and then Phil wants to grab dinner and talk about some bullshit promotion he wants me to head up. Sorry about this . . . and about this morning. Don't wait up, okay?"

Susan stared at the phone, the door, the dust that floated around the end table lamp. Turning off the Crock Pot, she swallowed hard, the taste of cinnamon and eucalyptol burning on her tongue. She walked to the bedroom and removed her black skirt and red blouse, hanging them up with the care of a ROTC respecting his newly pressed uniform. She unzipped her black boots and peeled them from her feet, catching a glimpse of her shiny, ruby toenails. She felt the hardness of the floor on her soles as she put the boots on the shelf. She stopped to glance in the full-length mirror at herself, clothed only in a bra and panties, but only for a moment. She walked over to the bed, lied down, and pulled the blankets up around her throat. She felt the warmth of them. She felt the weight.

3

CHARLES MINGUS HATES MY LILY-WHITE ASS

Being dead for twenty-five years, that didn't stop Charlie Mingus from busting down my front door with the business end of his stand-up bass. He heard the music playing on the stereo I guess. It was Bird, and he never could get enough of what Bird did with his horn.

When he saw me—skinny and pale—his interrogative gale knocked me to the floor. "Aw, man. What the hell is a cracker like you doing listening to 'Klactoveesedstene'? Who gave you permission? Who told you that you had the soul to understand the complexity of what Bird was sayin'?"

He filled the doorframe, eclipsed the sun. His teeth clinched a cigar the size of his ego, dripping ashes of indignation, setting my carpet aflame. Mingus lifted me by the throat and threw me to the top of the stairs. I landed and tumbled down in a percussive 5/8 rhythm that made him smile a maestro's smile.

He pulled a string off his bass and tied me to the kitchen chair; started rummaging through my record collection, old scratched up 33's and evens some 78's from the days of Savoy and Prestige. "Chet Baker? What is this shit?" His voice a mercurial roll, his fist curled, ready to give me the same toothless sag Baker kept in his final years. "Come on," I said, "his groove is warm, sparse—it makes me ache." I hoped to connect with him on an emotional level, knowing I could never spar with him on technique or style. "You want to ache? Listen to Trane's 'Alabama'. White men killed four little black girls in a Birmingham church, and Trane mourned for us all. That's anguish. Chet Baker. Shit."

How could I tell him that I could sing him every note of 'Alabama', if I weren't tone deaf? That the song haunted me in my sleep, but not like his own 'Goodbye Pork Pie Hat', the saddest dirge I'd ever heard, six pallbearers on an uphill march to Lester Young's inevitable peace? How could I explain Chet Baker, a zoned out white junkie who lifted everything he learned from Miles and Clifford, but still managed to make it his heartbreaking own? I appealed to his better nature, a logician's argument. "You know, Chet fell out that window, that's what made him a legend. Like JFK, dying before his time, lionized for his last fatal moment."

"Man, Chet Baker didn't fall out no window."

"Yeah, in Amsterdam. What, you think he jumped? Took his own life?"

"I was there." His eyes shrunk into his skull, his cigar hung from his lower lip. "I pushed him."

"You . . ."

"Pushed the muthafucka right off the ledge." His cheeks swelled like Diz's used to when he played "A Night In Tunisia", a wicked grin filling the hole where a mouthpiece should be.

Now Mingus had been dead some eight or nine years when Chet's frail frame melded with the cobblestone alleyway beside the Prins Hendrik Hotel, but I wasn't going to argue with him. After all, here he was.

"You got any wine?" He began to rummage through my kitchen, tossing chicken legs, hurling pears; then came the refrigerator door and a series of empty plates and Rubbermaid bowls, all licked pristine. Mingus came out sucking his fingers, so fat only one could fit in his mouth at a time. "What kind of host has a man over and don't even stock up on wine?" He opened my last beer with his teeth, drank it all and ate the bottle. He hovered over me like a cloud threatening a nestling with its hailstones.

"Well, if there ain't no spirits, let's see how else we can get high," he said, returning to my record collection. "Ahhh, Brubeck. Duke. Dolphy. Now we're talkin'. He was readying "Ellington at Newport" for the turntable when his eyes scanned down the alphabet to the M's. There, between Marsalis and Monk was a collection of some twenty or thirty sonic captures of Mingus' chaotic genius. His smile was a reprieve.

Mingus wrapped his hands around my forearms and lifted me out of the chair, though it still drug beneath me, my inflamed wrists still lashed to its backing. He pulled out my copy of "Blues and Roots" and set the needle on 'Wednesday Night Prayer Meeting'. "I'm gonna take you to church, boy!" He ripped the string from my wrists and restrung his bass in one imperceptible move. I was free, but I wasn't going anywhere, not with 300 pounds of righteous anger hovering over me, not with the Malcolm X of jazz reborn in my living room. Not with Mingus about to play.

While the record popped and hissed along the warm grooves, Mingus doubled the bass line not five inches from my face, driving hot nails of rhythm into my core, making my chest vibrate with each pluck-and-slap. For five minutes and thirty-nine seconds, he lifted me up to God's house, where Jesus and Buddha and Mohammed and Vishnu and Krishna all sup from the sweetest fruit on the vine, while Monk plays "Epistropy" on a newly tuned baby grand. Then, with a warning no longer than the crease separating the tracks, he shot me back down to earth with the opening licks of "Cryin' Blues".

For five hours, he played song after song, album after album—*The Black Saint and the Sinner Lady, Ah Um, Oh Yeah, Tijuana Moods, Tonight at Noon, Let My Children Hear Music.* His fingers were a blur of crimson and ebony, my ears numbed by the low moan and rumble of his sound. I was higher than Bird on his nastiest trip, escalated by an Ecclesiastic squall of joy.

Mingus jumped from octave to octave on his bass, never taking his eyes off of me. He saw the swelling in my eyes, the quiver of my lip, and he knew it wasn't from fear. He saw my feet moving, my shoulders swaying. He'd found his way, burrowing right past my shortcomings and into my heart. He tore through my chest and wrapped his callused fingers around it. Mingus fingers. He could've torn it out and left me to bleed out on my carpet, the needle skipping endlessly as the police outlined my corpse in chalk and tape. But instead he gave it a gentle squeeze, and starting it pumping with new rhythm, something in a 9/8.

"Feel that?" he asked. "That's soul."

"It feels strange," I told him. "Its always beat in 4/4."

"That's because you ain't never lived the music."

That was the coldest thing he could say to me, but he was right. The music was all around me, up in me even, but it didn't flow out of me. I breathed it in, but I couldn't breathe it into anyone else. I felt the paralysis of being in the front row at Minton's, tapping my clumsy fingers to Max Roach's rat-a-tatta-tat, knowing I'd never sit on that stage. In my hands, his thundersticks were so much kindling. I knew no rhythm-a-ning; blues, but no roots. I had the soul of an admirer, not an artist. I hung my head.

"That's alright, boy. Lightning's gotta have a place to strike." Mingus smiled, smelling my impotency over the bitter scent of tobacco and burnt rug. Maybe it was my obvious awe, my vulnerability, or just that in his final years, Mingus had softened. Maybe it was that he sensed that I'd carry him—bass and all—in my arms all the way to Orval Faubus' gravesite and help dig him up so Mingus could piss in his filthy segregationist mouth. Maybe it was that Mingus knew that I'd love his half-black/half-Chinese ass even if he struck me dead then and there.

Mingus slung his bass on his back and stepped toward the door. He extended his hand, and I mine. He shook it and grinned. Then, he put his cigar out in my open palm, singeing the skin off in a perfect fifty-four ring gauge.

I howled. "What was that for?"

As he floated down the street, he hollered, "In case anyone asks, you can tell 'em, 'Charles Mingus hates my lily-white ass!'"

4

KITE

The struggle began well before takeoff. He stood there on the beach, oversized bathing suit sinking off of his tiny hips, wrapped in a morass of ribbon and tail. No sooner would he liberate one strand before he'd have another caught up in what seemed an infinite spool of cord.

I could've helped him, but I didn't. He was dogged, all jutting chin and nimble fingers; for an adult to step in seemed treasonous. A life lesson, learned far from scornful eyes and wagging fingers, is perhaps the kindest of gifts.

The sun slipped behind the sky's lone cloud as he managed to unravel the components of his charge. He stood up, toes twitching as he studied his dance partner. She had to travel just right. Couldn't run too slow or she'd drag and bend, couldn't let her get caught up in a low tidal gust that'd push her into the sand. She required grace, a gentle and knowing hand that would give her room, a stride which would let her find her own way. He couldn't know all this yet, of course. He was too young, too clumsy. But he was on the verge of magic.

His first attempt, hobbled by an uneven gait and a whisper of wind, was quickly sullied. There was no judgment from the boy. He picked up the kite, unwound the line from around the frame and renewed his effort.

This time, the sky denied the kite harbor with a swift squall that sent the diamond sputtering into the seashore with a thrust violent enough to rip a lesser model. He studied the kite, relieved to find it still armored for its maiden voyage.

The third time was no charm, nor the fourth. He tried for mere minutes, but they snaked like painful hours as I watched. Yet, the boy never wavered, never sighed. Each failed flight a lesson in refinery, every disentanglement a cause for hope.

Finally, the breeze steadily rippling off his back, a headwind in from the east found favor with the nose of the kite. And so the climb began, wrists turning in rhythm, feet adjusting for his companion's wide berth. If you'd checked your watch to see how long it took, you'd have missed it, the ascent was that seamless. The kite had embraced the theory of flight, and he rode on her shoulders.

His kite and the sky: that was his world. Nothing else, not even the cry of the sea, could penetrate it. There was no sense of where the spool handle ended and he began. You cannot buy that in a boardwalk hobby shop. It's an attention we're born with and one we start losing so soon thereafter. The erosion is self-inflicted, and ultimately fatal. But for these precious moments, he was in possession of something no one could touch. Even my voyeuristic joy was only a shadow of what he must've felt, watching his sandpiper nestling open her wings to the world.

I left him there, kite still kissing the sun. I couldn't handle watching him rein her in, an inevitable retraction of freedom that comes when the sun sets, when a parent calls, when a small seismic shift reminds us we are earthbound. I needed to remember him at the height of his discovery. For that day, he learned to trust the wind and tide, the elements that have the energy to lift us heavenward if we'll let them. He himself flew. He took me with him.

5

STICKS AND STONES

The nametags were lined up alphabetically, an unintended tribute to homeroom seating charts. The hostesses behind the registration table were a bevy of former cheerleaders, homecoming queen finalists, and Student Government Association treasurers. Their faces hung at different levels, from the twice-divorced sag to pert Botoxian lifts. They all expressed the same phony delight, as if they'd lived the last nineteen and three-quarter years to arrive at this moment.

Greg could only imagine the small talk wafting around the ballroom. "Wow, has it really been twenty years?" "Whatever happened to who-the-hell-ever?" "You haven't changed a bit!"

The hitch was Greg Limpkin had changed. Back then he was fat, shy and awkward, and the Darwinian hell that was high school left him an alienated, insecure mess by graduation day in 1986. He'd been mocked by everyone from his gym coach to band geeks. Girls whispered when they passed him, bullies encircled him on the track during Phys Ed, elbowing and punching him as he gasped through the required one-mile run. Swirlies, wedgies, and Melvins were weekly rituals in his freshman and sophomore years. His final two years were spent, as often as possible, on the back row, preferably in the corner, doodling on his spiral notebook covers and imagining a world where the odd got even.

High school held no warm memories for Greg. He'd spent the last twenty years living down the brutal void his classmates made of his days as a teen. Now, he was here for the most civil revenge—a detached superiority that would fuel his next twenty years.

A tailored suit complemented his now Adonisian physique. His hair, once so greasy some underclassmen donned him "lube job," was a coiffed masterwork. Gone were the eyeglasses that had all the subtle presence of strap-on binoculars, replaced by a pair of Lasik-perfected, piercing hazel eyes that saw right through the whole filthy sham that was the Hampton High Class of 1986.

Greg breezed by the Welcoming Committee, opting to remain anonymous and name badge free. The muffled sound of Journey's "Separate Ways" served as a trail of breadcrumbs to the ballroom. The predictability was mind-boggling: the retro décor, the deejay egging guests onto an empty dance floor, and a roomful of bewildered faces, trying their damnedest to resurrect relationships built on lab partners and locker assignments.

Greg nestled into a corner of the room, beside a stanchion littered with rejected yearbook candids, and observed. He recognized plenty of his former classmates—some were merely meatier versions of their younger selves; others were replicates of the senior prom picture. Mostly, they were heavier, less gangly, stodgier. Whatever awkwardness accompanies the teenage years is at the least balanced by a hint of abandon, a willingness to look even a little foolish. You are, after all, a teenager, and with that comes a certain responsibility to behave like a loosed pup. No one here seemed to have that sense anymore. They were all tied to something, unwittingly anchored to their own lives.

Two women approached the beam Greg had chosen for his cloak, bobbing their heads about to view the old photos of Key Club car washes and swim meets. Greg recognized one girl—Jamie Penn. She was one of many girls he would've asked out at the time had he not felt like he belonged in the bell tower of Notre Dame. She had always been cordial to him, though in the same way a princess might be to a peasant who does his best not to offend with his wafting stench. She glanced his way and gave him a small smile; the same one, in fact, from school. But this time, he returned it with brazen certainty. She blushed, whispered to her friend, and they edged toward the line at the open bar. He could hear her friend's response as they shuffled away: "I don't know . . . maybe someone's husband?" How he loved his anonymity.

He kept patrolling the horizon for two faces in particular. He hoped that Elliot Gables, former halfback and "Mr. Hampton 1986," or Doug

Grimes, a bullish mutt as ugly as his name, had found time in their busy schedules to make an appearance. This unlikely duo—the beauty and the beast—were responsible for many of his pubescent woes. Elliot took glee in the verbal putdown, saving his most poisoned quips for large gatherings where he could do the most damage. Doug was the muscle of the pair, giving Greg everything from earlobe flicks to bruised ribs over the years. Even on graduation day, a day when all matters of teenage disparity are civilly buried, the twosome managed to swipe his shoes right off his feet, causing him to make his hallowed walk across the auditorium stage in his socks.

That was the day Greg decided he would die. He would shed his acne-scarred skin the minute he drove away from the grounds of Hampton High, and be born again. Upon accepting his diploma, he walked straight to his car, robed and sock footed, turned up "Thunder Road" on the tape deck, and drove away with the rest of the class still claiming their walking papers inside the gymnasium. With Hampton in his rearview mirror, and the chimes of freedom in his ears, college shone before him like a lighthouse cutting through rolling oceanic fog. It was a town full of losers, and he had to get out to win.

Two decades later, the man scanning the periphery of the Westin ballroom bore no likeness to the Greg Limpkin these people had known. He was everything he said he'd be that June afternoon and then some: an English professor on the tenure fast track, published author, marathon runner, and eligible bachelor. He coveted being the teacher that had female Chemistry majors signing on for Brit Lit just so they could stare at him twice a week. Mostly, he coveted feeling superior to everyone who brushed up against him this evening.

Greg felt eyes fix on him from time to time, and that fed his glee, almost as much as seeing his old classmates regrouping into their sophomoric cliques, a retreat to the awkward insecurities that initiated their bond years ago. When Greg's eyes caught those of an onlooker, he made a game of it—how long before they'd look away, shrinking into their own insecurities? Greg had out-gawked no fewer than a dozen of his former schoolmates when a spatter of applause caused him to turn toward the entryway.

There were Elliot Gables and Doug Grimes crossing the threshold together, bounding over it, really, with the kind of ebullience usually reserved for NBA All-Stars being introduced over loudspeaker. They mustered a few high-fives and bear hugs from those closest to the door, creating enough of a row to cause a gravitational pull from the rest of the room.

Time had been good to Elliot, and a real bastard to Doug. Where Elliot actually seemed better-looking than his senior picture—no small task—Doug had morphed into the ratty thug he must've dreamed of being in school. His suit, fresh from the discount Big and Tall store, pressed against his frame like cellophane over gelatin, and his face, once merely pug, was now flat and thick architecture.

Some six feet behind the returning heroes was a woman—date or spouse of one of them to be sure, thought Greg—doe eyes peering through strands of blonde locks. She seemed embarrassed, either by their loud antics or perhaps by the whole overwhelm. Her hand stretched out in the hope that it would be taken, but neither man obliged. She broke ranks with the twosome and cut over to the open bar.

Greg watched as she ordered a drink and sat at an eight-top next to Becky Wagner and Elise Nasam, who were both buried too deep in their chatter to notice the stranger in their midst. Greg also noticed it was Doug, not Elliot, who went in search of this wallflower. Finding her, he opted to bark rather than fetch. "Gloria! Get over here, will ya? What the hell?"

Doug and Gloria joined Elliot at a table near the deejay booth, where Elliot could periodically get on the mike and crack wise about whatever retro-hip tune was playing.

A small line of alums formed by the table, like a papal processional; Elliot entertained his long lost admirers, while Doug interjected the periodic punch line. Gloria stared a lot, at no one in particular.

Greg blanched at the way these people—grown-ups, all—sank back into the wake of Elliot's shallow charm and Doug's earthy presence. Most hated one or both of them when they were fifteen. Yet, they seemed eager to reattach themselves to Elliot and Doug's populist coattails and recount whatever blurred version of grandeur they perceived existed for themselves at sixteen. That "Glory Days" was blaring through the loudspeakers was not lost on Greg.

The balm of superiority was fading, and Greg felt the itch. It was an itch that started around his collar, causing him to twist his neck away from the suffocating top button of his Oxford. It was an itch that spread quickly to his eyes, causing them to lose their steeliness and retain their old flitter of paranoia, looking for the inevitable taunt around the next row of lockers. This time, though, instead of shrinking into a quivering heap, Greg curled his fists and walked forward, joining the line of hero-worshippers to greet his old nemeses. This wasn't what he had planned. He'd hoped to leave the room in anonymity within hour one, smugly satisfied with who he had become and, more so, who they'd become. But the sight of stunted evolution ate at something long dormant in him. The distance between himself and the boy who endured too many spitballs and bruises, underwear around his ankles in the locker room, had pulled itself inward until the two sides met. His crafting gave way to impulse, and he was now all of five feet from shaking the hand of the man who had magnified all his vulnerabilities.

Greg pushed through two men—he'd have recognized them if he'd taken the time, former footballers, he was sure—and stuck his hand out. "Elliot . . . how the hell are you, man? God, not a day goes by that I haven't thought of you." Things got quiet.

Elliot scanned for a nametag, and finding none, opted to blow off the stranger. "Hi. Good to see you." He tried to start his conversation up with his former teammates, but Greg kept standing there, grinning like he somehow completed the picture.

"Dude, do I . . . know you?" Elliot finally asked.

Greg ignored Elliot and turned his attention toward Doug. "Doug . . . you doing all right these days?"

Doug didn't like the vibe Greg was giving off. "Fine, man . . . can we help you? You part of the class reunion?"

" . . . and this must be—let me guess—your wife? Girlfriend?"

She started to answer, "Hi . . . I'm Glo . . ." Doug put his hand on hers, an attorney silencing his client.

"Gloria," said Greg. "I know. I heard Doug barking your name earlier. Very nice to meet you."

Doug's eyes shot to Elliot for guidance. Nothing had changed all that much in twenty years—Elliot still prompted Doug, still had to remove the leash. But Elliot shook his head, too mature now for games, and certainly too revered to let some rebel buck ruffle his tux cuffs. "So, you know all of us. Why don't you let us in on who you are?"

"I can do you one better, Gables. I can show you." Greg reached over to the deejay's rig, cluttered with Scotch taped photos from the Hampton *Sentinel*. He pulled off an old favorite from 1982, a school nurse comforting a fleshy boy as she tried to pull mouthfuls of bubble gum from his matted hair. The boy's anguish, even through ribbons of pink Bazooka and bulky lenses, was evident.

Doug grabbed the photo and held it for Elliot and Gloria to see. "Oh, shit . . . yeah! This kid was . . . what did we call him? Orca? Yeah . . ."

"You called me a lot of things, Doug. But Elliot was the master put-down artist: pantywaist, rump roast, limp-dick Limpkin, pockmark. You went home and came up with a new one each night, didn't you, Elliot?"

"Hey, man. That was a lifetime ago. We were kids." Elliot traced the rim of his cocktail glass with his finger, avoiding Greg's resolute gaze. But he couldn't keep from looking back up at him, not really convinced the man before him now could have possibly been sculpted from the waste and ruins that was Limp Dick Limpkin. "I don't even remember much of what we did to you. It was stupid. Let it go."

"You don't really give a shit about the damage you've done, do you?" asked Greg. "You either, Doug."

Doug started out of his chair, but Elliot's words stopped him cold. "Seems to me you should be thanking us." While Doug processed, Gloria gaped at Elliot's nerve. Though she didn't know Doug and his pal in their adolescent days, it wasn't a stretch to imagine them being absolute asses. "Looks like you got your shit together now, and if you show up here looking to take me on after twenty years, I guess you could say I was your, what's the word . . ."

Doug shrugged.

"Catalyst. That's what I'm trying to say. Me and Doug here, we made you."

Greg began to feel the crumble of the playground, the locker room, the hallways, the suffocating feeling of trying to claw out of a corner. Two decades had passed, he'd added "Doctor" in front of his name, and could bench-press his weight, but none of that cast off the stifling chokehold, the shortness of breath that came with a feeling he'd long forgotten.

Elliot smelled his trepidation and pounced as keenly as he ever had in his pre-prep days. "Just like those punks that go in the army and let some drill sergeant tear 'em down and rebuild 'em. Doug here was in the army, right, Doug?"

Doug was on board now. "Yeah. They suck every bit of humanity out of you, then they remake you in their image. You come out a different man than when you went in."

"Just imagine yourself—thirty seven years old, 300 pounds, bad skin, buckets of flop sweat. Still wishing you could kiss a girl, or even work up the nerve to talk to one." Elliot's persuasive tone was a familiar melody to his old classmates, many of whom had gathered around for what, so far, had been the night's only promise of a thrill. Their eyes slid with vicarious glee from Elliot to Greg and back again, taking in the work of a master demolitionist and his mighty wrecking ball, jettisoning toward a man whose foundation was now shifting.

Greg could produce nothing more than a syllabic stammer, rendered impotent by the hands of a ghost. Doug chuckled at Greg's livery lips, unmoved by the touch of Gloria's fingers, useless yielding digits. "That dick of yours still limp, huh, Limpkin?" The bodies leaned—some toward, some away—anticipating the once-familiar birth of a playground pummeling. This time, though, Limp Dick Limpkin could not cower. There was no shelter from the hailstorm that would follow him the next twenty years if he did. All impulse and muscle, Greg swept up a half-full bottle of Champagne and brought the heel of it down on Doug's scalp, sending blood and cheap hair plugs down his face. Before the glass shards could hit the floor, Doug was on top of Greg's chest, knocking him to the ground and bouncing his head between his fist and the floor with rhythmic precision. Elliot took his time pulling Doug off. By the time he did, Greg's nose was putty, his face a bloody roadmap. "Come on, Doug . . . he's had enough."

"He started it!" Doug stood up, boosting on Greg's heaving chest. A barely conscious Greg could only think how sophomoric Doug's protest was, how childish to point fingers in a fight between men. But as Doug walked away, and Elliot hovered like a specter, Greg panned the faces of those he once longed to call his friends. They smirked, some shook their heads, others lowered them to evade his eyes. He rested his head on the floor and started to fade into unconsciousness. How good, he thought, to see everyone again after so much time, so many changes.

6

SET THE TWILIGHT REELING

If I could just get my hands on five hundred dollars. Tonight. If I could just get my sax out of hock. If I could hold you one more time. If I could finish that line. That song. That thought that never made it out of my head and into your ear. If I could find the right drummer. If I could have pulled off what Oedipus did. If I could remove this guilt like a skin. If I could check in for 30 days and get clean. If I could get some junk in my veins right now. If you'd have listened. If I had found that hook when I needed it. If God was home and checking His mail. If grace had dominion and sway over these demons. If I could just get my hands on two hundred dollars. Tonight. If I could just find my Velvet Underground tape. If I had been clean when I met that agent in Soho. If I could forget your name, your face, your fingerprints. Your sex. If this crescendo would ever ritard. If there were a grace note. If I had been born somewhere east of here. A hundred years from now. Or fifty years ago. If I had been Bobby Kennedy. Or Malcolm X. Or even Bird. If I had been a gunslinger. If I could just get my hands on fifty bucks. Tonight.

I could take my words. Those notes. This moment. My battered faith. Your bruised heart. All the troubles of the world would rest just fine on my shoulders after I turn that corner. I can see that corner. This time, I can see it. You'd see, too. I'd make it all up to you. I'd gather up all the stars and the sun in my arms, and I'd set the twilight reeling.

7

CUTTHROAT ISLAND

I f you're wondering how I wound up here, all I can say is, I guess I'd had enough of Master Classes with runway models who wanted to find their inner-Thespis. That, and if I'd worked one more shift at the Sunglasses Hut kiosk, I was going to go on a rampage through the food court.

So, what the hell, it was an open call audition, and even though I'd rather have been reading for a day player spot on a soap, reality television is the wave. I finally succumbed to grabbing my board and riding it out 'til it foams on the shore.

The line ran all the way out the building. I saw my old roommate, some guy who does mime in the mall for tips, and a former child star—the now paunchy and sad Denny Trevino—up ahead of me. Behind me was a mass of bodies that made the trading floor of the Stock Exchange look like a ghost town. My chances were about one in six thousand, I thought. Of course, that's how every audition felt, and sometimes I was only reading against three other guys.

"We're looking for a Tony Robbins type," said the casting lady, a grotesque troll in full kabuki face, a fresh cig hovering between her lips. "You need to read the copy like you've just found the Fountain of Youth . . . but we need to *believe* you. Can you do that, shug?" It was the same old tripe: can you jump through a ring of fire with your feet on the ground? Can you sell me this oven cleaner and make me think its sexual aerosol? I was game.

What the copy had to do with reality television, I had no idea. Some babble about 'taking it to the next level' and 'right risk'. But I was golden; Zig Ziglar on amphetamines. Go figure, when I had my shot to read for a love scene with Jennifer Anniston, I shook like a wet dog. Now, I was cucumber cool. I was the iceman, and all for a one time stint on "Cutthroat Island".

So, two callbacks later, I found myself in a pool of about eight guys; my ex-roommate and Denny Trevino both now distant memories. The mime, God save us all, somehow made the cut. He could talk, of course, but every word was accompanied by a punctuated gesture, like he was translating his speech into sign language. In the end, they went with me. Christ, can you imagine losing a gig as a motivational speaker to a mime? I think I'd just perform self-immolation from the Hollywood sign.

Three thousand miles away, in Atlanta, Georgia, the dupes were being lined up for my arrival, my faux show. Here was the pitch: this company, Braxton Consolidated—a total fabrication, invented just for this show— was recruiting. Jobs in the South, apparently, are hard to come by these days, because 500 young suits and skirts showed up for this big job fair kind of thing. That's where I did my push. I was there to work them into frenzy about not only Braxton, but also Braxton's supposed philosophy of 'the biggest shark eats first'. I had to get them ready for the ride. I was Nietzsche with a wireless headset, infusing them with Darwinian dramatics and a fistful of pomp about walking through fire to forge oneself.

Those that made the cut, and signed an ironclad waiver boasting more fine print than a road atlas, would get a chance to move right into management. Of course, they were 'strongly encouraged' to take an Outward Bound style trip to test their moxie and capacity for teamwork under pressure. My job was to get them to sign on for that ticket.

The trip, in fact, was reality television's latest ruse—a show featuring a bunch of ambitious young executives put through their paces on some remote island while hidden cameras captured every fight, every disaster. It was "Survivor" meets "The Apprentice", with no one aware they were being filmed, including at the recruiting event, where I was making my debut.

Deceptive? Hell, yeah—but quite a good ploy of smoke and mirrors, given how desperate some reality shows had gotten. Sex and gratuity had replaced what little ingenuity the genre ever pretended to have. Luckily,

I'd parked my scruples at the California state line three years ago, so I was more than happy to sign my life away to this lark.

Look, I had to drop out of SAG last year—couldn't pay the dues, and wasn't making anywhere near the minimum for my insurance, and with no SAG card, auditions were rarer than snow in Mendicino. Besides, who needed real actors when people were tuning in to watch Joe Lunchbox eat pig ass and run Amazonian obstacle courses every week?

You learn to compromise a few principles to survive in this town. You also let go of the image that you'll be straddling Michelle Pfieffer in a sweaty love scene, a pulsating music bed riding beneath a well-choreographed tumble on silk and satin. That's some other guy, not you. You get to a point where you're praying you'll get a run selling long distance plans or playing Corpse Number Two on "CSI". One look at a guy like Danny Trevino, former child star, and you get the picture real quick. So, yeah, I was more than happy to lead this clueless brigade down to the corner of Delusion and Grandeur. I was getting paid to lie. No different than most of these schmucks in the trenches doing commission sales, lying to people about extended warranties and the durability of siding. We were all the same whore, just with different skirts, that's all.

The only hard part was always being 'on' around these people. I'm not effusive by nature; you probably figured that out already. They say scratch a cynic and you'll find an optimist fighting to come out. That's not me anymore, and the toughest acting job I've ever done—ever will do if I get out of here—has been behaving like Mr. Max Potential when my nature cries out for me to curl up with a copy of Rolling Stone, some Doritos, and The Clash turned up to eleven. I'm more apt to say "suck it up" than "live the dream", but here I was, and it was time for all those Meisner and Method classes to pay off; the classes, and about eighty motivational tapes the network couriered to my doorstep. Swear to God, I've never listened to so much talk about 'potential' in my life. My mom and dad, screaming in both ears over the course of my entire 'wasted' adolescence and subsequent theatre major at Northwestern, couldn't have kept up with these drones. My favorite was this guy—you've never heard of him, I promise you—who kept talking about "The Eternal Whisper". Apparently, we all are omniscient, but have let too much earthly noise block our synapses. For us to unlock the answers to our lives, we are supposed to sit in meditation every day for—get this—six hours. From what I've seen, most suits have to put taking a piss in their Palm Pilots. And I don't think many people are going to miss out on Must-See TV to sit in silent contemplation at home every night. God, I hope not, anyway.

Aaron Spelling is bound to have more answers than the schmuck on that tape.

So, they fly me into Atlanta, and the charade is already in high gear. These people have been at the Hilton all morning for this job fair, meeting the folks playing Braxton staff. Men, mostly, but women too, who know enough about the grinding of the machine to bullshit any wet-lobed kid still wondering whether to enter the sector or get his MBA.

And get this: I had bodyguards! Well, security, anyway—or handlers. Whatever you call them, they were flanking me, creating an air of importance about me as we strutted through the lobby. I was decked out in a suit I couldn't have afforded if I'd booked a whole season on "Law and Order". Headset microphone perched on my noggin, ear prompter in place, and an ominous black journal in my hand. Someone had transcribed my lines and bound them in this slick leather book—all typed up and everything.

Some actors might've looked around and realized that they were betraying their 'art', or that they were becoming a part of 'the system'. Me? I loved every frigging minute of it. In fact, I was ready to give these people every ounce of whatever talent I had. I knew in a month or so I could be back at the mall, hawking sunglasses to every Angelyne and Alan Smithee in the business. I was going to hang on this moonbeam for dear life, ride it with untainted bliss.

So, I get into the ballroom and there was no hesitation; the lights transitioned into a pulsating blur of blue and red, the sound guy hooked a battery pack up to my headset and clipped it on the back of my pants, some C&C Music Factory techno-funk started filling the room, and I was introduced by the "CEO" of Braxton. His name or pseudonym was Jed Rose. I was introduced by my real name. Who the hell knew who I was anyway? Peter Welbourne, "Success Coach".

The crowd roared—they must've been drinking some mighty strong Kool-Aid all morning, because they were ripe. Ripe. I thought, 'man, people must be hard-up for jobs, getting all worked up over a recruiting session.' I found out later that the incentives that had been presented to these people were huge—it was like a colossal pyramid scheme with a triple-woven safety net. Braxton, as it were, was promising monster commissions, bonus structures, and a benefit plan that would leave at least half of the Fortune 500 companies in the dust. They were putty by the time I got them.

And me? I was bulletproof. I fed off their energy like a remora, and gave it right back to them. I sweated and swayed like a giant in the sun, coaxing them to suck on the jugular, bleed out the nectar and devour the rind. They clapped, they cheered, they were a corporate mosh pit just waiting for me to stage dive into their churned up wake. It was nineteen minutes of messianic muscle, and I loved every shameful adrenal second of it.

They must've too, because getting offstage and out of the ballroom was like swimming upstream through melted chocolate—hands sticking to my sleeves, women pouring in my path. It was so vital.

The town car they had for me was waiting out front, and they got me out of the hotel in a hurry. There's a guy in the car, he's sitting in the front, offering me a cappuccino. I take it, and he slips me an envelope with the cup. "What's this?" I ask.

"Your check—you were phenomenal in there, kid."

"Man, it usually takes two months . . ."

"Yeah, well, this is different—we flew you to a right-to-work state, you're not union, we didn't go through your agent. You signed a contract. You did your job, so here's your check. What's wrong with that?" From the back seat, all I could see was his head, but I imagined that the rest of his body was spineless, with a writhing tail dangling over the floorboard. I thanked him and he turned around. Then, I pressed the window of the envelope and jiggled the check to see the amount. I was so used to having taxes and pension and shit taken out that I figured it was going to be simultaneously grand and disappointing. Without missing a beat, the man said, "Its all there—$8000. Not bad for nineteen minutes of work, huh?"

"No. Not at all."

"I'm going to talk to the producers about you, Peter," he said.

"OK . . . how come?"

"I'm starting to get a picture of how you might be a fit—maybe more than a day player. Would you like that?"

"Yeah. What have you got in mind?"

"Maybe take you to the island, let you lead some of the competitions. What do you think?"

I could only hope he wasn't bullshitting. "Well, I'd have to . . ."

"Think about it, naturally. And I have to take the idea back to the coast, but just don't go taking any on-camera work the next few days until I can get back to you." He said it like I was going to have to pick between a Coen Brothers script and a sit-com spin-off when I got back to my apartment.

When I got home the next morning, the first thing I did was flush all the Ramen noodles in the cabinet down the toilet. I just tore open every last one of those nasty packages and dumped the stringy little bricks down the shitter. I had eight grand in my back pocket, and I was damn sure going to raise my standard of living, even if only to a higher grade of pasta.

Don't get me wrong. I didn't go out and put a down payment on a Lamborghini or anything like that. The money wasn't burning a hole in my pocket. Hell, that was rent and groceries for a few months. But that first day back, I did live like a middle-class king: I took myself out to dinner, bought a bottle of wine and a fat twenty-dollar cigar. I figured I'd go home, lounge around in my robe, drink, smoke, maybe watch "The Sopranos". I always wanted to read for that show, ya know.

But, when I got home, I had a message on the service, a Mr. Tolan. Turns out he was the guy in the car with me back in Atlanta. Anyway, he said he wanted me to meet him and his 'associates' at their L.A. office the next morning at eleven. No need to call him back, he'd just see me then he said. It's amazing how presumptuous people in this town are, but then again when your presumptions are about a starving actor, I guess you can be assured they are usually right.

As for me, I was going to just enjoy my night. I had a guy who could make me rich wanting to have a sit-down in the morning. I was holding a glass of Chianti in one hand, and a smoldering Siglo Cohiba in the other. Meadow Soprano was in a state of near undress on HBO. God was in His heaven, and all was right with my tiny wedge of the West Coast.

When I woke up the next morning, the apartment smelled like a poorly maintained humidor. I turned on the exhaust fan in the bathroom, opened a window or two, and checked the time. 8:30. I needed to get in gear for my 11 o'clock. If all went as I hoped, I would also need to plan a stop by the Sunglasses Hut to turn in my notice to the owner. Hi and bye, Chris, you sucker. Hope you get melanoma.

So, I get to the meeting—it's Mr. Tolan, two guys who had to be brothers (or clones), and a little waif of a girl who couldn't have been more than twenty. One of the clones regurgitates Tolan's praise of my work. Then, he nods at the waif—Ally Mcbeal with a ponytail—and she slides a contract in front of me the size of the Torah.

"What's this?" Like I didn't know.

"Season-long contract for the show, you'd shoot thirteen episodes on the island, working with our team to keep the contestants in the dark and on edge."

"On edge?"

Clone number two spoke. "We have every intention of scaring the bejeezus out of them."

"Can't these people sue you for tricking them like this?"

"Legal has that all taken care of. They are signing releases that list us—in very guarded terms—as 'partners' of Braxton Consolidated . . ."

"Which doesn't exist," I said.

"On paper it does. We got our incorporation papers last month. It's a shell company, but we plan to generate a meager profit. Enough to keep our noses clean," said Clone One.

Clone Two leaned in. " . . . and if they do try to sue, it's just free advertising for us."

Clone One put the button on it. "And who doesn't want to be on television these days?"

Ain't that the truth, I thought. And here I was proving it. "Can I take the contract home, read it through?"

Mr. Tolan weighed in. "Sure. Show it to your lawyer. Take it to your agent. We're offering you a full season on a network show; you should check it out, naturally. But we need the contract signed and back on this desk by the end of the week." Lawyers and agents—two groups I didn't want pawing at my money belt. Besides, my agent would be pissed that I took this gig behind her back. And lawyers? Don't get me started.

All I wanted to do was get out of their office, get home, count the zeros on the payment line, and Hancock the sig page. We all shook hands and I assured them they'd have an answer in the next day or so.

I made it to the elevator, that's as far as I got before I decided I had to see what the payout on this deal was. The figure—page six, highlighted in pink—read $650,000; that was fifty g's per episode. The disclosure clause, the liability section, the thinly veiled legal threats woven in the rest of the document seemed so trite compared to those six numbers. They already had my answer but I'm sure they knew that. I guess I should be ashamed that I can be bought, but couldn't you be? Believe me, if I had known then what I know now, I would've shredded the whole thing up right in front of them, and then pissed on their rug on the way out of the lobby. Anyway, I took the contract home, where it sat on my kitchen table for the rest of the day. I thumbed through it that night, and there was so much mumbo jumbo, I would've needed an Attorney-to-English dictionary to wade through it all. If I had taken it to an entertainment lawyer, he would've scalped me for 20%, taken a week to get back to me, and probably gotten me into a stink with the network. I know, "my best interests". Whatever.

So, there I was the next morning, bright and early, contract under my arm at the network offices. Mr. Tolan just smiled. One of the clones took the contract from me and sifted through it to make sure I'd signed, dated, and initialed every last "here and here".

"Any questions?" asked Tolan as he shook my hand.

"Yeah . . . two, actually. Where is the island, and when do we leave?"

"We've got a location scout narrowing down our island choices, but it will be somewhere exotic, I assure you. You'll love it. And you leave after we get through some rehearsals on the lot—Studio F. You start next Monday."

"Rehearsing what exactly?"

The clone stepped in, "More motivational techniques, challenge guidelines, fire walking . . ."

"Fire walking?" I wondered if SAG covered reconstructive podiatric surgery.

"It's one of the first challenges, and it's really very safe. Once you know the trick, you'll be fine."

"See you back here Monday, 9 a.m.—just show your credentials to security to get on the lot," said the clone, handing me a package with the network logo beaming from the front sticker.

"OK, then." What could I say—I'd bought the ticket, it was time to take the ride.

The next few days were spent in a transcendent fog. Nothing seemed quite real. I decided two weeks notice for a sunglasses kiosk in the mall, when I had eight grand to live on until the half-a-mil started rolling in, was too generous for this town. I just clocked out on my next shift and told Chris that I wouldn't be back. His indifference only solidified my attitude. Good to know how invaluable I was to him.

I spent some of my time shopping, and it was really weird, because it was the first time—the first time since I used to get an allowance anyway—that I didn't put value on what I purchased. I wanted it, I bought it: an I-Pod, new duds, a new burner for the computer, DVDs—it was Christmas and I was Little Saint Nick's anointed one.

Once I got home with the DVDs, I just holed myself up in the apartment for most of the weekend, watching "Goodfellas", "Taxi Driver", "Unforgiven"—all my favorites. I ordered pizza and gave the delivery guy a five spot for a twelve-dollar pie. I drank a lot of beer. Too much, probably, but I knew that this was my last weekend of revelry before I became Mr. Enthusiasm on a pretty much full time basis.

I probably should've been reviewing more motivation tapes, searched the Internet for some kind of something to bring to the party—or at the very least been building up the calluses on my feet. But I figured I'd be earning my money soon enough. Besides, how often do you get to bask, I mean really bask, in the glory of the future? Hell, if you're an actor, how often do you even know what you'll be doing in three months?

Whatever solace I gained from my lost weekend, my nose was slammed onto the grindstone pretty hard on Monday. The network brought in consultants—coaches, really—to work with me on my presentation, performance, the whole caboodle. It was grueling—hear it, learn it, do it, read it, learn it, do it. Start with words on a page, and spin them into gold within minutes; exhausting, especially when the whole 'hail fellow, well met' energy is not my inclination. Trying to suppress an adulthood defined by pragmatism in a dog-kill-dog town, while simultaneously trying to tap into my inner-nurturer took massive redirection on my behalf. By Thursday, I had blended the best of EST with Eckhard Tolle, Dr. Phil, Dr. Laura, and about six other PhDs. The Power of Now, self-refuge, suck-it-up, your higher power, the edge, six strategies to blah-blah-blah. I was a walking talking bullshit machine, regurgitating parables and pieties with televangelical precision.

Friday was the shit, though. Friday was the day I had to overcome fears I never thought I'd face. The fire walking, I knew that was coming. Some little yoga guru came in and within thirty minutes she had me traipsing across a heated practice grid in the studio that was, as she said, 'almost as hot' as the coals would be. The trick, in case you ever get the urge to wander barefoot across a bed of 700 degree coals, is to keep moving, as the pain doesn't have time to register if you move across the bed at the right pace. You're feet might look like a couple of cindered garden gloves when you get done, and you'll want to cool them as fast as you can, but it's not mysticism, it's just science.

But crispy soles were the least of my worries. It was the snake man who almost sent me running for the door. I hate—freaking hate—snakes. So, the prospect of holding the head of one, while his scaly body wrapped around my body like a leather vise, made me piss and tremble. "He won't hurt you. He's harmless," said the trainer. He was talking down to me, acting like I was being childish, like he was trying to hand me a gerbil.

I tried to picture six-figures and a new place in Laguna Beach, bikini-clad groupies lining up to join me on the island, anything to make touching this spineless reptile worthwhile. Then my eyes locked with Mr. Tolan who had crept in the back of the room. Suddenly, the snake seemed like the second greatest threat in the room. I held its neck and let the handler wrap her around my shoulders. She lay there heavy on me and I just kept staring at her skin, a green and yellow maze of authority. The handler took her off me, grabbed her neck, and told me that I'd done well. He disappeared with the snake, and came back in the studio with a small glass terrarium holding a pair of tarantulas. Non-venomous, he assured me. This creepy crawler test of will continued until lunch with me enduring the threat of fangs and stingers from every phobia-inducing arthropod and reptile known to man, or at least the L.A. Zoo.

By the time the caterers were setting up the pasta salad and grilled chicken ricotta, I had lost five pounds in sweat. But something strange had happened too. The more I faced these little beasts—staring down spiders and letting a scorpion traipse across my shoes—the more I began to feel, well, not invincible, but certainly heroic. I'd never so much as taken on the school bully as a kid, and I was never one to go down to the creek to look for night crawlers and lizards, so maybe I finally put to bed some of that stigma I had as a boy about being a tenderfoot, about being in drama club and band camp when the popular kids were hitting free throws and bludgeoning tackling dummies. Whatever it was it left me famished. I ate like a true starving actor: two platefuls of catered goodness, washed down with what must've been a pitcher of pink lemonade.

After lunch and my little "Wild Kingdom" detour, I was asked to perform my "welcome to the island" speech one more time. I nailed it, and they sent me home early. Man, when I walked off of that lot, I felt immortal. Bulletproof. I had faced death twelve ways to Sunday, wowed the suits, and convinced myself I was a decent actor, all in one day. It was the first time, since I moved to California anyway, that I really felt right in my own skin. For three years, I'd been telling myself I belonged here, that it was a fit, but I knew I was a liar until that moment. Only then could I exorcise all that doubt, all the guilt that came with sending my parents postcards from the Sunglasses Hut asking for a little cash or lying about how many auditions I'd had that week. "Ooh, I met Debbie Reynolds, Mom" or "My agent wants me to read for the part of Gene Hackman's son!" Lame . . . very lame—but no more.

When I got home, I had a message. It was one of the clones. The first one, I think. He said, "Nice work today, Peter. We're in good shape for Monday. A car will pick you up then at 7am and drop you off at the international terminal at LAX. Someone will meet you there. You can pack one bag, but be sure to leave your script and any other network material at home. We don't want to let the cat out of the bag. See you then."

I think he enjoyed being portentous. He spoke in cloaked terms, like he was somehow superior to the rest of the Coast, and thereby easily over the rest of the U.S., which is viewed with a conceited empathy by most who sit over two-tops in Los Angeles bistros. But now, their arrogance was o.k., because he'd let me in. And the first rule of Fight Club is, you don't talk about Fight Club. So I was willing to play along.

I spent the weekend doing all those things you do when you're about to take a trip: dry cleaning, bills, emptying the fridge of any potential stink bombs, burning songs onto my Ipod: everyone from Dave Matthews and Miles Davis to Creedence and Johnny Cash, in case you're wondering. I like having a little bit of everything available for my many colored moods. Everything except hip-hop; I can't stand that shit.

I called my folks. It was the first time I hadn't called collect in almost a year, and they were floored. They were headed out the door to Red Lobster with the neighbors when I called, so we barely got to speak, but I did tell them I had landed the mother of all acting jobs, and that they could stop sending me money right away. Mom sounded a little incredulous, like I had actually just bagged a cable access infomercial. "As long as you're happy," she said. She always said that, like if I were to call her from a crack house some night, with a rock in one hand and a call girl's ass in the other, she'd still say it. She's so automatic.

So, they went off for their calabash shrimp buffet and I told them I'd call them when I got back. As I put the phone on the cradle I realized I'd never asked when I was getting back. How many days were they shooting? Did I need to go ahead and cover next month's rent too? Shit. And it was the weekend—I didn't know how to reach Tolan or his clones. They'd never given me cell numbers which is really weird for this town. Your cell number is your main contact, office is second. But these guys were playing the whole clandestine routine to the hilt. I thought it was funny, really. And so what if I was gone a couple weeks or more? I was coming back rich enough to get out of any bind a barely furnished apartment could cause.

So, a limo—yeah, you heard me, a limo—pulled in to pick me up Monday morning. It was so righteous. Mrs. Glendale, who lives in 8A, just about dropped her Bloody Mary when I strolled by and hopped in the back of that long black ride. I blew her a kiss as I got in. Inside the limo, I fiddled with the radio, found Ryan Adams and cranked it. I played with the sunroof and highball glasses, and called the driver "Chuck" (his license on the dash said "Charles"). I was a sophomoric asshole to be sure, but how often do you get chauffeured on someone else's dime?

At the airport, I was greeted by a woman, which surprised me. Not that I'm a chauvinist or anything, but I just figured I had been dealing with men all along, except for the skirt in the network office who barely said 'boo', so it took me back. She was the talent wrangler, and a production assistant on the job. Kelly Reuben was her name, cute enough in her little khaki shorts and ankle high hiking boots, and smart as hell. You could tell that right off.

She talked like someone who had been in the business for a lifetime, though I don't think she could've been thirty yet. She reeked of street smarts, the kind of person you'd want with you when things go south.

She helped me get through security, the whole passport ordeal, and to the gate. It was only when we got our boarding passes that I found out where we were going. "Where the heck is Seychelles?" I asked, likely mispronouncing the hell out of it.

"It's an archipelago off the coast of Kenya. Over 100 islands, only about half of them inhabited," she said with the steady objectivity of a National Geographic documentary.

"And we're headed to one of the uninhabited ones, right?"

"You got it," she said. "Let's find our gate."

She must've known I had a million questions, from 'are there really snakes?' to 'is there a pool?', but she was too about the business at hand for me to feel comfortable asking. Besides, we had a daylong flight ahead of us, so I could hit her with my slate of queries once the beverage carts starting hitting the aisles.

We actually chatted very little on the flight over, though. She pulled out her cell phone and laptop, oblivious to the rote 'electronic devices' warning they give at takeoff, and began typing away on shooting schedules, approved revisions, and other logistical stuff. Every passing statement I made seemed interruptive, so after a while, I just shut my mouth and settled in to watch the in-flight movie, Nicholson and Adam Sandler in "Anger Management": funny, but not that funny, especially in the claustrophobic trappings of a long international flight.

I picked up the in-flight magazine, thumbed through it. I wasn't much of a news hound so I was blissfully unaware—until we were airborne—that Kenya had been on a flight restriction for the U.S. for most of the previous year, with all the terrorism and shit that had gone down over the last couple of years. "Great," I thought. "We're just off the coast of a Hamas theme park."

I slept, but not well; I ate, but not with much enthusiasm, airline food being what it is. By the time we were descending, my head was a throbbing ache, my shoulders two hunched tombstones, burying my neck in a pinched hole. Kelly was shoving her laptop and spare battery back in the storage bag. I asked her what was next. "We catch a connecting flight to the islands, then a boat to Cutthroat. Then, you get some rest," she said.

"So, I never got a script for the island stuff. Is that cool?"

"You'll get notes onsite, but you'll have to be sequestered while you review them. Hope you're as quick a study as they said you are." She was so businesslike, but with a real approachability, like every statement was accompanied by an unseen wink or half-smile. She also seemed to lack the façade most of the other players in L.A. had affixed over their hearts. It was refreshing, seeing authenticity make it through the mire of backstabbers.

Of course, what the hell did I know about her yet? Maybe she was a failed actress, and just fell into this production thing—maybe all her bitterness and pretense just fell away the day she traded in her drama mask for a clipboard. I don't know about people anymore, except that I prefer seeing most of them in my rear view mirror. I guess you could say my misanthropy outweighs my self-loathing just enough to allow me to be my own best friend, for lack of a better choice. How sad is that? I wonder if I would feel that way if I were doing summer stock in Kansas. Oh well. Neither here nor there, because there I was, about to touch down on a landing strip in East Africa, getting ready to portray the kind of con-artist every actor dreams of playing. Come on, think about it. Actors—at least most male actors—live for this kind of shyster role. From Ratso Rizzo to Kaiser Sose, we all wanna be the mythic enigma, the one with something going on behind his eyes. That's how I told myself I had to look at it, maybe so I could forget I was actually a shell-game huckster on a yet-to-be-optioned reality program.

Ninety minutes later, a puddle jumper skidded to a stop on the shore of one of the islands. We hopped a small boat and skated through the archipelagos, past islands of stilled beauty. Finally, two islands converged to form an oceanic ravine, which our boat clipped through, leading us to a piece of land that loomed with desolation. Unlike the rest of the islands we'd passed since Madagascar, all brimming with an aura of vitality, this one seemed foreboding, the kind of place that might get tagged with a name like "Devil's Lair". Perfect, I thought, schooner them through paradise and dock in purgatory—only on television.

When we went ashore, Kelly led me to the center of the island. A full crew was racing around under Klieg lights, rigging minuscule cameras in trees, patching microphones the size of dust mites to rocks. The island, it seemed, had been converted to one big CIA surveillance site. You could almost feel the satellite hovering overhead.

"How the hell you gonna pull this off?" I asked Kelly. "I mean, can you really use . . ."

A voice cut me off. "They'll believe what they want to believe. Most likely, they're fish who can't see the hooks for the bait. Dag Esbjorn, producer. You must be Peter."

Dag Esbjorn? This guy had to be kidding. He looked like Aryan dream spawn—blonde, blue-eyes set deep in a pale Swedish face, chiseled features. And that accent, Sweet Jesus, it was so thick you could pour it over pancakes.

"Hi Dag. Good to be working with you." What else was I going to say?

"Yup. Now, go get some rest, we'll stir you when we're ready for you." I started to ask him about the schedule, but Dag had already turned away from me and began barking orders at some of the crew. Kelly took me by the elbow and said, "Any questions, just come to me. Dag isn't someone to bother. He's . . . not a people person." I was thrilled to hear my superior on this desolate rock was a misanthrope.

Kelly led me through a thicket of trees to a clearing. My little bamboo hut shone like one of those houses in the woods in a Grimm's' tale—a beacon amid the big, scary forest. My bed was a makeshift cot, my nightstand a cut of plywood cradled on a mound of dirt. I guess they couldn't snazzy up the place too much, in case a Braxton wannabe walked in for some reason. If I was living large, they'd question my intent. Castaway vibe and all though, it was still better than my first apartment in Los Angeles.

I expected to pass out the minute my head hit the low-budget pillow, but once I settled in, I started hearing all those sounds one associates with Africa: the bugs, the beasts, the howling primate in search of a late night hump. That, coupled with the sound of the film crew chatting over walkie-talkies, was just too much. I finally had a chance to think about where I was, and it started to gnaw at me. I must've laid there an hour or more before exhaustion finally conquered anxiety, and I faded off to the sound of a primate gangbang in the trees overhead.

The next morning I awoke to a gentle tickle on my thigh. In my groggy state, I thought of a girlfriend from a year or so ago who used to wake me up with the lightest scampering of fingers on my skin. I may have even said her name as I brushed at what I believed to be her hand. Instead, the dancing on my leg transferred itself to the back of my hand and I realized I was getting my first Seychellois wake-up call from a hair-laden spider the size of my fist. It resembled a McDonald's hamburger patty with legs—flat, brown, and meaty. I flung it across the hut with a panicked backhand before it could get its teeth in me, thank God. I kept a steady eye on it while I looked for something to kill it with. Had there been a newspaper to roll up, it wouldn't have done the job. Not unless it was the Sunday Times, dropped from a helicopter. No, this bitch required a spear, or the business end of a snow boot, neither of which was handy. I finally found an extra tiki torch in the corner of the hut, and drove its stake through the center of the spider causing, I swear, an audible screech from the damn thing.

I got my boots on quickly, after checking the insides of them, of course. This was no place to wander barefoot, I had surmised. Then, I stepped out to see what the crew had constructed while I slept and, more importantly, when the catering team would have some breakfast ready.

I opened the door to the hut, and found myself staring out over a vast coppice of hibiscus and fruit trees towering over the clearing. A pair of lizards scampered across my line of vision, giving each other playful chase. I followed the closest thing to a path I could find in search of civilization and, hopefully, eggs. I had a set of 3x5 cards that Kelly had given me to review one last time with her before the 'fish' arrived. I also brought a book with me. Figured I'd have plenty of downtime to read during this adventure—so I brought Huxley's "Brave New World", the only book I read all the way through in high school.

There's a reassuring silence to the jungle in the early morning, as if all the serpents and carnivores have settled in to nap through sunrise. It's only when you listen too closely to the lack of noise that it becomes disquieting, and as I walked I began to feel that sense of unrest. The more I wandered the more I realized I should've waited at my hut for Kelly to retrieve me. It was as I was turning to retrace my steps back to the hut that I finally smelled something cooking. It was strong, like the waft of meat from a grill. That was all I needed to pull me through the maze. The thought of bacon alongside the eggs I'd been pining for would've carried me past Godzilla himself should he appear. I plodded through the trees, navigating by nose, until I reached the edge of the palms and looked out over an abandoned bonfire. The crew's belongings were scattered around the perimeter of a keenly organized collection of timber. As I got closer, the smell that had once seemed so delectable began to burn my eyes. I peered into the maze of crackling branches and trunks and saw something long and sinewy. A bird? A fish, perhaps. Then, leaning in, I saw the extremities—the burnt toes, the roasting calve. It was a human leg, from the knee down, left to burn off like autumn leaves in someone's backyard. *My God, what have I gotten into?*

I looked behind me quickly, expecting a cannibal, a boogeyman who would push me onto the pyre and start flipping me with a palm frond spatula. But there was no one there. There was no one anywhere. The clues were sparse and ominous—abandoned equipment, a hat here, a pair of shoes there. Notebooks and a shooting script scattered along the sand. A part of me wanted to flee back to my hut but fear kept me shackled to the shore. Whoever had made off with the crew was now gone and this spot, despite the portentous hints of danger, felt safer than any unexplored tract on the island. After all, 'the fish' were coming today. A boat had to show up soon, full of Braxton wannabes, and I'd simply hop on board, call the Coast Guard, the Seychelles Police Department, whoever it is you call when Americans go missing, and go home. I wasn't about to play Robinson Crusoe and start looking for folks on my own. My life, I thought, was surely worth more than what was left of theirs. Besides, how exactly would I save captives from a band of guerillas or cannibals? Nope, the paralyzing fears I felt down inside was plenty to keep me company.

I settled on the sand, my back to the embers and flesh, and watched the horizon for some hope. None came all morning. I tried to keep the visuals at bay, the ones of Dag being roasted over a spit, or Kelly—sweet Kelly—fighting off the advances of some savage tribal king. I sifted through the belongings strewn about me, and came across enough sustenance to pass for breakfast: two Powerbars, a Thermos of water, and a Ziploc baggie of dry roasted peanuts. It wasn't a three-egg omelet, but then it wasn't a cameraman's fried foot either.

I gathered up the papers peppering the shoreline and scoured through them. They were mostly production notes—a loose shooting schedule, notes about food prep, and bios on each of the Braxtonians who were to arrive that day. Paper-clipped to a manila folder was a waiver, signed by Dag and the Seychelles authorities, basically absolving the governing body from any injuries or deaths that might occur during the filming of "Cutthroat Island". The list of lethal high-risks read like a who's who of explorer phobias: snake bites, shark attacks, piranha schools, primates, arachnids, reptiles, elephants, lions, cheetahs, wildebeests, rhino, buffalo, hartebeest, hippo, crocodiles, vultures, hostile natives, terrorist groups, guerilla factions, typhoons, riptides, black widows, leeches, blister beetles, tsetse flies, sleeping sickness, ticks, tarantulas, wild dogs, wild cats, wild egrets, improperly ingested fugu, poisonous plants, leaves, and herbs, food poisoning, anti-venom reaction, jellyfish, and pinching crabs. It was an all-inclusive protectionist's guarantee that would make a Hollywood lawyer proud. To sign this was to insure one was on his own. I'm sure the fine print of my contract had something equally binding in it. Damn, I wish I'd called an attorney. I was on the shore without a paddle, and after hours of thumbing through belongings, nibbling on peanuts, and siphoning the last drops of water out of the Thermos, I was getting edgier than Pacino in "Dog Day Afternoon". I sifted through the papers again and reviewed the shoot schedule for the day. It listed the 'participants' arrival at 8:30 a.m. My watch read 10:22. This wasn't good.

By noon, the sun was a fat blister in the sky; a red, puffy sore taunting me and draining me of my energy. I had to get out of the heat and into the cool refine of the trees. It was midday now, and surely once these castaways pulled ashore, I would hear them. They would scour the island for the crew, and I would come running to greet them. After all, I wasn't going far, just enough offshore to sit in the shade. I certainly wasn't going to sleep. I walked down the beachfront for a mile or so and spotted a pair of trees—one harbored coconuts, the other some sort of exotic fruit, a thin spongy date-like orb. The coconuts were a bitch to open. I had to hurl them, Randy Schilling style, against tree trunks until they busted open and then race to get the milk before it all spilled out. I'm sure there was a better way, but I remembered little from "Castaway", except for that damned volleyball. That and "Gilligan's Island" reruns were the sum total of my island survival knowledge.

The milk was sweet and surprisingly cool. The dates weren't dates after all, or if they were, they were a damn sight less sweet than the dates I remembered as a kid. Whatever. The mere thought of being without food—my Powerbars and peanuts now depleted—was all too consuming, and I planned to feast off of these two trees until they were bare, just in case the boat didn't show today.

The boat, in fact, did not show. Fuckers. I spent the afternoon and evening hovering between the shore and the grove of trees off the coast, sweat running off my skin hot and cold. As the sun sank into the sea, I knew I had to make my way back to my hut. It was a sheltered haven, and even if I didn't sleep a wink, I'd be safer under a roof than out in the open. Better the spider you know. I found the hut again, with some difficulty, as night fell quickly upon these cursed little islets. I did find one of those long barreled grill lighters in my hut which allowed me to light one of the tiki torches. Only one, I thought, as too much of a glow might attract those ignoble flesh eaters that had a crew luau on the beach last night. The flicker of the light was enough to keep an eye on my immediate surroundings, and I laid there surveying the earth, the walls, the space under the doorway for hours, nodding off only a couple of times. This night, the slightest scuffle of underbrush could not be rationalized away, and the monkeys' screams sounded eerily human. I was a paralyzed child, clutching my Huxley paperback like it was a teddy bear.

I welcomed the morning. The silence crept over the land, and I found an hour or two of semi-conscious sleep in the earliest hours of dawn. I awoke when I heard the sound of shuffling through the brush outside my door. Be they legs with four feet or two, I couldn't say, but the hope that salvation might be scampering by was enough to light me from my cot. I peered through the slats of bamboo, but saw no one, and the footsteps, retreating from the beach and heading deep into the trees, were now faint. I stepped out to see who or what had crossed my path, and saw nothing but a swarm of bugs hovering around a patch of greenery. If this was an ally, one of the fish from Braxton Consolidated, they were running away from the shoreline, and that meant the rest of their crew would be waiting there for their search party to return.

Boots still on from my quasi-sleep, I high-stepped it through the trees toward the beachhead. I jumped over earthbound vines, wove through branches like a running back finding his way through the defensive line. The closer I got, the more certain I was that there was a boat full of hapless job candidates sifting the sand for the whereabouts of Peter Wellbourne, faux motivational speaker and life coach extraordinaire. I would be more than happy to break my contract, rebuke my oath of chicanery, and come clean with these good folks once they pulled me aboard their vessel. I'd take the lawsuit from the network, sure. After all, extenuating circumstances, right? One crew member cooked, the rest escaped or abducted on this Godforsaken soil. I'd take my chances in civil court, believe me.

I sprinted over the rise and began my descent down the sandy hill to the shore, and looked to where the tide meets the land. What I saw next shook my foundation. Floating out into the deep was a small bamboo raft, big enough to harbor perhaps one man. Instead, there were three lifeless bodies on it. The tuft of blonde hair hanging over the edge of the raft's starboard side was Dag's, no doubt. The other two were likely film crew members. I called out to them, hoping against hope that they were all taking a short siesta or the morning sun had merely sapped them of their strength. But as the water splashed against my ankles, I could see patches of red adorning their skin, like huge chunks of flesh had been removed from their stomachs and limbs. The red trickled into the blue water, giving off a purplish hue. I couldn't imagine going into the water to retrieve them, but that's what I felt my body doing. All those hours on the soundstage in L.A. handling snakes and tarantulas must've instilled some untapped heroism that was longing to emerge. Either that or I just had nothing much to lose, like the audition you know you aren't right for.

I waded out hip deep, and was perhaps fifty feet away from the drifting raft when my peripheral vision caught the emergence of a great force. It moved with the violence and grace of the sea itself. A dorsal emerged, racing not twenty feet in front of me, and on past to the floating buffet that dripped liquid chum into the creature's wake. The shark—a sleek, massive blur of blue and white—rammed the raft, taking half of it and one of the corpses down with it. Dag and the other crewman rolled off like butter sliding off a pancake, sinking into the sea where they would undoubtedly be finished off before they could hit bottom.

I ran to the shore, gasping and wheezing like some asthmatic infant. Sitting in the sand, I sobbed for what felt like hours, curled up on the beach. I reveled in self-pity, truly earned for perhaps the first time in my life, as I realized there was little hope, the water and land both home to killers. The ones in the ocean I knew. National Geographic had shown me all too well what sharks do, and how undeterred they are in their pursuit of a meal. As for whoever shared this tract of land with me, all I knew was what I'd seen: the remnants of a cannibal's cookout, and the disemboweled crew sacrificed and cast out to the gods of the deep. It was only a matter of time, I thought, and I wondered if there was a way I could end it all painlessly, hang myself from a coconut tree, or find some poison plant to ingest with my coconut milk. The thought, the merest figment, of being terrorized by a tribe of natives, or lying paralyzed in my bunk as the venom of a cobra ran its course through my nervous system was too much to bear. If I believed in a benevolent God, I would've prayed for a quick miracle or a quicker death. There are times when agnosticism has its liabilities.

I was exhausted, hungry, and feeling a touch of vertigo. Given my acquiescence to fate, walking back to my hut in the middle of this death camp was nothing to me. There was a bit of food, and a place to lay down without the stench of blood coming off the surf. Maybe the walk, the feeble attempt to rest, would do me some good and shift my mindset from fatalist to survivalist. I'd read some Huxley, I thought, and take solace in a vision more bleak than the one before me.

A spider—another hairy burger—crossed my path. I stomped it with a certain aplomb that comes with adrenaline and hopelessness. It didn't scream, but I felt its syrupy ooze splash on my leg, and breaking the karmic camel's back, I threw up. Every bit of coconut milk and island fruit came pouring out of me like a sieve. I was disgusted with myself, losing what little nourishment this hell tank had seen fit to serve me, and all to appease one of my mindless little tantrums. It was this kind of shit that use to cost me jobs—walking out on callbacks that ran too long, whining about stilted dialogue with the writer in the room. But those were jobs, bit parts in indies that never saw the light of distribution. This, this was life, and I realized as I watched that spider's very soul running down my shin that I'd better get my shit together. It's impulsiveness that does us in. Like I learned on one of those damn motivational tapes, if you focus on the telephone pole, that's what you'll crash into, even if it's the only goddamned thing on the stretch of road.

I found a thick green leaf and scooped the spidery remains from my leg. I had no sooner disposed of the slimy foliage than I heard a scream, high pitched and primal. My first thought was that it was another monkey on the prowl for a mate, but as it echoed out, bouncing through the tundra, all I could hear was the cry of a woman. I thought of Kelly; sweet Kelly who bid me adieu the night we arrived and had yet to resurface. I thought about the myth of rescue. It only happens in the movies. And then I thought how good it would feel to have an ally—someone to work with to find food, to devise a plan, build a boat. Someone to hold onto when I got scared shitless, which presumably was going to be a fairly ongoing condition. Someone, let's be honest here, to have sex with, a mutual attempt to be somewhere other than here, if only for 15 minutes a day. The scream echoed again and I followed it through uncharted undergrowth and the thicket of trees. I followed it until the screams no longer echoed. I was hearing them in real time now, and through a web of branches, I could see a clearing; an open tract where a group—no, a tribe—of men and women stood. They were all but naked, their privates covered only with vines and leaves. Their skin was a golden color. They were huddled around what appeared to be an altar of some sort. I could just make out the shape of a raised plank, and the tops of two wooden poles which must've been connected to the altar. There was another scream, and they stepped back, laughing. It was then I saw that this altar was actually a restraining device, which held Kelly, her head dangling like a wet mop. The scene was archaic, right out of a Tarzan flick, but there it was . . . a bound damsel, a clan of tribal sadists, and the lone adventurer, in over his head, and stupid enough to stay for the fight.

But there was to be no fight. I was tip-toeing through the jungle in size 11D boots. I was about as dexterous and sly as a crippled bison. I didn't exactly have home field advantage. So, the sting that I felt in the back of my neck was really no surprise; nor was losing consciousness as I peered up at the painted faces of my soon-to-be captors. I just remember thinking I hope this isn't the big sleep. For all my pessimism, I still wanted to live . . . or so I thought as the world grew small and black.

It was the best sleep I'd had on the island, but the wake-up call was a bitch. Things were fuzzy at first, like a whiskey hangover. My eyes began to find focus and I could tell that I was floating on a tiny bamboo raft, lashed to a second raft. My hands were tied behind me, a slimy knot of jungle vines. Sitting on the adjoining raft was one of the tribesmen, who gave me a huge grin when I came to. He waved a long knife in front of me, as if to say he'd just as soon cut my raft loose from his as he would sheath the blade. I flinched, until I realized he was guiding my view to the other end of his raft. There was Kelly, hands and feet tied, unconscious. The slightest sudden move from her and she'd drop into the ocean. There we were, the three of us, bobbing in the African abyss. I knew begging was futile. All I could think of was "The Deer Hunter" and how the Vietcong reveled in watching DeNiro and his comrades bob up and down in those swamp-set tiger cages, gasping for air over the filthy water. This guy would get off on watching me squirm, and I didn't want to die like that. I'm a coward, but I'm not a pussy. A pussy would plead for mercy. Not me. I might change my mind if I saw a dorsal fin, or if Kelly teetered over into the water, but for now, I was relying on pure stubborn stamina.

I took my time working against the vines. A slight wriggle here, a calculated tug there, until I finally got my hands free. I guess I must've learned something in acting school, because I just continued showing my poker face. Hannibal Lechter paid me no never mind. Now, I just had to look for an opportunity, one that I thought would be more capitol if Kelly were conscious.

It must've been fifteen minutes or more before she started to stir. Her eyes met mine and I saw sheer terror. Whatever dark shit she had been through on the island must not have prepared her for this, because I thought she was going to bust into tears right then and there. I gave her a slight, firm headshake, as if to say, 'hush . . . trust me'. That did it. She began to sob and heave so frantically that the tribesman, suspect of sedition, reached over to the rope tying their raft to mine and began to cut. He was emotionless, like he was coring an apple. He looked up at me, a smirking villain right out of "Raiders of the Lost Ark". This was my chance, I thought. I dove underwater. I came up on the opposite side of his raft, wrapped an arm around Kelly, and rocked the makeshift boat enough to send him overboard. He splashed and flailed as I climbed onto the raft and reached for his knife, teetering on the raft's corner. Kelly let out a scream, begging me to stop. My adrenaline was flowing and I had no time for her cowardice. Action had to be taken—swift, direct action. I grabbed the knife, and as he tried to climb back onboard, I drove the blade deeply into his neck. That is to say, I thought I did. For some reason, the knife didn't penetrate. It was as if the blade retracted back into the handle—a reverse stiletto the size of a machete. Still, the blunt thud of the metal on his neck deterred him long enough and I went for the next best bet for a lethal blow, the wooden oar.

Again, Kelly screamed for me to stop. But I was now in irreversible motion, bringing the oar to the side of the man's skull with a swing that could only be described as Ruthian. Kelly began to sob as the poor bastard dropped into the sea, lifeless. I'd never so much as given a guy a black eye before, but I had to admit after all I'd been through, a little justified violence felt damn good. Kelly continued to weep as I started to work on her knots, tugging the vines away from her chaffed bare ankles. For the first time since I saw that empty beach two days before, I began to feel hopeful.

"Don't worry," I said, "we're going to be alright." "You don't understand," she said. "You don't know what you've done. Oh God . . ." She was a hysterical mess. I lifted her hair back from her face, trying to get to her reddened cheeks to wipe them, comfort them, and I spotted a small bud in her ear. I recognized it immediately as an ear prompter, like the ones actors use on the set to have lines fed to them. Through it, I could hear a tinny voice. I pulled it out of her ear, as she buried her head into my shirt, now acquiescing to limp despair. The voice was Dag's, screeching in a shrill Aussie accent, "Dammit, get out there now! He damn well may have killed Joseph!"

I pulled Kelly's head out of my chest and asked her what the hell was going on, but before she could answer, a pair of speedboats seemed to come out of nowhere, skating our way. After that, she didn't need to say anything. I knew.

Later that afternoon, the local authorities dragged the area and found the bloated corpse of one Joseph Utumi, a character actor from San Diego, who had signed on to be a part of the biggest ruse in reality show history. Kelly the P.A., real name Sandy Fleming from Los Angeles, sat beside me at the Seychelles P.D., and tried to explain how the whole thing got out of hand. Dag Esbjorn, real name Dag Esbjorn (who could make that up?), was on his cell phone, talking to network legal, trying to save the show and his job. "I know it didn't go according to plan, but it's really a great ending, mate. We got it all on film. Death is a part of life, mate. Now, we can shoot the trial! It'll be huge!"

Now, I'm in a holding cell a hemisphere away from home. Even if I get to walk, I'll be known as the actor who killed another actor on a reality television program that will likely eek out four episodes. There could be a book deal, talk show appearances, live engagements with other reality show alum.

Or I could sit in a cell until I'm almost sixty.

You tell me which is worse.

8

ONE HORSE, NO RIDER

If I only hear it at night, it must be a dream, right? That's what Matt Dobbs told himself with his eyes wide open under the buttery canyon moon at 3:15 in the morning; hooves churning up the dust and splashing through the ravine, then fading into a stillness that wrapped itself like a shroud over the low plains. And the thud right before the water, like a body tumbling from its saddle, spurs on lifeless heels spiking the air with one last chord.

Matt thought he saw it one night too: the gait of a stallion, moving along the horizon, an otherworldly tinge around its mane. But then, Matt's fondness for Knob Creek whiskey made some nights foggier than others. Drunk and alone, holed up in a little one room farmhouse in the middle of Abilene, he'd howled at the moon on more than one occasion, fired his gun just to hear it echo, cursed God just to see if He cared. So, Matt might be entitled to write off a four-legged specter as a Kentucky aged apparition.

But then, Matt's horse must've heard it too. Every night as the galloping drew in on him, his mare Acacia would whinny and bray like she'd caught a stone in her shoe. Then, like the sweeping pass of a hard rain, it was over, and the plain was as silent as rolling fog.

Matt could only take it so many nights. The loss of sleep was starting to affect his already poor eyesight, and he was only a few days away from

his next cattle drive along the Chisholm Trail, so rest was precious. He'd
decided if it happened again tonight, he'd go into town and see his brother
Hyatt, the preacher. He needed someone to talk to, and he couldn't
imagine telling this tale to the town doctor. Besides, Hyatt rarely
judged, at least not with the sulfurous fury associated with most of
God's men in the West. Hyatt even brought Matt a bottle of Tullamore
Dew—a rare Irish drinking whiskey—when their mother died a few
years back. Hyatt never tried to save Matt's soul; he just kept living like
the man Matt wished he could be.

There was plenty for Matt to confess, should he choose to. He'd
cheated a man out of his life savings in a rigged poker game last winter.
He had the draw on a horse thief outside Riggs' Saloon once, but holstered
his gun and grinned at the man as he rode off on the Marshall's day man's
steed. Then, there was the kid. The kid couldn't have been more than
twenty. On a cattle drive up Chisholm a couple months back, this kid
Henry fancied himself quite the wrangler. He'd stir the cattle up just so
he could chase them back into their herds, flaring the tempers of the
other men on the ride. They'd put up with him all the way from Waurika
to Oklahoma City, and then a few of the men devised a plan to put a scare
into the kid; once he dispersed and regrouped the cows with his
showboating, they'd all pull their guns and fire in the air, creating a true
rampage among the herd, really scaring the hide off of him, settling him
down for good.

The wranglers had barely made it past Yukon when they stopped to
let the cattle graze in a field overlooking a swale. The kid started in with
his whooping and hollering, trying to create another heroic chase for
himself. As he got the handful of cattle back under his control, one of the
men—Charlie Caldron was his name—said, "On three." About half a dozen
of the men drew their guns, Matt included, and when Charlie gave the
count, they fired. The one that got spooked the most was Henry's horse.
She reared back and began to buck, sending the kid off his saddle and
over the pinto's head. This chain of events, coupled with the staggered
spray of half a dozen bullets, left the kid lying on the hillside, a gape in his
chest from one of the shots. No one said anything as the kid lay dying
looking up at the confused faces of cowboys and cattle, but everyone
figured it was Matt's bullet that got the kid. He was the last to fire by a
good three seconds. Not that anyone cared. They'd give the kid a Christian
burial and tell folks he'd caused a stampede, which is what he'd been
bucking for anyway, and got trampled underfoot. But then Matt started
talking like he was going to go to the law in some kind of nervous act of
contrition. Charlie took him aside and reminded him of what guilt could

do to a man, and that sometimes, it was better to live with it than to act on it. Then, Charlie muttered something about how he'd hate to hold two funerals in one day, just loud enough for Matt to hear him.

Matt never said another word to anyone. He buried it deep the minute they laid that kid beneath three feet of Oklahoma clay. He even managed to convince himself that he didn't fire the fatal shot; must've been Bo Ward, who wore glasses as thick as liquor bottles, and talked with a stutter that made him sound—not retarded, necessarily—but certainly slow on the uptake.

Matt lived with that notion deep inside him for quite a few months, quelling its arbitrary tickle with the whiskey until he couldn't recognize its itch anymore. So, in his mind, he had nothing to offer Hyatt in the way of profession. Matt would just start talking, and Hyatt would somehow make him feel better. Hyatt would offer some Bible verse to chase the mare out of his nightly visions, giving him the false comfort of one who embraces salvation to wriggle out of a malaise, only to deny it the minute the serpent releases his grip.

Matt rode Acacia into town at noon, having only gotten to sleep at daybreak after the deafening hooves visited upon him again the night before. This time, he made it out the back door and into the potato garden with his rifle. He felt the wind stir up, the mare passing not ten feet from him, and again, he saw it riding away from him. He dropped his rifle as a crack of dry lightning seemed to create foxfire around the horse's mane. Then, like the lightning, it was gone.

Matt prayed that night, something he hadn't done since he saw the kid hit the ground that summer. He could count on both hands the times he'd talked to his maker, and every instance was one of reconciliation, a quick fix for peace of mind. Matt promised God he'd go see Hyatt that next day, and he'd talk to him about finding some true redemption this time, like it was on a shelf at the General Store, he just needed someone to point him toward it.

Hyatt was fixing lunch when Matt knocked on his door. Hyatt invited Matt in, but seemed less receptive than in the past, his face a veneer of skepticism. Over a bowl of beans and a heaping mound of scrambled eggs, Matt shared his story of the apparition, and how he'd asked God to deliver him. Hyatt asked him when he had done this, and Matt told him just that night. "So, you're already coming to me? Didn't even give God one night?" asked Hyatt.

Matt assured him this was part of his pact. He'd come to Hyatt for God's answer. Hyatt looked away, drawing in a deep breath. "You been drinking?" he asked.

Matt squinted, ready to go on the defense about his deepening habit. Instead, Hyatt put his hand up. "Never mind. I don't wanna know."

Matt told Hyatt that he had a grip on his drinking, even as the scent of Knob Creek drifted across the table, cutting through the thick odor of beans and eggs. "So, you gonna help me or not?"

"Matthew, I can't keep being your confessor. Seems I see you maybe three times a year, and it's usually to borrow money or have your burdens lifted. If it ain't the whiskey that's causing you to see crooked, maybe God himself sent this thing you way, you ever think of that?"

"What kind of a God haunts an innocent man?"

"Ain't none of us innocent, Matt. You less than most."

Hyatt's candor was unsettling. His tenderness seemed to have grown calluses since Matt last saw him. He was hard, unflinching, like Matt used to fancy himself before he started second guessing his good sense.

They kept talking it out, tempers flaring time to time. Bottom line, Hyatt said, was Matt had to give up the bottle, period. Matt seemed to think Hyatt could perform some sort of Christian hoodoo, exorcizing the demon with the right Godly incantation. Vice and virtue could find no compromise, and Matt finally stormed out of his brother's house and headed straight for Riggs' Saloon. Hyatt trailed Matt, finding him two shots into a line 'em up of three, straight Tullamore Dew. "So, this is it? Your answer is to crawl deeper in the bottle?"

Matt spun around on his stool and gave his brother a glare Hyatt hadn't seen since they were kids. "Why you got a problem with me all of a sudden, brother man?" asked Matt.

"You come to me for clemency from the Lord Almighty when all you really want to do is ease your own guilt." Hyatt was close up in Matt's face, closer than Matt cared for. When the customers heard the preacher's voice rising up in the saloon, they leaned in, making Matt all the more uncomfortable.

"Guilty for what? Taking a drink every now and again? Yeah, I do, and so do these people." Matt gestured to the patrons, as if they'd all ridden in with him on Acacia's back. "But I bet their asses are in the pews on Sunday morning, and you don't question their reasons."

"They ain't my blood!" Hyatt was shouting now, his face flushed burgundy.

"Lucky, ain't they?" Matt was feeling the surge of the whiskey in his head. It tingled with heat and he felt alive.

"Blessed, I'd say. Blessed they ain't kin to a murderer."

The room hushed over the accusation, the saloon suddenly as silent as a church in prayer.

"Mur ... what do you mean murderer?"

A few months back, a young man went on a cattle drive with you, but he didn't come back, did he?"

Matt was frozen by the public revelation, his eyes darting the same way they did in that Oklahoma sun when the smoke rose from his Cimarron.

"You didn't have the decency to tell anyone, or come to me then and ask for God's mercy, but one of the other shooters did. He knows his bullet didn't even graze the boy, and he still came crying to the altar from guilt, because he still had a conscience, and a soul worth saving. You don't want salvation. You just want someone to hush the demons."

Matt looked around, realizing his bar mates were now his jury. "I didn't kill nobody. Never have, and anyone who says different is a liar."

Hyatt grabbed his arm. "I'd swing from the gallows in your place if I felt there was any honest remorse in your soul. Until there is, I venture to say you won't see a good night's sleep or a peaceful waking hour."

"You pious son of a bitch."

"Still too proud to get on your knees," said Hyatt, still gripping his arm with a strength Matt didn't know his frail fingers could muster.

"Find your own knees, preacher man." Matt swung hard, connecting his free fist with Hyatt's left jaw. The punch sent him back over a stool, striking his head on the bar's edge as he crumpled to the floor.

There was no lawman in sight, and no one was willing to draw on Matt, so he met no resistance as he leapt onto Acacia and fled into the plains.

He didn't stop riding until he was back at his farmhouse. He put Acacia in the barn and holed himself up in his house until nightfall, swigging from his last bottle of Knob Creek as he sat at his supper table. He'd pulled out the bible his mother had given him when he left home; it's binding pristine and unbroken for over twelve years now. In a fog of anger and hurt, Matt flipped from book to book, Old Testament to New and back again, looking for something to offer hope, or fuel his resentment. The random patchwork of verses stitched a quilt of contradictions: a God both merciful and spiteful, who hastens the sinner, yet smites the innocent. A savior who turns over tables in the temple yet offers no fight as he's nailed to a tree to die for people who'll only use his name in vain.

Matt threw the bible on the table, and reached for his Cimarron. Instead, he picked up the whiskey bottle, a blind habit at this point, and walked outside into the thick night air. Full of liquor, and exhausted from too much scriptural deliberation, Matt sat himself down on the back porch and passed out.

He lay there, still as a dog in the sun, until his nightly visitor made her presence known; first, a low din in the distance, then a crescendo of hooves, rattling the planks on the porch beneath him and causing him to rise up, just in time to see the mare buck and a body in silhouette, rising and falling. There was a shallow splash in the ravine, then the horse crossed and headed through Matt's pasture, leapt over the stable gate, and stooped her head as she ran toward him. The bottle slipped from Matt's fingers, shattering into chards at his feet. He reached for his gun, whatever good it might do, only to realize it was inside, probably resting next to the Good Book. He fumbled with the door and, tripping over his own boots, fell forward into the house just as the horse trampled over where he had stood.

Breathless, Matt scrambled for his pistol, but rather than chase after the apparition, he clutched the gun close to his breast and laid low, a ball of leather and flesh on the floor. His swiped the droplets of sweat from his upper lip, and began to sob. This had to end. He laid there and thought of the prospect of turning himself in, going to jail for a crime he wasn't even sure he committed. He thought about going back to Hyatt, but after that little show in the saloon, he knew he'd lost his only ally. His only choice was to move on—leave his farm, and what little he called his own, and head up north, away from the rumors now likely swirling in town, away from the sight and sound that reminded him, night after night, that hell was real enough and patiently awaiting his final breath.

Too full of fear and whiskey, Matt rationalized that the best way to put things to rest was to burn down his farm, leaving at least a slim reed of belief that he'd perished in the fire. Then, he and Acacia would ride away in the night, the heat of the flames and all of Texas at their backs. So, a kerosene lantern, kicked onto some dry straw by the porch, fueled by a few final drops of whiskey he found in a bottle by his bed; that made about as much sense as any answer he could think of. He went about his business: the lantern, the hay, the alcohol.

The flames rose faster than Matt had anticipated. He was almost singed as the straw tumbled onto a burlap bag by his feet. It was only now that he realized he would need a few things—some things in the house, which was now aglow from floor to frame. He grabbed his holster off a post not yet alight, and what money he had was under his bedroll. He drug the bedroll out of the house, one end already ablaze, reached into the slit— just wide enough for two fingers—and pulled out what he had to his name: sixteen dollars, and a gold coin inside the fold. He left the mattress to burn, spreading an even more hungry fire to the garden, dried from the summer's drought; his potatoes, his onions, his tomatoes and corn wilting and reshaping in the fingers of the flames.

Careless a plan as it was, all was going well. Matt hurried to get Acacia out of the barn and make their way up the first leg of the Chisholm Trail. Pulling open the barn door, Matt found his faithful mare bucking and braying with a fear that the nightly apparition had never caused. The fire had her panicked and riled. The opening of the door was all she needed to make her escape. She charged toward Matt, knocking him to the ground, his head striking the stump of a tree he had chopped down not one month earlier.

As Acacia fled down the ravine, Matt lied unconscious on the ground, a small circle of blood forming under his head, a flickering of flames snaking around his limp shoulders.

As the sound of Acadia's hooves faded into the night, others galloped closer to the farm. Driven by stubborn love, Hyatt had come to reconcile with his brother in the cloak of the moonlight, and to try to help him get to another town, so he could start fresh—away from his demons real and imagined, the blow Matt gave him in the saloon forgiven as a cry of despair. In the distant night sky, Hyatt could see the glow of the fire. He feared the worst, prayed for the best, and rode like God's messenger to cross the ravine that separated him from his brother's reconciliatory kiss.

As Hyatt's horse reached the water's edge, slowing his gait to cross, Hyatt heard a frantic gallop, and saw a mare, charging toward him in a maddened rhythm of fear, silhouetted in a glow of orange and red that engulfed the distance. She carried no rider. Hyatt knew he needn't chase her down, for he'd see her again the next night, and the next. Matt had unburdened his demons on him for the last time.

9

THE BOY FROM TUPELO

Before he was Salvation and The Devil, and before he was yours and mine, a postage stamp, a svelte army brat and a bloated corpse on the toilet and the victim of "Clambake" and a recluse and a velvet painting; before he was ten feet tall and bulletproof, before he was weak from the pain and the poison and the search for something that would make it matter; before he was a punch line and a prophet, before '56, and '68, and '77; before you swore you saw him in a Burger King in '84; before the blues and the reds and the station at the cross; before he trusted too much and lined his body with a fleshy armor to keep out the insidious truth; before he did or didn't say 'nigger', before he collapsed in Reno, before he dropped to one knee and held that holy note on the Battle Hymn, before all his trials; before Priscilla, and The Colonel, PBJs and TCB and twelve million flashbulbs and the weight in his face and the weight of the world, he was Gladys' boy.

He stood at the edge of a gravel road, the paved highway out of Mississippi winding out in front of him like an endless ribbon. He wanted to record a song for his mother's birthday. Nothing more. So, he climbed into his pickup truck, four dollars stored up in his torn pocket, and he drove toward Memphis.

It wasn't the speed that killed him, it wasn't letting go of the wheel. What got him was forever looking in his rear view mirror, trying to catch a glimpse, one more sight, of that Boy from Tupelo.

10

GOD BLESS YOU, MR. VONNEGUT

"This is my sister's Pet Rock. She got the last one in the whole mall." God, what innocence—a pigeon-toed third grader causing all of us to covet a freaking box with a beige beach stone in it; show and tell brought out the naiveté in all of us, bringing things from home that perhaps would've best been left there. Charles Ward brought a National Geographic, native edition. Ellen Goshen brought one of her mom's Tampex. And me, I brought "Breakfast of Champions" by Kurt Vonnegut. The year was 1976, our nation's bicentennial, and you'd have thought I peed on the commemorative Spirit of '76 school flag.

Like all eight year olds, I just wanted to bring something cool for show and tell. I wasn't allowed to take my autographed Willie Mays card out of the house, and my older brother Eddie wasn't about to loan me his Stratocaster. All I had was a Frito Bandito pencil eraser and this book, also my brother's, which had a really great name, like the one from the Bruce Jenner cereal commercials. So, I slipped the hardback into my book bag and sneaked it off to school. Where was the harm, really? I'd be home a good hour before Eddie, and return it to its rightful station.

Gabe Puckett went right before me. He had brought his new goldfish from home, unaware that the bowlful of water was a prerequisite for survival. Gabe pulled 'Mr. Chico' out of his pocket and got his first lesson in life's fragile transience. As Mrs. Denton escorted Gabe out the door, his face sodden with tears, she cued me to go ahead and start my Show and Tell presentation.

I wasn't sure how to begin, after all I hadn't read the book; couldn't have if I wanted to with all those big words and transcendental subplots. I talked about how Eddie snuck the book home from a friend's house, and that it was named after Wheaties. I talked about the cover, and that the book had some drawings in it, but my cohorts were unimpressed. The combination of the teacher being out of the room and my presentation being sub-stellar left me clamoring to keep their focus. Finally, I blurted out the one fact I knew to be true about the work of fiction: "there's a picture of a butt in here!" It grew so quiet; you could hear the air conditioner whir.

I flipped to page five, which featured Vonnegut's amateurish rendering of an asshole. Actually, it was an asterisk, but how was I to know? I didn't really even know what an asshole was. Eddie just told me it was a 'butt', and that was funny enough for me. Funny enough for the class too, who got off on the idea that the picture, abstract though it may have been, represented a taboo orifice.

Now, you know as well as I do that if you want to encourage a child to be deviant, all you have to do is give him the warm acceptance of laughter. A lad will poke at a rabid dog with his bare toes if he thinks it'll get his peers tittering. So I continued, sharing other childish renderings by the author. Page 24 featured a doodling of women's underwear, the page before it, a funny looking beaver with some hairy bug underneath it. I was oblivious to the notion that both were 'beavers', but when the door flew open and Mr. Bullock, our assistant principal, came to see what all the unchecked frivolity was about, I learned, from Mr. Bullock in fact, that 'beaver' was rude slang for a woman's reproductive area. I cannot say it enough: I was eight, I was Episcopal, I was vastly naïve.

Mr. Bullock took the presence of Mr. Vonnegut's work in his school very seriously. The phrase he used to describe him was 'rabble rouser'. I only knew this phrase from a story we'd read in Sunday school, where the Romans referred to Jesus and his disciples as rabble rousers. It seemed a compliment. After all, from what I'd been taught, Jesus was one of the good guys, like Batman or Mannix. But no, rabble rousing was bad; bad enough to have me suspended for three days.

My mom—a tearful heap of 'why me's and 'what did I ever do's'— brought me home and sent me to my room. I was sequestered there long enough for her to peruse "Breakfast of Champions", make a detour into

Eddie's bedroom to tongue-lash him for owning such a book and then, for act two, pay a visit upon my door.

"Do you even understand what you've done, young man?" she asked, holding "Champions" at arm's length as if it might get venal cooties on her blouse.

"Yes."

"What?" She wanted an answer. I hadn't expected the follow up question.

"I . . . uh. I took Eddie's book to school, and it's a bad book."

"It's worse than bad, little man. There are things in this book. Do you know what the word 'subversive' means?"

I would like to think she knew I didn't. I shook my head just in case.

"It means you question God, your parents, your teachers . . . you try to hurt what is built up around you, when what is built up around you is good. You don't want to do that, do you?"

I didn't want to hurt anyone, that was a given. But that my taking a book to school would somehow cause so much collateral damage didn't make much sense. I didn't have an answer, so I stood there silent a moment too long. Mom hated silence, and rather than seeing it as a mandate, she usually saw it as, well, being subversive.

My punishment for taking a book which was not mine, and then displaying cartoon renderings of beaver and BVDs was to pray for God's forgiveness and write letters of apology to my class, my teacher, and my assistant principal. Some would say I got off easy, but Mom had a sadistic streak that I couldn't really appreciate until I studied de Sade in college. She said I had to stand up in front of the respective parties and read my letter to them. I had only seen one person have to stand guilty before his peers and read a prepared statement, and that was Nixon in '74. I may have been six at the time, but I knew shame when I saw it.

Most third graders understand authority. Authority is the life-sized finger that presses down on you, but since that finger also keeps you safe from a few thousand unknowns, you accept that. You're willing to take the swipes and scrapes dished out by the finger, because you know that ultimately, the finger knows best.

I was a good kid, a good kid suddenly feeling fingers coming at him from everywhere. My teacher had a finger in my face for getting her in trouble with the school, pulling out political propaganda while she was playing Florence Nightingale to a traumatized lad who'd committed involuntary agnathicide. My assistant principal had a fistful of fingers in my face for my being the Wee Belo equivalent of Abbie Hoffman. My brother had his finger in my face for lifting his book. My mom had her finger in my face because that's what moms do. Dad didn't need to put a finger in my face. He'd already put a belt to my backside. That was how he dealt with dissention. At least that got it over with. He'd give me three to the soft cheeks and then we were buds again. Mom held a grudge, and drew the punishment out like she was turning the crank on the rack, one notch at a time. She wanted me to read my apologetics to her, rehearse them, then practice what I'd say *before* I read them. That's how I spent my three day suspension, honing drafts of letters like Emerson in Concord.

I returned to school on a Friday, a blessing in that it meant I'd only have to suffer one day of abject humiliation before the billowy cushion of a spring weekend that would help put the slings and arrows I was sure to incur behind me. I don't remember a lot from third grade. I remember hitting my first home run, actually a sad trickle of a single that made it through too many legs on the playground. I remember having a crush on Lynn Buttermere, a missionary's kid. Not much else. The single most resonant experience from third grade, however, one that stays with me to this day, is having to read those letters to my friends and 'The Fingers'. As I stood before Mrs. Denton with sweaty palms and gelatin legs, I felt small. Small in a way no youngster should have to feel. That feeling was multiplied by a dozen in front of my class, by a hundred in front of Mr. Bullock, who sat with this indignant smirk on his face that reminded me of a Halloween decoration we had, a smug skull who knew what it was like to be dead, and relished that you'd soon know yourself.

That night, I went home and sobbed into my pillow. Though I was content to wallow in my own self-pity, I was comforted by the solid hand of my sibling. Eddie began to pat my back, asking me to sit up so we could talk. He had the book in his hand, 300 pages I'd wished I'd never laid eyes on, all those shitty drawings of flags, tombstones, and banners.

"Hey, little buddy,' whispered Eddie. "You're taking this way too hard. Come on, sit up."

I nestled into his side, letting him cradle me under his wing while I wiped away a face full of slobber. "I'm sorry you got busted for this book. But ya gotta not take things that don't belong to you."

Between huffs and sniffles, I told him that I knew that if I had asked, he'd have said, 'no'. He complied. "Yeah, I would've, but not because I don't want to help you with show and tell. This book isn't for kids. In fact, it's not for a lot of grown ups." I gave him a glance. Who was left, I wondered.

"Remember when you wanted to read my copy of 'Catcher in the Rye' because you thought it was about baseball, then I sorta told you what it was really about? This book's the same way. You gotta understand things aren't what they always seem, and a lot of people . . ." He paused to gather his thoughts. I remember the space being chiasmic. " . . . like, you know the way some of your bedtime stories are too scary for you. Some stories scare certain grown ups too."

"So, it's a scary book?"

"Not exactly. Let's just say this book makes people think, and some people don't like to think." That made clear and perfect sense to me. Given the choice, I liked to think. But Tony Nettles, who sat behind me in school, he didn't like to think. He was a bully, and never did his own work. No one liked him. I figured, 'people don't like non-thinkers'. It would be more than a decade before I experienced self-correction on that childish assumption. Of course people like non-thinkers. They rely on them. Certain people build their empires around them.

Eddie stood with the book dangling beneath his gangly left arm. "Someday you will be ready to read this, though, and when you are, it's all yours." His footsteps faded as he went to his room, followed by the muffled sounds of "Tangled Up in Blue" bleeding through our adjoining wall. Eddie was the only one I truly needed absolution from, and he was the only one kind enough to offer it.

The next week at school, the incident was all but forgotten by friends, who had moved on to the next opportunity to tease someone—a ragamuffin named Cathy Roth who made the mistake of trying to give herself a haircut over the weekend. My humiliating incident was past tense, and I was happy for it. As for Mrs. Denton, I never could get a read off of her, but I stayed in line more than ever to assure she wouldn't ever see me as a rabble rouser. I still hated seeing Mr. Bullock in the hallways. He now looked on me like a lost sheep he'd single handedly brought back to the fold. He'd go out of his way to pat me on the head, to smirk when he caught my eye. I didn't understand it then, but I knew it irked me; made me feel worse than I did for getting busted in the first place. Still, I marched on to the cadence of obedience, an unwitting conformist now smoothly assimilated into something small and finite. At the age of eight, I learned that my spirit, when challenged by authority, crumbled like rotting slate.

My remaining years in elementary school were spent on the Principal's List, where all "A" and "B" students with good conduct reside. I was a safety patrol. I never misspent my milk money.

My halo followed me to high school, and it was there I learned that it wasn't just adults that wanted you to fit a certain ideal. I spent the best days of my youth trying to get into ill-fitting cliques and folding what few ragged edges of individuality I had under my collar to assure I'd ease into the precise mold popularity required. I was a ship adrift again, navigating to anchor at the port others told me I should. Trying to feel good felt like hell.

By the end of sophomore year, I'd had enough conforming. I burned my Izod shirts in effigy, pierced my ear, and started hanging out with the freaks, the kids who copped cigs from each other outside of shop class. I found mild violence, when well-timed and carefully measured, came with few repercussions. I found certain girls like guys who appear dangerous. Then, after another suspension, this time for fighting, I found that all I had done was trade one form of orthodoxy for another, a clique for a posse, my ideals for a hollow rebellion that was no more authentic than my black pleather jacket.

I dropped out of the freak zone, gave up my three month old smoking habit, and decided to cruise under the radar for the rest of high school. I was hesitant to speak out in class, unsure of where I was supposed to fit in, or if fitting in was even the point.

I felt even less at home at home. Mom and Dad had now split, they just hadn't bothered to recognize it, so the house widened like a canyon, with me dangling in the gulf between their loveless silences. Eddie had long since moved out, and the ache I felt whenever I walked past his closed bedroom door was tangible. More than ever, I needed my big brother.

While self-awareness is rarely a teenager's strong suit, I did realize that things weren't supposed to be the way they were. It all came to a head the night my mom sent me to church because she and Dad were fighting. It was a Friday and there was nothing going at church, but she dropped me off anyway and said she'd be back to pick me up at 8:30. I just walked around the playground, the ball field, sat inside the chapel and stared at the stained glass. That was the night I realized that I didn't want to be a grown up. Pete Townsend was right. But then, I didn't want to die, so what were my options? I didn't have the answers, and even if Minister Dave had been at church on Friday night, I doubt I would've liked his solution. So, I picked up the phone late that night and called Eddie. He was living in Maryland, and only came home once or twice a year. I couldn't wait 'til Thanksgiving.

I got his answering machine. We didn't have an answering machine yet, so at first, I thought it was kind of cool, but then realized it meant we wouldn't get to speak. He was probably with a girl, or out of town on business, doing consulting work. I left as succinct a message as I could. "Eddie, hey, it's me. I . . . uh . . . I can't seem to figure it out. Life, I mean. I dunno. I just wanted to talk. Things are weird here. People are . . . ya know? So, uh, call me, okay?" It wasn't Shakespeare, but come on, I was fifteen.

I stayed home all weekend waiting for Eddie to call. The afternoons drew out like a blade as the silence of the phone careened off the vacuum that was my parents. Really, it was like a mausoleum, only with HBO. I sat in my room and listened to Pink Floyd with one ear, the other ever hopeful for the chirp of the phone. It never came, and the letdown from the one person I knew I could count on hurt more than anything. Spending an entire two days listening to "The Wall" probably didn't help either. Uncomfortably numb.

I stumbled through the beginning of the week, resigned to the machinery of my life: breakfast, school, lunch, more school, home, dinner, bed. It was best to look at it in those terms, benign labels serving as road markers to get through another day. I wondered if that was how Mom and Dad had finally decided to navigate through the rest of their relationship: morning silence, breakfast, work, the clinking of silverware accompanying a pin-drop dinner, post-gelatin-and-Cool-Whip quarrel, bed. Maybe they'd just keep doing that until I moved out, then go ahead and put the ugly beast they called a marriage out of its misery. It seemed pitiful, but I figured they made their choices. They were adults, and I assumed free will was abundant once you got out of high school. But then if that were so, then Eddie was choosing not to call me back and that was something I just didn't want to accept.

When I got home on Wednesday, still stinging from a pop quiz on World War I, there was a package in the mailbox with my name on it. No return address, but the postmark was Bethesda, Maryland. I tore it open right there at the curb. Inside was a frayed and tattered copy of "Breakfast of Champions" and a note from Eddie that simply read "I think you're ready."

I'd honestly forgotten all about the book, but the dust jacket, the sophomoric renderings, the highlighted passages brought all those memories from third grade flooding back on me; not in a bad way, though. The festering feeling, the nagging dark tugging at my shirt tail, a kid about to be thrust into adulthood, was exactly what I felt back under the judgmental gaze of Mr. Bullock and his puritanical ilk.

Paper clipped to the back cover was an envelope, which read "Don't open until you've finished the book. I mean it." I didn't need extra incentive, but if I had, that dangling carrot certainly would've started the pages turning. I retired to my room, coming out only for dinner and school. It took me only two days to soar through the eccentric world of Kilgore Trout and Duane Hoover. The hypocrites, hung from their flagpoles, were there for all to see: the self-righteous, the jingoists, the soul suckers and self-appointed drill sergeants of life. The burning bottle rocket of imagination was engaged by someone who understood that the best way to fight authority was to let them think they were winning. My mind fired off in a thousand directions. I'm not going to tell you I began to understand it all, but what I did understand were the possibilities, the ones that intertwined in Vonnegut's fertile imagination and the ones that lay before me as I stood on the cusp of self-reliance. It was a cosmic wake-up call. It could've just as well happened with Flannery O'Connor, or "On the Road", but for me the seismic shift came through a wiry little mass of moral madness named Vonnegut.

The last words of the book, a cry from Kilgore begging the author to 'make me young', stung me. I'd been trudging my way through my adolescence, looking for something further down the road of life that would help it all make sense. The fact was, someday I'd be looking back to my youth and realize that now was all I ever had, that I wasted a lifetime of *nows* looking toward an elusive *when*, a slippery *what if*. Zen masters say enlightenment comes in a moment. That was mine. Instant dharma.

The envelope held a long letter from Eddie as eloquent and life changing as the novel itself. Eddie told me he knew about Mom and Dad, that Mom had been calling him, weeping into the receiver long after Dad had gone to bed, spilling her sad resignation through the wires. "I think you're ready to know all this, because my hunch is, you already do, it just becomes easier to cope with when you know someone else knows." He told me that Mom and Dad loved me, but neither had the capacity to help me find the answers I was likely searching for. "Adults are too self-absorbed, little brother. They've embraced the rut, and confuse their compliant goosesteps for the dance of life. Don't let it happen. Find you now—your terms, your life. Don't let the bastards get you down."

Eddie signed off there, but there were three more pages clipped to his epistle: a trio of handwritten notes, a tyke's most earnest scribbling. The letters to Mr. Bullock, Ms. Denton, and my classmates were brown around the edges, but the message hadn't faded. Taped to each letter was a solitary match. I knew what Eddie was telling me, and few things had ever been more tempting than igniting them right there and then. Instead, I decided to keep them, hung them on the bulletin board in my room, in fact, with the matches still taped to them.

Mom often asked why I'd want to keep 'those old things' around. She also asked me where I found 'that dirty old book'. Most of all, though, I think she wondered what happened to her son, as I went from zombie to "A" student. The notes that were sent home by teachers no longer reflected a kid who seemed uninspired, but by one who seemed too much so. Some hailed my spirit; others told my folks I needed to just accept what I was being taught as fact instead of questioning it so much. A Sunday school teacher pined that I'd worn her down when she tried to convince a roomful of high school juniors that the world was only 6000 years old and dinosaurs never existed. I dismantled her with Vonnegutian glee. She was one of the robots Kilgore Trout talked about. Everyone is a robot except me, that's what Duane Hoover believed. While I wasn't that delusional, I did accept that the robots walk among us. You can't miss them, they are usually the ones pounding loudest, trying to drown out any hint of that 'different drum' Thoreau spoke of. That I was quoting Thoreau back to my Humanities teacher in eleventh grade scared the shit out of her, by the way.

I would go on to turn many more corners in life: college, marriage, a job that allows me to sleep at night, fatherhood, and even the inevitable divorce of my parents once Dad hit retirement age. But I never lived in fear. Fear, I found, was the most crippling defect to ever plague mankind. Let the locust siege, let the floods come, but never let fear into your heart. It finds root quickly, and nothing short of an exorcism can extract it. I like to think Eddie and Kurt performed that exorcism on me, and I've lived every day since keeping the beast at bay.

11

FREE REFILLS (FIFTY CENTS)

It was burnt dishwater, but he was on his third cup of it. A little sugar and some half-and-half did the trick, even with the nastiest of diner coffee. He didn't need it to taste like it came from Starbucks, he just needed its warmth, the reassurance of steam floating heavenward.

Her nametag read "GINA" in all caps. She'd been at The Grittle #559 on Buckeye Road for fourteen years, that's what she'd told him when she poured his first cup. By his third, he'd learned that she had a teenager at home she was raising, her ex was in Dallas, unemployed, and shacking up with the sister of some Busch League NASCAR racer. Gina said that she hadn't seen child support in over a year, and that her ex was hustling souvenir maps at Dealey Plaza to try and come up with enough money to send her way.

"Pathetic," she said. "How many maps of the book depository you think he'll have to sell to pay for Ashley's braces? To help us get a car that'll run?"

On any other night, he'd have looked right through her, or given her an obtuse response to shut her down. He was, after all, a tenured philosophy professor with an understanding of the human psyche that far outdistanced her capacity to grasp her own path of self-sabotage. But tonight was different. Tonight, he needed her.

"Why don't you hire a lawyer?" he asked.

"You know any that work for free, 'cause with tips and $2.10 an hour, that's about what I got to offer."

"Legal aid? Social services? There's got to be somebody."

"Sugar, there never *has* to be anybody, no matter what they tell you."

He liked her directness, her earthiness. For the first time in a long time, he felt as if he was talking to someone who lived without apology. It was refreshing to hear candor delivered with such warmth. He tried to keep her talking. "What does he do? I mean, what did he do before he sold JFK maps?"

"He installed cable TV, satellite dishes, that sort of thing."

"Seems there'd be plenty of call for that these days."

"If he could get a referral, maybe, but he was hooking people up for side money," she said. "Got caught, so they fired him. He can't even list that job on his resume."

"So, he just ran off to Dallas?"

"You ask me, I think it was all part of his plan anyway. He just got busted before he could get enough money to leave. He was already sleeping with this Andi girl, I knew that."

"How'd you know?"

"Aw, hon, he left a trail like he was begging to get caught. That's why I never called him on it. It was pathetic."

"You never confronted him?"

"What's the point? You think it woulda made him stop?"

A truck driver saddled up to the counter. Gina excused herself, but said she'd be back with more coffee in a minute.

The professor studied the restaurant, every detail he could absorb: the flooring, the arc and crest of every gaudy orange booth, the seeming contradiction of residue and sheen on the stools at the counter. He stood up and walked to the jukebox, passing behind the mountain of a man that was the trucker. He smelled of nicotine and sweat.

The professor's senses were alive tonight, for the first time in ages. He took in all that was around him. He was aware of his very heartbeat, and thought it ironic that it is our final moments that bring everything to the surface. If these sensations came earlier, he thought, maybe people wouldn't end up numbed beyond repair.

He reached in his pocket and pulled out just short of a dozen quarters, which he'd grabbed out of a mug in his office before he left the university for the evening. His eyes danced down the row of selections. There was no Sinatra here, and certainly no Vivaldi. The classicists in this diner were Haggard, Cash, and Strait; broken hearted songs for broken spirited men and women who used music not as a societal stripe but as a balm. At three in the morning, a jukebox isn't a music lover's luxury; it's a friend to the lonely, the weary, and the lost. The professor slid a handful of quarters in and picked songs based on his curiosity of their titles: "Pancho and Lefty". "The Weight". "The Long Black Veil".

He stared through the slit in the blinds at the parking lot, empty save his new Saturn, a purchase that failed to lift the fog, and the eighteen wheeler that sprawled across close to a dozen spaces. The side of the truck had "McGibney's Foods" along the side of it with a small Ichthus, the "Jesus fish", underneath the logo. The professor smiled. How nice to have a faith strong enough that you care to advertise it to the free world. How assured one must be to align his livelihood with his creed.

He'd often joked that the best part of being an agnostic was that he could sleep in on Sunday, but the downside was, sleep rarely came easy. The professor had spent his life wrestling with philosophy, theology's bastard cousin. He studied it, mastered a certain knowledge of it, and then served it up to students as objectively as a chemist pours compound into a beaker. To him, philosophy was vast, but religion somehow felt narrow, a God-in-a-box approach to life that robbed the seeker of the joy of the hunt, putting their feet on solid ground rather than treacherous cliffs. He'd been willing to trade assurance for adventure, until recently.

Between the gypsy strum of Willie Nelson and the hum in his head, he could hear the waitress making small talk with the trucker. She called him 'hon', but that didn't mean she knew him. She talked about how she makes eggs over easy at home, and how she'd always wanted to see Chicago, but never made it past the Mason-Dixon. The professor went back to his booth, and pulled the menu from behind the napkin dispenser, a flare to Gina that he might actually be more than a table camper sipping refillable buck-a-cup coffee all night.

Gina broke away from the trucker, his shoulders now a slouched mass of plaid hovering over the counter as if he might fall forward into slumber at the mere mention of sleep. She was back at the professor's side. "You wantin' to order some food, hon?"

The professor studied the menu. "What do you recommend?"

"IHOP," she laughed. She must've used that line a thousand times, but that he gave her cause to make a joke made him smile.

"Tell you what. I'll have the pie. Whichever is the best."

"One slice of pecan pie it is, and a refill on coffee..."

"Thanks." He stopped her as she turned, searching for something to keep her close. "Hey, you like this song?"

"Guess so. 'Pancho and Lefty', right? I'm more of a 'Blue Eyes Cryin' In the Rain' gal myself."

"Why are we all so drawn to sad songs, I wonder?" The question was designed to launch something lengthy and metaphysical, something that would open a Pandora's Box of understanding. Instead, his words dropped to the floor with a thud. It came out sloppy, like a pick-up line. He sensed his misstep.

Gina's eyes rolled. She turned, heading back to the counter. To stop her again would seem desperate, so the professor just feigned listening to the song, a story of fraternal betrayal and an odd sort of kindness in the Old West. He realized he rarely listened to music with lyrics, and hadn't in what seemed decades. In grad school, he traded Lennon and McCartney for Liszt and Mozart and never looked back. In moments of quiet reflection, he could pull the lone oboe out of a sixty instrument orchestra, but he couldn't tell you what happened to Bob Dylan since his motorcycle accident in '66. Was he even still alive? Did he still matter?

The professor stared at Gina. It was the first time he'd noticed her in any physical sense. Her hair was blonde with roots she obviously wasn't hiding, and her figure was supple, with legs lithe from what must be a daily twelve-hour anaerobic workout. Her face seemed to be a mix of light and shadow, a hint of radiance eclipsing a well of ache. He wondered how a woman lives in this world without coming unhinged by it all. Why do people keep going when this is all there is, third shifts and deadbeat spouses? His stare was harmless, but penetrating, as if he were trying to unravel her and her history with one stony gaze.

Gina sensed the look, she'd felt something similar to it many times. Those other men, however, were more apt to be wondering if her skirt might hike up than if she had ever reexamined her choices. The professor was broken from his gape by a whisper from the side of her ruby lips, and a sudden motion from the trucker, a giant awakened. He walked over to the professor, looking as solid and stoic as a curled fist. "Excuse me, friend. The lady would appreciate it if you'd stop staring at her, alright?" His voice was steady and terse.

The professor was horrified. "I'm sorry. I didn't realize . . ." His words trailed off into his half-empty mug. An overwhelming despondence seemed to rise up in him, a latent shame that, from time to time, coiled around his chest just to test its infiniteness. He felt ashamed for trying to loosen the thread of the blue collar, the mystery of a woman he did not know, the peace of mind that comes with blind faith. His face was his obituary, an open wound splayed out on a vinyl seat cover.

"Hey, buddy. You alright?" The trucker slouched a bit, putting his hands down on the table to get a closer look at the veritable implosion in booth number three.

"I'm fine. I . . . I wasn't trying to leer. I'm not a letch. I'm just . . . my mind isn't all here tonight."

"Have some food. Always gets my head out of the clouds," the trucker's gut was a testimony to a life primarily lived squarely beneath the clouds. "No harm done. Just gotta look out for the lady, alright?" As he turned away from the professor, it was as if his body retreated in two movements; first his head and legs, then his torso, struggling to catch up. The trucker sat back down on his stool and mumbled something to Gina to the effect of 'that's that' or 'harmless'. The professor couldn't tell which.

He could feel sweat starting to form on his forehead. He knew it wasn't from his brush with The Mountain, but rather that rising dread that comes with facing something that's bigger than you, something that can knock you off your center of gravity. To some, it might be that 300 pound mass of flesh calling you out for being a pig, but to the professor, the trucker was just the steady reminder, the ever pulsing light that alerts a ship that it's going way off course, that the rocks are perilously close.

A hand placed a piece of pecan pie in front of him, and he longed to reach out to clasp that hand in his, relieving vertigo and vast disconnect all at once, but instead, he looked up to find reassurance in Gina's eyes, to start talk again of the grassy knoll and Country songs. But his eye followed the bend in her wrist to her arm, then her face. This was not Gina, but another waitress who must've just returned from break. She was pale and odd-looking, her teeth a mangled row of yellow stubs, her breath a stream of nicotine. She placed the dessert plate down with a graceless clatter.

"Anything else or you want your ticket now?" Her eyes pierced him with judgment, daring him to request anything other than the check. It was clear that Gina must've passed him off to this girl, deciding that whatever signal his stare gave off damaged an irreparable nerve. He'd lost his connection, and was too tired to pursue a new one, especially with someone so obviously unconcerned about her own place in the world. "Just the check, thanks."

Gina continued her conversation at the counter with the trucker, now erupting into titters of laughter that made the professor ache with envy. How could she turn on him so quickly, how could one innocent look reverse something that had unfolded so naturally, so gently, on a night he sought only a word of reassurance? Not a touch, just a word. Is this what we had devolved into? A civilization so hungry for a moment of honesty, yet so frightened by it that we recoil whenever we brush up against it? We live beneath shells and shields, he thought. Places to hide behind when we feel the fresh breeze on our raw skin. The security of hopelessness defeating the white light of the unknown. All the philosophers in history look down on us, he thought, and they shutter at what we've become. He'd never fancied himself to need God, but now he understood why so many did, and he regretted ever holding them in intellectual contempt. They were, after all, just trying to feel that breeze, to follow that white light, and they couldn't recognize that it was here among us, in tiny moments. God is the thread, if He is anything at all. Tonight, for the professor, that thread was found, only to slip away again.

He tried to catch Gina's eye, but the more he looked her way, the more he could sense her angling her body away from him, and almost like a magnet, the trucker turning toward him. This time, the Mountain would not be so magnanimous. This time, he'd come with a curled fist, ready for purification. Though the professor didn't fear the idea of being beaten bloody, it seemed too much trouble, just a detour from the inevitable. So, instead, he cast his gaze out the window again, staring at the night, the pooling of light underneath the telephone poles, and the shimmering fish on the side of the truck. On the jukebox, The Band sang "The Long Black Veil", a western tale of a man who died for the wrong sin, who chose to keep quiet and hang for a murder he didn't commit. That's Socrates, he thought. That's the Christ. That's all of us. Dying for the wrong sins.

The professor stood and emptied his pockets. Twenty seven dollars and about three more in change. A sterling silver money clip and a gold St. Jude pendant on his keychain. He placed them on the table, car keys and all, and wrote on the back of the bill: "Title in glove box. For you."

His eyes met hers one time before he walked out, and she looked to see the pile of belongings he'd left behind on the table. Before she could speak, he dropped one quarter in the jukebox and, turning to the trucker, he smiled. "Play something upbeat, for Chrissake's, alright?" He walked out of the florescent light of The Griddle and into the dusk.

Gina stood over booth number three, silent as she took in what he had done. The trucker watched the professor as he walked past his car and out to the highway. The Band's dirge faded, and the jukebox fell silent. There was one selection left to be made. Someone just had to choose it.

12

GET BEHIND THE MULE

I'll say this for him; the boy's made quite a name for himself. That guitar made him a lot of friends, and he ain't livin' too shabby neither. He calls us from the road to tell us where he's at each week. Chicago, New Orleans, St. Louis, the boy gets around. I'm glad for him, I really am. This bunch he fell in with isn't exactly my cup of tea, or his ma's. They're too busy on Saturday night to be where they should be on Sunday morning. They drink too much; think more of themselves than they probably should. Still, that seems to be the way of things now. People don't lay down roots, they just want out of where they came from, and don't seem to care much for staying put long, like if they had to be still, they'd have to stop and think too much. None of these kids take time for thinking.

He sends us money now and then, piece of a check from records he sold, or some cash from a show. I wish it made me feel proud of him, but it don't. Sort of shamed, not because he's helping us get through the month, but because I don't like how he makes his money. Don't like that he don't work for it. People pay him for fooling around on that guitar of his. Sometimes I'm sorry we ever gave him one when he was a boy. It didn't make a man out of him.

When he comes home, I look at his hands. He always had my hands; large, strong. Impressive bones, muscular too. Hands meant for the land. Sometimes I tell him that God gave him my hands, but he turned 'em into his ma's. They're soft to the touch, almost feminine. He's quick to show me the calluses on his fingertips, but they're like tiny thorns in a bail of cotton. I show him my hands. They are leather, scarred and healed a hundred times over. Soiled hands that will never come clean from the land.

I tell him that's what a man's hands should look like. He just smiles, pulls out his guitar and picks a song. It's pretty. He could always play real pretty. But he's never worked a day in his life. That boy never would get behind the mule. Tell me, what good's a song when the harvest comes?

13

ME AND THE DEVIL BLUES

For Charly Lawson, a good night of singing the blues at Three
Forks consisted of six broken strings, a table's worth of tearful
women, and at least one legitimate jook brawl borne from vicarious despair.
Anything less than that was deemed a reprehensible failure.

Tears and violence were always hovering low at Three Forks, a
rundown shack of a roadhouse, specializing in warm beer and fried anything.
It was where local inhabitants of Greenwood, Mississippi came to sooth
their tattered bodies and spirits with cheap ale, conversation, and lethal
doses of Delta blues, courtesy of howler Charly Lawson.

Charly stood 5'5" in his stocking feet, which is how he might as
well have performed his sets, for the lack of canvas left on his worn
work shoes. He was hardly an imposing figure—short in stature, 140
pounds, and shoulders as narrow as the neck-width of his six-string
Vega.

Yet, when he stood onstage, Charly was a behemoth. Somewhere inside
that brittle frame was the enraged voice of a Siren betrayed. When Charly
sang, it was said that so much pain and catharsis filled the air that couples
would fight, break-up, and reunite with one another during the course of
one verse, without even so much as a word spoken between them. Charly
could channel so much angst through his guitar that even common licks

were met with mournful silence. Charly didn't just make you feel knocked down, he made you taste the dust.

For most at Three Forks, Delta loam was an all too familiar flavor. These black men and women spent the better part of their days working on farms, in fields, or, if they were lucky, in a heat scorched warehouse. Hours were long, money was scarce, and the Three Forks was the one social catchall in town: decent food, friendly prices, and nights of music that somehow made the grueling days bearable. If you think you've heard of it, it's probably because Three Forks was also the place where, on an August night in 1938, blues pioneer Robert Johnson was poisoned by a jealous man with a bottle of strychnine-laced whiskey.

For weeks after Robert's death, the Three Forks was a hollow cavern of its former self. While Robert had only been a passing presence in the roadhouse, he left a mark so indelible that no one dared to take the stage again until late that October; Halloween, to be exact. The man who finally had the courage and the chops to pull up a stool to sing was none other than Charly Lawson, a drifter who had just moved into town from parts unknown.

Comparisons to Robert Johnson were inevitable, but they soon faded as Lawson proved he stood in no man's shadow. When locals would ask Charly where he came from, he'd simply state, 'up the road a piece'; asked of his awareness of local legend Robert Johnson, he's just smile and say, "I never had the privilege". Yet, over the period of one year's harvest, Charly Lawson had managed to do what no local blues aficionado could've imagined. He had created music so honest and bone chilling that the thought of missing Robert Johnson was seen as merely sentimental rather than essential.

Like Johnson, Charly had his fair share of female admirers. The women saw him as raw and unguarded, a rare trait for a poor man in the South, especially a poor black man. Yet Charly never left the Three Forks with a woman on his arm or in the company of men friends, for that matter. The mystique led many to speculate his origins, and his intentions in Greenwood. Stories connected to other drifters began to get attached to Charly. *He could be that child killer from Tutwiler. Or maybe he's that singer from Chicago, whose family was killed in that fire, coming down here to start his life over. Or is he Robert reincarnate?* Superstitions ran amok in the rural south. No one knew this more than Charly, who seemed to take all the gossip mongering in stride. Only one rumor intrigued Charly, and he pressed his ear to the wall every time the topic surfaced.

The story goes that, on a dark Delta night, Robert Johnson stood at the crossroads of Highways 61 & 49 and came face to face with the devil.

He promised the devil his soul in exchange for the ability to play and sing the blues above all others. Whether this actually happened or not was suspect. Bluesmen were seen as hosts to demons by most right thinking rural Christians in that day anyway; and Robert himself did little to dispel the myth, what with songs like "Hellhound on my Trail", "Crossroad Blues", and "Me and the Devil Blues". This legend followed Johnson to his grave, follows him today. Some say his demise at 26 was proof positive of his deal with Satan, who was too impatient and stony hearted to let Robert enjoy his mastery for long. Others believe it was a carefully crafted yarn, designed to give Robert a legacy, a fame he was never afforded in life.

Charly was interested in a Faustian bargain of his own. He had already proven himself to be Johnson's peer in ability. Fame and money were Charly's ends, and two specialties of Satan, he was sure. So, Charly Lawson continued his gigs at the Three Forks, and leaned in when bar talk turned to the Crossroads. It didn't take long for him to find out exactly how Robert Johnson met The Devil. Buy a thirsty man a whiskey and he'll tell you your tale of choice.

Most agreed the events played out something like this: Robert went out to the Crossroad marker at Highways 61 and 49 with his guitar in hand. A murky veil of fog hovered around a sliver of moonlight. Frogs croaked, crickets chirped, bats claimed the air. As the hour approached midnight, Robert commenced to play a fierce dirge that jettisoned from tree to tree. He improvised a verse or two to sing over the stinging licks:

> *Goin' to meet the devil, 'cause I ain't 'fraid of him*
> *Goin' down to meet the devil, ain't afraid of him*
> *Trade my love of Jesus, my mama and my friends,*
> *Jes' to meet the devil and show him how to sin.*
> *Preacher say he live way down in the hole*
> *Preacher say he live way down in that hole*
> *With a heart so mean and greasy, and eyes as red as coal,*
> *Come on up, sweet devil, I got for you a soul.*

Robert sang and strummed patiently, as if the keys to Scratch's manifestation were mere tenacity and endurance. As the moon skimmed its path over the wooded terrain, a sinister stillness began to pervade. The wind steadied to a near halt, and the sounds of night crawlers and tree nesters subsided to an unsettling hush; only Robert's dancing strings permeated the paralyzed air. Then, suspecting his time was at hand, Johnson stopped his snake charming and waited for the serpent to emerge from his hole.

There was no conflagration, no foreboding fanfare to pronounce his coming. Satan simply appeared before Robert. Assuming the presence of a faceless angel in black, the devil stood no taller, no thicker than Johnson. He had no gothic glow, no supernatural signifiers. Yet, his cartilaginous hands and wart-encrusted face let Robert know he wasn't being duped.

"Nice night," said a voice stenciled with flecks of broken blades and uneven stone.

"I figured you'd come."

"Your proposition caught my ear."

"A soul?"

"Your soul."

"Yes."

"And for possession of your soul, you want me to grant you the talents befitting a peerless blues man?"

"Already got that. I wanna play like I had two guitars going. I wanna be so good that people know I must be in legion with you."

"How have I earned such devotion here in God's country?"

"It ain't about you . . . or God. It's just about playing like one of you got possession over me. I gave up on God when he took my wife and child. That leaves you."

"By default."

"You kill my wife and baby?"

"No."

"OK, then." Robert extended his hand to meet with Lucifer's. The Devil was taken aback by Robert's brashness. There was no trepidation, no grating questions about the afterlife or lakes of fire. Johnson wanted what he wanted, and accepted the brutality of sealing such a deal. They shook hands, a gentlemen's agreement.

The Devil then asked to see Robert's guitar. He turned each of the tuning pegs a quarter notch or so, ran his barbed nail down the strings, and handed it back to Johnson. "So it is," blessed the beast, and faded into the Mississippi night.

Robert, willing to trade away the only piece of himself that folks believed survived past ruination, had done so with unwavering confidence and only a speck of carelessness. He neglected to discuss the duration of his contract. His soul's surrender was for eternity, but the length of his musical dominion on earth went unmentioned; and the devil lives in the details. Robert was only 26 when he succumbed to poisoning. They say the three days he hung on between the bar scene that planted the lethal seeds and his actual demise were ravaged with fits of dementia and vomit.

Robert, however, never once invoked God to intervene. He was resolved. The devil had won. He could only hope that the music he made would reverberate longer than the time he had been given to play it.

That was the patchwork version of the story, anyway. Upon sorting through all the sureties and hearsay on Robert's demonic tryst, Charly Lawson began to prepare himself for a journey of like purpose. *Johnson, thought Charly, had missed the point. It wasn't about bargaining for skill . . . it's where that skill would take you and for how long that would keep the Devil at bay.* Charly was confident that if he just timed his trek well, following the mythic maps and blueprints, he too would have his chance to barter for immortality.

One scalding Mississippi Summer night at the Three Forks after a fiery set of music, Charly packed up his Vega acoustic, stashed his slide in his breast pocket, and headed for the door. Two women cornered him by the jukebox on the way out. As the women clamored over the size of his hands and the might of his honey and vinegar voice, Charly reached in his pocket and produced two coins. "Play something nice on the jukebox, ladies. I got another gig to get to." Without so much as a grin over his shoulder, Charly moved through the doorframe and into the graveled street. He would not slow his pace until he came to the crossroads.

Upon arriving at Highway markers 61 and 49, Charly looked around for what the best vantage point might be. He settled himself on a knotted pine log, still gummy with sap, thicker than it was long, and began to play. He started off with a traditional blues progression, nothing fancy, and peppered the riffs with some fine finger picking, including a clean alternate bass line that gave the illusion that a stand up bass player had come along for the journey.

Soon, Charly had unearthed his mojo, and locked in on a pentatonic fury of bends, vibratos, slurs, hammers, slides, pull-offs, and licks so precise, even he glared in amazement at his own hands. Then, he summoned up the spirits:

> *Woke up this mornin', on a hellbound train*
> *Woke up this mornin' on a hellbound train,*
> *Well, I cry out for Jesus,*
> *But I know I cry in vain.*
> *The devil he got me, on a long black chain*
> *The devil he got me, on a long black chain,*
> *One end's 'round my ankle,*
> *The other's on this train.*

Charly looked around as he segued into an instrumental riff. Nothing. No devil, no hushed wind, even the woodland creatures were still about their business, hooting and scurrying over the dried leaves. Charly was undeterred, and continued his requiem:

> *The devil he got me, on the 503*
> *The devil he got me, on the 503*
> *Ridin' on a slow train*
> *Toward eternity.*
> *When I meet the devil, gonna kiss his shoes*
> *When I meet the devil, gonna kiss his shoes,*
> *Cause God may give us life,*
> *But the devil gave us the blues.*
> *Ain't no need in prayin', try to save my soul*
> *Don't you worry prayin', you can't save my soul*
> *Cause when you play the blues*
> *You got to pay the toll.*

"The blues," a voice said.

Charly looked up, expecting an apparition of evil incarnate. He was stunned when he found a white man in a chalk-tinged suit and an ivory pork-pie hat.

"That's some mighty fine picking, young man."

Though Charly's contempt for most white Mississippians ran deep, he knew the game. "Thank you, sir."

"What are you doing out here past midnight playing and singing like that for?"

"No harm done, is there, sir?"

"No, none at all."

"Good, 'cause I wasn't aiming for no trouble. Just wanted to play where I wouldn't bother nobody," said Charly, turning on a humble Jim Crow act that made him sick to his innards.

"Do you, uh, know who I am, son?"

Oh, damn, here we go, thought Charly. *Truant officer? County judge? Grand Wizard?* "No sir, I reckon I don't," said Charly.

"Nick Moloch. I'm a local . . . used to play music around town. Then I moved up North and got into the business end of it. I run a record company up there. We handle mostly popular artists, but some blues and jazz acts too. I came back to town looking for new talent; visited three jook joints this very night, with no luck. That is, until I started to walk back to the train station."

"Sir?"

"Son, what I just heard was some of the finest blues playing of my life. I'm not kidding you either. That was fine, fine picking and singing. Best I've heard in a long while. Now, the question is, would you be interested in doing some of that playing for money? Nothing big at first, but if you caught the ear of some of my business partners, maybe it could be. You could have a couple of sides released, maybe a recording contract."

Charly's mind was alight. He had come out to offer up his very being to the underworld, and through fate or good fortune, got all he bargained for with no more sacrifice than a blistered forefinger and a broken high E string. "Sir, I'm . . ."

"Stop right there. I don't feel comfortable with a man of your obvious talent talking to me like some Steppin Fetchit. You call me Nick, and I'll call you . . . what do I call you? Never got your name, son."

"Charly. Charly Lawson."

"Charly Lawson. Hmm . . . that's alright, I guess. 'Reverend Charly Lawson' maybe, or 'Gentleman Charly'. Yeah. Something nice. 'Lightnin' Lawson'. That kind of rolls off the tongue, don't it?"

"Sir?"

"Just trying to think of a name that'll sell."

"Oh. Well, uh, Nick. What I was saying was, I'm a blues singer, but don't get me wrong. I don't wanna die broke in some one room farmhouse. I got my sights set on bigger things, using my music to get me somewhere. You saying you're the man who can make that happen?"

"Me and some other friends of mine, yes, we can; if we can come to terms on some things."

"Things?"

"Like I said, maybe a new name, find you an image, some songs to sing."

"Songs? I got plenty of them. Write 'em myself."

"Charly, will you walk with me to the train station? I gotta catch the next ride home, and I dearly would like to talk to you about all this. Might be our only chance." Charly slung his guitar over his shoulder and ventured toward the depot with his newfound companion.

"Charly," said Moloch, "fact is, we got people whose job it is just to write songs. Can you believe that? Songs for fellas like you that play and sing so well. Now, I'm gonna tell you a little story. I'm sure you heard of Robert Johnson."

"Oh yeah. Hear about him lots."

"Well, see, he wanted to sing and play his music his way. Only reason he got to record anything was 'cause he spent his own money to do so.

Then, after spending all his savings to record it, didn't have any money to market it rightly. I'd say he'd be known all over the US if he'd done that differently. Hell, the old boy might even still be alive."

"Uh-huh." Charly wasn't sure what to make of this, but if he was being positioned to eclipse Johnson, he was willing to keep an open mind.

"Bottom line, Charly. Robert Johnson ain't gonna be remembered outside the Mississippi Delta, and even hometown folk will forget about him soon enough. You, on the other hand . . ."

"Go on."

"You seem like you got the smarts to recognize a good thing when you see it." The fat man pulled out a pair of four dollar cigars, extended one to Charly: "You smoke?"

"Nah . . . never could justify spending the money on 'em."

"You will. Here."

Moloch lit up Charly's cigar and then his own. They shared an inaugural draw and continued their journey. "You see, Charly. These blues you and your people play, they're raw and filled with passion . . . am I right?" Nick gave Charly a knowing nudge. "Now, that's good, but blues music, that ain't all there is. The music people are listening to on the radio every day ain't blues. Oh sure, there's some blues down underneath maybe, but there's also lots of what we call *mainstream* music. You know what I'm talking about?"

"Guess so."

"Now, I ain't saying take the blues outta your music. I'm just saying you might think about making it more presentable to the white folks who have the, excuse me for saying so, but have the money to invest in buying records every month."

"How I go about doing that?"

"Did you hear what you were singing back there, 'bout the devil taking you to Hades and such? White folks don't want to be hearing 'bout all that sadness and evil. Hell, we just now are recovering from the depression."

"*We* ain't." Charlie tilted his head back toward Greenwood.

"Yeah, and you never will, going on like that. Hell, you revel in it. The idea is to smooth over your blues. Temper it with some Dixieland or swing to perk it up a bit."

"That ain't really blues, is it?"

"Look here, if you wanna keep on singing for poor folks who are aching from their woes, so be it, but I don't see how you're ever gonna rise above your station that way. You wanna inspire them to do better? Do better for yourself." Nick rubbed his chin, angling for a way to say it delicately, but the best he could muster was a blunt "That means music that has an appeal beyond the local jook."

"Lemme ask you this, Mr. Moloch. Why would white folks wanna listen to a colored singer anyway?"

"Your people's music is starting to permeate the air up our way. Trouble is nobody white will go to a colored club to see you sing. Race relations are better up North, but hell, it ain't exactly like we're kissing cousins."

The train station was just apiece up the road. The conversation had frittered by quicker than their strides. Charly knew they were nearing the end of their trek. "That being the case, how do I go about making music for money?"

Nick grinned like he had just plucked the long stem of the wishbone. "You let me surround you with some musicians . . . white musicians. You let my people select your repertoire, book you some gigs, and let's just see what happens, Charly." A gentle clinch of Charly's shoulder punctuated the offer.

"And what do I do?"

"You sing. You play. Well, maybe you play. We'll decide that. You might just vocalize. But, if you do, you work on a smoother way o' playing. If you can play the dickens out of a guitar like I just heard you do, I know you can turn it down a notch or two, right?"

"Mmm. I guess."

"And we can just as easy take some of the piss 'n vinegar outta your voice. You sing with a lot of feeling. We don't wanna lose that . . . we just wanna change the emotion behind it a little. Little taste of the big city life will give you all the inspiration you'll need."

The two now stood on the train platform, in front of an eight car passenger train, fires stoked and ready for boarding. The engineer passed by, pocket watch in hand. "You sure have given me cause for thought, Mr. Moloch," said Charly.

"Well, hell, Charly, what's to think?"

"I guess just sleep on it so when we talk again . . ."

"Charly, we don't talk again. I'm leaving in three minutes. I had every intention of taking you with me."

"Right now?"

"You got your guitar. I'll get you a new set of clothes and a place to stay. You got anything else you can't live without until you pass through again?"

"I reckon not, but . . ."

"But nothing, Charly, if you do this, you might be in a recording studio by next week. You could be signing papers by Monday lunch." Charly surveyed the station, east to west, in pregnant consideration.

"What's it gonna be, Charly? I can't come back for ya. And if I have to send for ya, it could take a week or two. It makes a big difference, me telling my associates about the next big thing and me showing up with him in tow."

"Yeah, I can see where that'd be true."

Nick handed the porter his ticket, and stepped on board. Charly stood at the platform's edge, letting his gaze run the length of Nick's anticipatory stare, the 'Colored' car at the end of the train, and the wooded pathway he had just traversed. Charly's eyes met Nick's again and locked. Nick puffed his cigar and smiled a twisted smile that Charly ultimately could not deny.

"I guess you gotta grab me a ticket for the Colored car, then," said Charly.

Nick's smile widened. "Already taken care of, just go on back to the last car. Sorry 'bout that. Them's Mississippi's rules, not mine."

Charly welcomed one last ride on the cultural caboose. The milk and honey would flow soon enough. He tipped his hat to Nick, then to the Porter. Charly turned one more time to give Greenwood a fond valediction. He pulled his guitar off his back and clutched it in a gracious hug. Here he was, ready to give away his very soul for what was coming to him all along. *Maybe Robert Johnson wasn't so foolish after all. Maybe it was a matter of being unlucky. Bad timing. Poor bastard.*

Charly was ready to shake the Delta dirt off of his shoes and claim his portion. He pinned his guitar under his arm and stepped aboard the car. As Charly cleared the last step, he looked across the car; before him sat two dozen black men, each clutching guitars, each burdened by a look of assent. Their eyes were gaunt, unflinching. They cut right through him. Charly stood silent in the aisle, as the 503 pulled away from the station.

14

OPENING DAY

You can smell the promise of Opening Day—the bouquet of the newly shorn turf, the slight hint of lime down the foul lines, the powdery cloud of Gatorade as it's dumped into the dugout cooler. Stand behind the plate and the expanse looks like God's promise to a chosen few, the 750 men who call The Show home. It is Easter Sunday after a winter of Good Fridays. Unfailing as an equinox, the nine hometown boys take the field, the last warm-up pitch is tossed, the lead-off man steps into a chalk-rimmed box of perfect proportions, and rests the bat on his shoulder, just for a second, to survey the wonder, the possibilities. A whole season of hope stretches out in front of him like a chiasmic yawn, and when he lifts the bat from his shoulders, the gentle weight of ten thousand little boys' dreams takes its place.

The pitcher, too, holds 10,000 wishes, held between the 108 tightly woven stitches of the ball. He is the thinking man's hero, calculating the inches, the precision of his dipping curve, his elusive slider, his heat so brutal that no man's stick could lay claim to it. He stands in the eclipsing shadows of Koufax, Gibson, and Spahn and prays his arm has a tenth of their elegance. This first pitch sets the tone for the game, for the season.

There is symmetry to baseball that eludes us in life. Away from the diamond, as perfectly chiseled as any jeweler's stone, our days long for the simplicity of throw, hit, and catch. But God is no more in the dugout guiding our game than Casey Stengel. God's up in the cheap seats now, with binoculars, doing His best to just score the game properly.

At best, for those of us who must watch from afar, the game is a metaphor. But baseball is also the one great peacemaker. When my father and I, estranged as two warring tribes, would go to see the Sox play at Fenway, all conversation of broken curfews and C-level grades fell away and we worshipped together at the altar of all that was true and good in our lives, in the taste of a hot dog smothered in golden mustard, in the enviable joy that came with having field level seats where Fisk could hear me call his name. My last good memory with Dad comes not in us holding hands through his mire of IV's and tubes at Mt. Sinai, but of our palms slapping together as one when the Sox clinched a playoff berth a few months before he died.

Today, it is baseball that brings me a tenuous balm with an eleven-year-old boy who doesn't yet know that when his father takes him home today, Dad will drive on to his new apartment, and see him on weekends and holidays. There was no defining moment for Trisha and myself, no clumsy one-nighter or careless fist. It was an almost imperceptible series of tiny pin pricks, rather than a mortar shell, that bled us out and lead to a weary admittance that love, in whatever form it had taken for us, had morphed into some sort of hideous complacency; a complacency we promised each other we would never tolerate should it find its way past our door. Maybe it was losing both my parents within a year's time. Maybe it was how the years had drained the passion out of Trish's shoulders when we embraced. Maybe I was just a lesser man than I wanted to believe.

Joshua sits in the car, the trunk packed with suitcases and clothes, and waits for me to drive us to the game. His playful honking of the horn is, for the first time in our lives, not funny to me. What used to be a gentle teasing of my own impatience before family trips now only bellows as a shrill reminder of my inadequacies. I stand in the kitchen, fumbling with keys and words, trying to find something to say to Trish that will lighten the burden for her, wishing suddenly I could make everything all right again. But I cannot. That I took the initiative to suggest my moving out, that I found an apartment a couple of miles away; these things were a death knell of sorts. She wanted me to stay, see if counseling would help us work things out, but I wanted a trial separation, a temporary split that I knew would only cause the rivulet between us to pool into a widening gulf. Each visit would become more formal, every conversation more guarded until one day we'd simply see that it made more sense, seemed more practical, to keep separate homes, separate lives.

"Coming, Josh! Stop honking please!" I yell as he taps a shave-and-haircut rhythm on the horn. "Look," I turn to Trish. "I'll just tell him the truth, but I'll leave it open, open that I might be back soon."

"So, you'd reconsider if . . ."

I cut her off before she could angle this into another quest for compromise. "I'm just saying, I think me moving out is enough for him to digest for a while. We won't talk about duration, or consequences. He'll just know that we'll get together again next Friday night and that I'll try to drop by for dinner once a week or so, that's all I can promise."

Trish's eyes well. The closer we've come to taking action, the more I realize that I am more invested in this change than she. Perhaps I was the only one who fell out of love, or maybe I just didn't have a healthy idea of what love should be, I don't know, but there was no turning back now. The deposit and the first and last month's rent were paid, and we had reached a peaceable agreement not one week earlier.

I kiss her on the temple, another sign of our flagging affection, and walk to the car. Trish doesn't follow me, leaving me with the image of her quivering lip, her eyes tinged with pink, her bare feet shifting on the linoleum floor in anxious dread. This, I think, is the last time I will live in my own home, the home I helped build, and I have no reason to give for it other than that there is a thin cage of ice around me now. Why I blame Trish for not being able to pry me from it, I do not know, but I do, as much as she blames me for being resolved to live in it.

We back out of the driveway and, sensing something is amiss, Josh poses a baseball trivia question, our traditional way of passing time en route to the stadium. "How old was Sandy Koufax when he quit the show?"

"That's easy," I say, "thirty." I toss it back to him. "Why did he quit?"

Josh wrinkled his nose. "He got hurt, right?"

"His pitching arm," I answered. "It felt older than thirty."

"How could he just quit like that? He was at the top of his game," says Josh.

"He had to save his arm, and I guess there were more important things to him. You know he refused to pitch in the opening game of the World Series because it fell on Yom Kippur."

"What's that?" asks Josh.

I give him a smile. "The holiest Jewish holiday. It's like Easter or Christmas for us."

Josh watches the traffic backing up on I-95 for a while as we drive into Boston. While his mind drifts from thoughts of Maysian catches to the steam from a fresh Sabrett, I grapple with the inevitable admittance that lay ahead, seeking some gentle precision as I raze a young boy's world. I will tell him, I think, as we are making our way home from Fenway. No man, no true father would deprive his son of the enchantment of a Major League game. This means that we'll have to push through this awkward silence and get on with the business of being fans, just a couple of buddies who swap lore and share a pretzel as we watch the luckless wonders of Beantown slouch toward almost.

Today the sun is a crimson wonder, sharing the sky with a hitter's wind that is decidedly pushing toward the Green Monster. Josh and I find our seats along the third base line and watch as the groundskeepers put the final touches on the field. It truly is majestic, and that Josh can see this makes me proud. He marvels at the diamond the way some kids his age stare at a new Gameboy or one of those X-Boxes through a store window. He sees past the labor disputes, the bloated egos, the steroid-strengthened muscles that help push regulation Rawlings into the cheap seats. The holiness comes from the total picture, the history that brought the game to this sun-drenched day, the formless legacy that assures him the game will still be a constant when he brings his son to Fenway. He knows where the game has been, and believes in where it can go. Mostly, for him, there is today, and all the promise Opening Day brings with it.

I am loathe to leave Joshua for even five minutes while I run to the restroom before the first pitch, but he assures me he will stay put, and I go. I come back with quickness in my step as I hear the public address announcer welcoming fans to Fenway and asking the 30,000 plus to rise for the presentation of the colors. To Josh's right is a black man now, sixty, perhaps older. He stands with his Kansas City Monarchs cap over his heart as local boy Steven Tyler sings—howls, perhaps—The National Anthem. The crowd cheers as if he has just performed "Dream On", and baseball prepares to birth another season of wonders.

The Red Sox take the field to a legion of hands echoing the percussive opening strains of John Fogerty's "Centerfield". Nine men in red and white scatter into a formation so familiar, so geometrically perfect that no logician could call it into question; the sun cascades off the foul lines, and the shadows drop like a swath of satin over section 153 where we are stationed. It is perfection.

Joshua sits with his glove in hand, naively certain a foul ball will have his name on it. "Whose foul you gonna shag today, Josh? Nomar's?" Josh gives me that look I used to give my dad, the one that says I need to back off the 'that's my boy' routine. But I have to keep my mind active, keep my head in the game. I cannot afford to sink into a morass of worry over talking to Josh about his mom and me, not if I've got nine innings and a walk to the car to wait through. So, I turn my attention to the man sitting at Josh's elbow, his head buried in his program, as he scribbles the line-up for the visiting Seattle Mariners on the scorecard. He finally feels my gaze.

"Oh hi." I am thrown by his steely glare. "I was just admiring that you were scorekeeping. It's a lost art." Josh gives me an eye roll.

"Kept score at every game I've been to since I was as young as this one here," says the man, nodding toward Joshua, who brashly responds with a headshake. "What? You don't keep score, little man?"

Josh is candid, but his tone respectful. "I miss too much of the game. Then, I get home and all I got is a sheet of paper that looks like a math test."

"Heh. Yeah, you can miss something if you're not careful, but you really learn the game when you keep score. The strategy, the science behind every play." The man jots down another name or two and cracks open a peanut shell with his free hand.

"Hey dad? What's his hat? That's not the Royals." Josh whispers. But his voice carries on the wind like a lifted fly ball.

"Now, I know a bright young fella like you has heard of the Kansas City Monarchs," says the man. I feel a history lesson coming on, though it is one long overdue.

"Are they a Triple A team?" asks Josh. I blush, like he's just asked the man why he isn't eating fried chicken instead of peanuts, but the man is a patient sage. "No, son. They were the finest team that ever played in the Negro Leagues." The second wave of redness came on as I anticipated Josh's next question. "What are the Negro Leagues?" Time stands still as the old timer looks to me. I give a weak smile, eager for Josh to learn about the history of the game, but really hopeful that he can enjoy the one at hand, given the post-game that lies ahead. Today, of all days, I want Josh to see something spectacular: a sliding catch, a triple play, a ball hit so hard it sails over the Red Seat in right field, shattering Ted Williams' Fenway distance record.

"You know, Josh should learn about the Negro Leagues. Maybe you could tell him about them. You know, between innings." My statement feels like a peace offering rather than an earnest request. The man laughs. "Son, the Leagues were as rich and textured as the Majors in their day— I got more stories than your boy here has patience. I'd talk his ears off." I give him a pursed-lipped smile, clean closure to our banter. That is, until Josh says, "I know who Jackie Robinson is."

"Do you now," says the man. "Yes," says Josh. "He was the first black man to play baseball." The man shook his head, "No, son, he was the first black man in the Majors, but the Negro Leagues were filled with black men playing baseball. Jackie broke down the wall."

"What wall?" asks Josh. The man points out toward the Green Monster. "One at least two times bigger than that one there."

His metaphor is lost on Josh, and the first pitch is imminent. "Tell ya what, we'll pick this up later," said the man. I smiled and nodded on Josh's behalf. We watch together as Kurt Schilling sends a fiery screamer past Ichiro, twice baptizing the Fenway faithful with the tailwind of the pitch, the gale of the swing. Our annual constant is launched, with no site of labor strikes or rain clouds to stop the splendid machination of the next six months. Perhaps this will be the season when the Sox watch the World Series from the Fenway dugout, rather than from a sports bar.

Where will I be by post-season? Six months is an eternity—so many decisions made and executed in half a year, between the first and last pitches of a season. Players overcome slumps, find their stride, and contend for the title between April and October. All of that is put in motion today, by one pitch.

I am where I said I wouldn't be, lost in my thoughts, and find my way back only when the Sox are coming off the field after an apparent 1-2-3 top of the first. Our new friend thumbs his program, scanning player bios and earmarking an ad for Thornton's Fenway Grill. Josh watches him curiously, but never speaks. Fine with me, I think. He doesn't need to shoulder the white man's burden on my account. Not today anyway.

"Dad," says Josh. "What's going on?" I ask him what he means, putting on my best game face. "You've been staring at the foul pole for the last five minutes," he says. The kid doesn't miss a beat, I'll give him that. "You've been acting weird all day—you and Mom get in a fight?"

"Um, sorta. Yeah." The admittance of the slightest static between Trish and me seems to alleviate a soreness in my chest, and I only hope that this slight revelation hasn't transferred the ache to Josh. Josh pushes onward, unaware of the rocks poised to fall in his path. "You fight a lot, or you did. Then, you stopped. Now it's just real quiet all the time. Is everything o.k.?"

"Yeah, Josh. It's fine. Grown-ups fight sometimes, it's how we work things out."

"You've just been really weird," Josh says.

"I'm fine, Josh. We're all fine. Hey, tell ya what. Why don't you go get us a couple of hot dogs?" Josh's face shines, and I hand him a twenty-dollar bill. "Get whatever you want with the rest of it, o.k.?" My son, so earnest and concerned just seconds before, is on his feet, bounding over his aisle mate with the clumsy exuberance of a foal. He hollers back an obligatory "excuse me" as he tramples up the stairs and out the entryway.

I stare out at the infield and take in the New England air, but can feel the old man's eyes on me. I turn. The slightest hint of a smile curls at the corners of his mouth. "Got out of that one, huh?"

"Yeah, well, we came to watch a game, not have a family counseling session. He should get to enjoy the game."

"Mm-hm," the man returns to his scorekeeping, and I feel the air leave my mouth, a weighted sigh that makes my chest tremble. I had gotten out of 'that one', but it was just a stall tactic. I couldn't keep buying Josh hot dogs the rest of the day. I've no sooner thought this than the man says, "When you gonna tell him?"

"When am I going to tell him what?"

"That it's over." The man has folded his program and is now giving me his full attention. A lifetime of scoring every at-bat suddenly tossed aside to play therapist. I remain resolute. "I guess that's really none of your business, and who says it's over anyway?"

"You. I seen it before. Seen both of my sons do it to their kids. You get this faraway look like you'd rather be anywhere else, and you carry that with you wherever you go. Gets so you wanna shed your own skin, but you don't. You shed theirs." He kicks his head back, alluding to Josh.

"Yeah, well, every marriage is different. Every family is different." I hope to sound more indignant that I likely do. By now, Josh is headed back down the stairs with two hot dogs and a souvenir cup of Coke big enough to have an undertow. "Let's just drop it, alright?" I say. "Dropped," the man says, and Josh slides back between us, aglow with excitement over the taboos he's about to break. Trish is a bit of a health nut, and hot dogs rarely make it into our fridge. As for cola, it's regarded with the same disdain as tobacco and firearms, so this is a pure criminal activity for Josh, and I am all for it.

As Josh takes a chunk out of his first hot dog, the man leans in and says, "Wanna hear about Jackie Robinson now?" Josh shrugs, wiping the mustard from his chin with his free hand and, after a premature swallow, concedes, "Sure. You ever meet him?"

"Meet him? Yes, I did, but not at a ball game. I met him on an airplane some years later. 'Course, I'd watched him play all those years, so I felt like I knew him already."

I am grateful for the man fulfilling his promise to Josh, and for getting off my back about our personal woes. It's funny, but when the weight of the world is on you, there's a real war that goes on inside between wanting everyone to give you help and everyone to just keep to themselves. Even strangers. I caught myself more than once over the past few months getting into such conversations at work, at church, even over poker with a group of guys who haven't had an emotional revelation since their first orgasm. I'd ask "Why do people stay together?" and that would open up all kinds of psychobabble. Most of the comments leaned toward not wanting to be alone and how being comfortable was equitable to being happy. I didn't buy it, but I liked hearing people talk about it for a while, then I wished they'd stop. At some point, the talk always crossed a threshold that went from theoretical to personal, and then I'd recede.

I listen as the man tells Josh about how gracious Robinson was when they met, and how Robinson was as pivotal as Martin Luther King and Rosa Parks for the Civil Rights Movement. "To refuse to get up and go to the back of the bus, that was huge," he said, "but to be dropped in the middle of some fifty-odd white men on the field, and another few thousand in the stands, most of whom would just as soon see you beaten with a bat as hitting with one, that's something else."

Josh is well into his second hot dog now, and the two have totally lost sight of the game, mired in the stuff of which legends are made. Schilling is throwing fireballs past the Mariners, but Josh and his new friend are decades away, in a time both simpler and more small-minded. The man tells Josh about seeing Jackie in a major league uniform for the first time and standing silent as crowds jeered his mere presence on the field. He talks about a game where he watched Jackie turn even the vilest of bigots into rabid fans with his hustle and verve. He paints a picture of a man, half-way down the third base line, taunting the pitcher as he goes into his stretch, daring him to pick him off, then breaking for home and beating the pitch across the plate. "Stealing home, that was his trademark," he says. "You had to either be brave or crazy to try it."

"We steal home a lot in my league," says Josh. This is where I jump into the fray. "Uh, Josh, that's on a passed ball or wild pitch. Jackie Robinson stole home on perfect strikes."

"Your dad's right," says the man. "See, Jackie knew that to get through all that hate, he'd have to take his game to a new level. He'd have to play the game better than every white man out there, and he did, even with people yelling horrible things and throwing pieces of watermelon on the field. Josh furls his brow. "It's a myth that black people like watermelon," I tell him. "It's a stereotype, and they were making fun of him." Josh seems befuddled by this, and I am glad for it. Racism shouldn't make sense, and kids will be the first to let you know it doesn't.

A loud cheer pulls us back to the game as Garciaparra drives one to the centerfield wall and makes it to third after the ball takes a wild careen toward right field. We are rapt in the anticipation of a man-on-third, no out situation—a much-needed insurance run at odds with the many ways a team can leave a man stranded ninety feet away. But today, the diamond gods are smiling, and on an 0-and-2 pitch, Manny Ramirez faithfully drives a sac fly to left, giving Nomar plenty of time to tag and cross.

Putting what appears to be a button on our Jackie Robinson discussion, the man confides to Josh that Jackie would've been dancing and bouncing on the third base line, giving the opposing pitcher such fits that he couldn't have found Ramirez's strike zone with a roadmap and a compass. "Jackie would either have taken home, or helped Brooklyn load the bases. He made pitchers that nervous," he says.

Josh and I watch as Boston goes on a tear, piling up seven hits in the next two innings, including two long balls that give us a commanding 7-0 lead over Seattle. By the eighth, I am thinking about the talk Josh and I must have, and I start getting my head around it again. We have managed, thanks to a Sox blowout and our didactic friend, to breathe in baseball for the three hours we've spent under the Fenway sun. Now, the magic is coming to an end.

As the Sox take the field for the top of the ninth, the man leans in to Josh one more time, speaking loud enough for me to hear, too. "You know what it takes to play baseball, son?" Josh gives him a puzzled look. "For those men out there, it takes talent and determination. For Jackie Robinson, it took something more. It took a kind of courage most men don't have. Only the thing is, they do, they just don't know it. You know the kind of courage I'm talking about?" Josh nods but his eyes broadcast his naiveté. I begin to feel uneasy with the man. The time has come to move on, and I want Josh to enjoy the end of the game; the thrill of the final out, even in a lopsided game, is to be cherished. Instead, this old timer is breathing his hot breath in Josh's face, giving him a life lesson to accompany his baseball history. "Look," I say, "you've been real nice, but Josh is trying to watch the . . ." He cuts me off, spitting his words right over Josh's head and into my face with a voice as steady as rod iron but eyes that reveal a fury that must run deep. "The kind of courage I'm talking about is the kind that gets handed down because someone showed it to you. You think Jackie Robinson walked out on Ebbets Field alone that first day? He had the weight of all of Negro America on his shoulders, praying to God he'd get a hit that first at bat, and you know what else he had? He had the good sense to know he was right where he belonged. That's why he couldn't stay on third base for too long without dancing down the line. He knew he was meant to cross that plate—to steal home. It was the bravest thing a player could do, and that's why we spent half this ball game talking about him instead of one of those men down there right now."

I give the man a cursory nod, the sermon now ending, but then he quips, "Takes courage to know where you really belong. That's the kind of courage little boys take with them into manhood. All the 'go home, nigger' chants and watermelon rinds in the world can't take that out of you." The man holds his stare until he senses my shame, then he tips his hat and says, "Good to meet you both. Take care now." Josh, who ignored all that just transpired in favor of the game, turns away from the field and offers a goodbye. The man smiles back at him and nods, then gives me a parting look, takes a breath, and heads out into the walkway.

I find it absurd that this man would try to chisel away at the complexity of a marriage, tying it up in some cinematic sermonette on sports heroism. To think he could somehow change my heart with one swelling 'Field of Dreams' speech seems ludicrous to me, and there is a part of me that wishes I'd told him I saw right through his quixotic pining. Courage, I think, is knowing when to walk away, like Sandy Koufax did when his arm gave out. Courage, like everything else in life, is subjective, and cannot be relegated to broad ethical blueprints. It is situational, as much as we hate to admit it, and sometimes the bravest thing one can do is hang up his spikes.

The game ends with a long fly ball that teases the Green Monster but ultimately drops like a sandbag over the warning track and into the faithful glove of Johnny Damon, who drifts from center to shag it. Already on our feet to watch the trajectory of the drive, the fans give the Sox a cheer as the teams gather around the mound for high-fives and glove slaps. Josh jokes that they ought to make Major Leaguers line up and say 'good game' to all the opposing players, like he is required to do in his pony league. This makes me smile, and I pull him to my side and give him a squeeze.

In the parking lot, I start to break the ice. "Josh, you wanna go get some ice cream? There's something I'd like to chat with you about." He is mildly suspicious—Coke and ice cream in the same day means something, though he is not sure what. "Sure, Dad."

"Let's go to Ben and Jerry's," I offer, and we slide into the front seat to caravan with the snaking line of cars out onto I-95 again.

Figuring we're in for quite a meltdown, I begin to broach the subject, trying to get handle on my opening farewell. I had structured it all in my head, at least I thought I had: start with the generalities about how people sometimes don't stay together, about how some of his friends have parents who have split, and then whittle it down to the inevitable specifics, the dance around the 'd' word. But as I try to stack the words in my head, they are nudged out by the indelible image of a pair of cleated feet, dancing over chalk dust. The damn man stuck Jackie Robinson in my head and, stubborn player that he was, Jackie won't walk away. Instead, he jitters back and forth, channeling all that fear—a fear he must've felt in some deep down part of him, wondering if someone in the third base bleachers might throw a brick or fire a pistol. That fear is melted down by an alchemist's hands into pure courage, and thrown back into the fire again, illuminating the trail for those brave enough to get close to the heat. I see his feet start to settle and then, like a train, surge down the line toward home plate. He is alive in the moment, and his slide, a mere half-inch under the catcher's swiping tag, is what happens when pressure succumbs to grace. No matter how hard I try, I cannot release the image, the majesty of one man, carrying dreams on his shoulders, down the third base line and finding himself, finally, safely home. The words I'd constructed, once so inevitable, will not come. They have come too close to that heat.

I don't know what Jackie looked at when he started his run homeward—the pitcher's footing, the catcher's mitt, or maybe the ball as it raced him to the plate. I'd like to think he had his eye on the only thing that mattered: home.

I am not sure what I will do tomorrow. I could find myself putting my shirts and jeans on crappy metal hangers in my new closet on Willoughby Lane. I could be calling a marriage counselor and asking naïve questions about the therapeutic process. No one knows what lies ahead when the next pitch comes along. Today—at this moment—I do know where I am supposed to go. I am carrying a little boy's hopes on my shoulders for one more day. Today, I am stealing home.

15

CAN I HELP YOU?

S he'd checked me out with my groceries twice before—frozen dinners, shaving cream, a carton of Pall Malls, that kind of thing. She'd managed to scan two and a half week's worth of food without ever speaking to me, not even eye contact.

In my day, people didn't treat you that way. A firm gaze, a warm smile were part of what you were buying. These kids today, though, they've got little interest in paying attention to just about anyone who can't do them some good. I'm just an old man to her, to all of them, I suppose. Still don't make it right.

Her face reminds me of Ellie's old bulletin board in the kitchen, plugged full of shiny pins, creating some sort of punctured symmetry. This girl's got earrings in places I'd never imagined I'd see them, outside of some National Geographic special on aborigines. And her eyes, did she paint them that dark, or is she just not sleeping? Maybe she smokes. Smoking will do that to you. Ages your eyes. Aged mine. I wonder if she's still in school.

I'm going to play a game today. Try and get her to talk to me; direct questions, teasing questions if I have to. I'll get her riled if I can't get some courtesy out of her. That's how I used to get Ellie to open up. Even when Ellie was sick, and knew she wasn't leaving the hospital, I could get her to talk if I teased her about the tubes of food running into her arm. We joked up to the last minute. Her last breath was more like a laugh. Or a sigh. You know that kind of sound when you exhale, but it sounds light, like a titter of laughter. It was like that. I was glad for that. I hold it in my grip every day. No one can take that.

Maybe I'll tell her that joke I heard on the country station yesterday morning. Do kids still tell jokes? I don't know what moves this generation. They're so damn different. They're like foreigners to me.

She needs to talk to me today. She can't keep to herself forever. Bad for business.

16

MEAT IS MURDER

Tofurkey. Not Dogs. Veggie Joes. It's not like you couldn't find ways around eating meat if you really tried. The flesh of God's creatures doesn't have to be systematically, voraciously destroyed for people to survive, even thrive, on this planet. And yet, there they were over in the produce section, scavenging over cuts of pork shoulder and veal shanks, chicken necks and ground round, like some sort of carnivorous brigands. Superior; higher on the food chain with their opposable thumbs that help them clip coupons for marked-down rib eyes and kabobs. A warped sense of entitlement.

These thoughts permeated Harper Peet's mind every time she visited the pedestrian grocery store rather than her usual vegan-friendly market. From time to time, she had to go where the flesh-rippers roamed in order to procure items that just weren't available elsewhere. It was also a decent place to meet her next convert.

Harper didn't have any PETA stickers on her car. She'd never tossed red dye on a fur-wearing diva in the streets of Pasadena. Yet over the course of less than two years, she had converted nine people to a chiefly vegetarian lifestyle.

Harper reformed men: fattened, breathless men who she'd see waddling through food courts with their orange trays of orange glazed chicken or saddling up to the burger bar at Shoney's. The flash of a slender calve, a wry smile while spooning croutons on her salad, and the ice would be broken. Then, she'd saunter over and introduce herself. Nothing forward, just a 'hey, don't I know you' or 'I'm sorry, I couldn't help but notice . . .' For a single, stout gentleman in Texas, this was all the energy Harper had to exert. She was seated at his table within seconds.

Harper kept sex out of the equation; she was nobody's whore, not even Isaac Singer's. But, the visit rarely ended without the setting of a dinner date—she'd cook, her place.

Once her portly quarry would arrive at her duplex, she'd treat him to a vegan meal so analogous to its brute kin that her date wouldn't know the difference. In fact, so delectable were the servings that the men never questioned the animal-friendly ambrosia. It was only after two heaping platefuls of Fake Steak, Tofu Chops, or a fresh soy and black bean half-pounder that Harper might let the recipe out of the bag.

More than likely, though, she'd hold the cards to her chest. She'd learned this after a too eager attempt at conversion a couple of years ago, which resulted in a huffy exit by a mill worker who was none too pleased to find his stomach had been firmed with a five-alarm chili composed of soy protein and wheat. His "fuck you, hippie freak", as he stormed out almost made Harper quit right then and there. Instead, she refined her approach, streamlining to a less aggressive tact.

Now, she'd actually court these men, feed them, watch them trim a few pounds, and boost their self-esteem. The education went virtually undetected, like the sound waves on a subliminal tape. True, it could take weeks or months, but only when she felt they were truly on a path toward a better way of living would she gently let them go. It was, she believed, a win-win: the reformed men, the pardoned beasts, and her own conscience. Somewhere, she knew her daddy was watching her and giving his blessing. He orphaned her when he was just 44, but the coroner's report said his arteries appeared closer to eighty when he had his fatal heart attack—an episode she witnessed and then relived throughout her teenage and collegiate years. Group therapy and an empathic grief counselor helped, but it was only when she read a flyer for a wellness seminar, titled "Change the World, One Life at a Time" did the conflagration of her grief get regenerated into a small flicker of hope. She became a vegetarian, shed twenty-nine pounds of fleshy despair, learned what animals do to our bodies, and what we do to theirs. Meat was murder—for all involved. From this spark, the enduring fire arose, and Harper set out to win souls to a lengthy, cruelty-free life, reaching out to those who turned deaf ears to rhetoric, who ignored doctors' pleas. She sought the unreachable.

Tonight at Food-Co, Harper shone her candle on the butcher himself, a stout, unshaven fellow whose stubby hands likely reeked of raw meat. He'd take some work, but she was feeling cavalier.

A stunning woman, Harper had learned that she had to look more the urban cowgirl than Berkley grad. Gone was the knitted serape, the worn Birkenstocks that revealed her unpolished toes, the mala beads around her wrists. Instead, she now sported bright yellow and orange Oxfords, faded Levis, and bovine-friendly cowboy boots encasing her now cinnamon red digits. Her hair, once carelessly pulled back in a simple ponytail, flowed freely over her shoulders in a fiery red cascade.

She approached the counter, masking her disdain for meat. The look of it, glowing up all bloody red and fatty white from its cellophane and Styrofoam shells, made her innards churn. She kept her eyes level with the chunky meat peddler.

"Hi, can I help you?" His cheeriness belied his grizzly look. An easy smile shone from his unimpressive mug.

"I'm sorry, are you Marty Scones?" asked Harper.

"No . . . no. My name's Larry . . . Larry Getz," he said.

"Oh . . . my gosh, you look like Marty. I went to high school with him in Luchenbach. Of course, that was forever ago . . ."

"You don't look like you've been out of high school all that long," said Larry. The first compliment; the jaws of the snare trembled.

"Why, thank you."

"How can I help you?"

"Err, a half dozen shrimp, please". She had no intention of actually buying the shrimp. She'd ditch it on an end cap en route to the checkout counter.

"A half dozen?"

"Dinner for one." Her answer provided more entryways than a gazebo.

"Oh." He cast his eyes away from her, embarrassed.

"Hard to meet the right fella, I guess." She took the shrimp from him, clumsily secured in a sheet of butcher's wrap, then she lingered, keeping the conversation alive with talk about hating the singles scene, her wariness of dating services, and the ennui of eating over the sink while watching reruns of 'Andy Griffith'.

An awkward silence, followed by an awkward attempt: "I like shrimp." It was weak, but she knew it was his best shot.

"I guess I'm going out on a limb here, but . . . would you like to have dinner sometime?" She asked.

He was fat, lonely. She was lovely, sweet. There were no other pre-qualifiers for Larry. He lived alone, ate alone, watched movies alone. "Yes!" Stray dogs couldn't jump on his meat scraps any quicker. The jaws snapped shut.

"Saturday night, around six?" she asked. She scribbled her address at the bottom of her grocery list, tore it off, and handed it to him.

"What can I bring?" He suddenly had the hopeful innocence of the chubby kid just asked to the Sadie Hawkins dance by a cheerleader.

"You like wine? Bring a bottle of red."

"Will do . . . . uh . . . I never got your name."

"I'm Harper." She extended her hand, and Larry met it with his, trussed tightly in a slimy Laytex glove. As soon as he realized his breach, he pulled back, horrified. "I'm so sorry. Really." He gave her a paper towel and she said a polite goodbye, then she raced to the ladies' room to scour the meaty residue from her hand. The stink, she thought, would stay with her all day.

That Saturday, Harper created a banquet for Larry. The appetizer was Roquefort tartlets and tomato pesto toasts. The main course a tender tagliatelle with spinach gnocchi and homemade tomato sauce gently seasoned with oregano and fresh garlic. Dessert was a vegan chocolate mousse, lighter than hummingbird wings.

Larry arrived a little before six, but drove around the block twice to make sure he didn't show up too early. He spent the better part of the afternoon looking for the perfect combination of clothes. Too casual and he'd seem flippant, too formal and he'd come off stuffy. The compromise of jeans with a button down shirt and sport coat, he felt, was perfect. Harper had seen this first-date ensemble so many times that she had to resist snickering when she opened the door for Larry.

Harper welcomed Larry in, accepting a bottle of 1998 Coppola Merlot and a long-stem rose as he entered. She pecked him on the cheek, and turned on her two-inch heels to the kitchen, where she was putting final touches on the inaugural feast. "Make yourself comfortable," she said.

"This is a nice place, Harper," said Larry, admiring the amalgamation of photos and artwork on her walls—O'Keefe and Ansel Adams sharing space with Grandma Peet and Papa Rose.

"Thanks. Can I pour you some wine, or get you something? A beer?"

"I don't really drink. Not anymore."

"Oh . . . well, there's Diet Coke, tea."

"Water's fine. I need to drink more water," said Larry, patting his bloated stomach.

"We all do. They say that 80% of Americans walk around dehydrated most of the time. Can you imagine how much more energy we'd have . . ." Harper caught herself. Such lectures were landmines for this early in the relationship. She handed him a glass.

"Thanks," said Larry. "Yeah, we'd be better off, I guess. I tell ya, I get home from work sometimes and it's all I can do to stay awake through a ball game. Of course, I'm on my feet all day." He stood in the middle of her living room stiff as a cadet, an awkward ox too worried about the china shop around him.

"Really, Larry, get off your feet! Sit! Hell, take your shoes off, I don't mind. You can relax, honey," said Harper. Her guarantees soothed him some. He sat, Buddha-like, on the ottoman.

"Thank you. I'll leave my shoes on."

"Whatever you like. And I hope you like tarts, because that's our appetizer." She served him a small plate brimming with delicate pies, small enough to rest in a child's palm; each carefully filled with the finest non-dairy gourmet cheese on the market. The faux Roquefort, she was assured by the market, was imported from France.

Larry wouldn't have known if the cheese was real or not, or whether it came from Paris, Texas, rather than Paris proper. He liked it because Harper made it. And he liked Harper because he sensed Harper liked him.

The entrée was equally appreciated. The gnocchi was one of her finest creations, and not a bad introduction to vegetarian living for Larry. The fake beef and such would come a date or two down the line. For starters, the sheer pleasure of a hearty meal that never assumes the need for meat is the strongest and subtlest tact.

After a dinner's worth of flimsy conversation about Texas, family, and a delicate dance around world events, they retired to the living room. Harper held up a DVD she had rented for the occasion—the latest Robert Duvall movie, a western. Larry had seen it before, but would never tell Harper that. Harper slid down next to Larry on the love seat as the previews rolled. For the first thirty minutes of the movie, Larry hardly moved. He sat like a paralyzed bear cub, arms hugging his belly, a barely perceptible twitch from his head now and then.

Harper wasn't looking for any crude advances, but she did hope that Larry would show enough interest to put his arm around her, or at least shoot a gaze her way now and then. She slipped her shoes off and tucked her silky bare feet underneath her, just inches away from Larry's lap. Foot flirting, she'd found, was a very non-threatening lure—the physical contact was minimal, while keeping her beau entranced and entangled. For some men, it wasn't mere foreplay; it was unshod sex, pure and simple.

Larry, however, just scooted over a bit to give her more room. By the end of the movie, Harper was feeling soundly rejected. She turned down the volume a bit as the music over the credits swelled. Then, she gave Larry another glance and saw that his brow was caked with a layer of warm sweat. At that moment, she realized, he was afraid of her. Her closeness intimidated him, the promise of her bare feet brushing his thigh perhaps the most sexual contact he'd had with a girl.

He felt her sympathetic eyes leering at him. When he realized the sweat beads were evident, dangling rivulets of liquid failure, he wiped them off and leapt from the love seat. "Oh . . . oh. I have to go," he said. Harper's heart ached for him. Her goal was to heal these men, to help them achieve a higher level of humanity, not to send them reeling to therapy.

For a moment, she thought she might just come clean and relieve the pressure on them both. Then, thinking better of it, she realized this would only cripple him further. This was their first date, and he, more than anything, needed a second one. She grabbed his shoulders, easing him down from his panicked lather. "Hey, hey. It's o.k. You don't have to be so nervous around me, Larry. I'm the one who asked you out, remember? I should be the basket case."

"Yeah. Yeah." He took a swallow of air and regrouped. "I haven't done this in a long time. Dating, I mean. I was never any good at it." He looked around, still a bit disoriented. "Can I sit down?"

"Sure, sweetie," said Harper. They sat and she took his burly hand in hers. "Look, honey. I'm in no rush. We had dinner—that's all. We can move nice and slow. No pressure. Let's just take it easy and see where it goes."

"What you must think," he said. "What a wimp, huh?"

"God, no. It's sweet, getting nervous around me. It means you like me, right?" She wanted to do the work for him, get him out of this painful hole he'd dug.

"Yes, I do! I really do."

"Tell you what. Let's go ahead and make a second date, and you just forget all about tonight. Go home. We'll start fresh next time."

"Really?" He sniffed, childlike.

"Really." She walked him to the door and gave him a lingering peck on the cheek. "How 'bout a weeknight? Wednesday? Around 6:30?" He nodded, thanked her for a beautiful dinner, for being sweet, and walked the narrow sidewalk to his truck.

Harper locked the door and turned to survey the stack of dishes, the leftovers needing to be stored, and the love seat stained with a ring of perspiration on one side. She was troubled by what Wednesday might bring. All the men who she'd dated on this vegan conversion trek were a bit headstrong, stubborn. It was watching them come around that gave her joy—seeing their minds open to the possibility of trimming down, the hope of meat-free meals, the gentle unfolding of a new life. But Larry was different; he was soft, clingy. His flop sweat was like flypaper, ensnaring her pumiced heels. He required the softest of kid gloves.

Wednesday came and went with a more casual dinner—vegan sloppy joes and fresh red potato wedges with a drizzle of olive oil and brown mustard. Harper, too, was more casual—a Bonnie Raitt t-shirt, denim shorts, and Keds. The atmosphere seemed to work with Larry, who was calmer, chattier this time. That he was working to relax was often times evident, but his exertion made him all the more pitiable to Harper. When he gathered up the nerve to ask for a third date on the way out the door, she'd have to have been a Gestapo to say 'no'. This time he pecked her cheek. And this time, as he cleared the threshold, she could've sworn she heard him mutter, "Love you"—the phrase dropped and abandoned like a teenager leaving a stink bomb on her doorstep. Before she could be sure, though, he was gone, bounding down the sidewalk like a gleeful little leaguer.

This was a problem. Infatuation and lust she could handle. She knew how to two-step through that terrain, but "I love you" had never come up before. The tough Texas men were always too proud to invite such constriction. She could depend on it like true north. But Larry . . . he was different.

Rather than dwell on the minefield that was date number three, she sought distraction—journalistic schadenfreude. She kicked off her Keds and curled up on the love seat to watch the news, the world's woes a strangely welcome reminder of how truly untroubled her tiny life was. There was the car bomb in Bali; the pizza deliveryman who was trussed up with barbwire, his neck injected with kerosene in some gang initiation in Ohio. And then, there was the big local story: a new slaughterhouse was about to begin operation in Tyler.

That morning, a tiny cluster of activists from New Mexico had made their way up to protest. Nothing new; slaughterhouses have always been targets for radicals. Earlier in the year, two killing floors in North Texas were under heavy scrutiny for continuing the practice of slaughtering wild horses for export of equine meat to Europe. Animal rights groups turned up the heat, getting injunctions against them. This next chapter was bound to cause a stir.

What created the media frenzy this time though was a bizarre string of events that unfurled at the protest. While the dozen or so vocal opponents of the slaughterhouse hup-two-three'd in front of the corporate overseer's main office in downtown Tyler, a handful of rapscallions—fans of "The Dutch Leamer Show"—showed up to stage a counter-protest. Leamer, a far-right regional radio host, announced that the protest was underway and that 'faithful followers' should head down there with handfuls of cheeseburgers and chicken fingers in hand, ready to hurl their bounty at the 'meatheaded mob'.

A small band of louts took Leamer at his word and upped the ante, showing up with raw meat in hand, and hungry canines on leashes. After pelting the 'granola bars' (Leamer's term for environmentalists) with bloody cuts of flank and topside, the pranksters let their pups loose to give the lefties a harmless, hilarious scare. The crowd spread as if dodging gunfire.

The beagle and retriever were innocent enough—they plodded toward the chunks of beef and gobbled them up, oblivious to the mayhem. The rottweiler, however, was another story. He smelled the fear, and despite weeks of obedience training, devoted himself to the removal of a college student's left forearm. Only the business end of a protest sign was convincing enough to bring him down. An animal rights activist had to drive a stake into the dog's back to save his friend, a final impulsive irony.

The news covered the story from all angles: the victim, who required 51 stitches; the hero, who had to stab a dog to save a colleague, too shaken to talk; the slaughterhouse spokesperson who talked of unassailable rights to operate their place of industry; and Dutch Leamer himself, who had no comment. Instead, the news showed a still of Leamer, his plump visage emblazoned on a billboard for a local steakhouse, a little cartoon balloon leading to his lips, pronouncing, "Have a cow, man!"

Harper felt her toes curl around the fabric of the love seat. Her hand gripped the armrest with feisty indignation. Here was the man she should have set her sights on; an icon whose conversion would create a trickle-down effect that could ripple throughout the Southwest. He could be her truest conquest, a peak experience that might even allow her to retire from her quixotic activism and live a dullard's life again, her karmic charkas at long last cleansed of obligation. Though he'd be tougher than gristle, Harper had found her last repair.

Harper didn't sleep very well that night, her mind a river of images—the raw meat dripping off of people's clothes, the dog following his instincts, the violent consequences for man and beast, the glowing teeth of Dutch Leamer hovering over a filet from Dottie's Steakhouse. Larry—fat, sweet, Larry—and his peck on the cheek, his hurried promise of devotion, never crossed her mind.

The next morning, a weary Harper hoisted herself out of bed for another day's grind at Java Juice. There, she served coffee and pastries three days a week to counter the dip in business the economy had invited upon her corporate writing job, penning newsletters and brochures from home. In the days of the Bull, she was able to sustain herself and her meager needs on her stay-at-home job alone. Now, though, a recession had most businesses in town putting Harper on hold.

She turned on the radio—A.M. talk this time, rather than her morning dose of NPR—in hopes of finding Dutch Leamer scuttling over the airwaves. She found him on his East Texas home, KRTX. Harper was aware of Leamer peripherally, but had never heard more than snippets of the man at work. As the coffee brewed and the water in the shower plunged on her skin, Harper gave audience to the man who woke people up with "a damn good dose of common sense" every morning.

Asked by a caller if Leamer felt his supporters went too far, he declined to comment, saying, "I hate lawyers, but I trust mine, and he tells me to keep my mouth shut on this one." Before each station break, however, Leamer made his feelings clear. The bumper music was accompanied by sound effects of cattle mooing, an ominous grinding sound, a lone dog growling, and most distastefully, an effeminate sounding man sassing "oooh, bite me, bitch!" Harper had heard enough, and found Steely Dan on a classic rock station while she finished her breakfast.

In doing so, she missed another ninety minutes of rhetorical theatrics. Leamer was the kind of man who celebrated the greenhouse effect, who sponsored trips to the Amazon to "chop down an acre or two of rainforest". He once taunted the Taos Pueblo tribe in New Mexico by sending them a box set of John Ford westerns on Yaqui Pagean—an Indian holy day. It was all in kidding, of course—a cry for America to 'get the stick out of it's thin-skinned ass', as he once said in a magazine interview.

Dutch Leamer hated the PC movement, and fed upon the 'mealy', as he called them; those that cried out for sensitivity in a world where only Darwin's most strapping survive. The majority of clear-thinking right-wingers had distanced themselves from him, finding him too bullish and extreme. Yet, he was there, with an audience as faithful as Pentecostals, heeding his flock to "educate the clueless, eradicate the useless". To some, it sounded like a fascist cry for eugenics. In truth, it was a desperate attempt to shock in a world where Howard Stern and reality television had raised the bar on what crawls beneath a listener's skin. Anne Coulter redux.

Harper's ire gnawed at her all day, a rottweiler clinched fast to her conscience. How could she woo and win a man so cruel; a man who'd sooner have Thumper on his plate than as a pet? The plan would involve some research, the first of which required a trip to the local bookstore to buy a copy of Leamer's first publication: "Why I'm Right".

She felt like she was renting a skin flick in the Disney Store when she walked up to the checkout with Leamer's tome in hand. The kid behind the counter appeared plucked right out of some commune in Aspen. His eyes gave her the once-over as she pulled out her debit card. Harper wasn't one for handling false scrutiny. "It's for my brother . . . his birthday," she lied with a blush.

"Oh," said the boy. Harper couldn't tell if he was relieved or indifferent. She wished she'd just kept her mouth shut.

Harper was so eager to sift through her new purchase that she just dug out some hummus and pita bread for dinner and, settling in with a half carafe of port, she sprawled out on the love seat to read about her next conquest.

She read Leamer's views on all things political, from abortion to unions. It didn't take long for her to realize she was taking on a straw man in behemoth's rags. Leamer wasn't a Republican, or a Libertarian. He was an opportunist. In print, all his hyperbole fell with a thud. His work showed no research, no logic—just self-aggrandizing rhetoric, scribbled with a fist tightened by anger. The white yahoo's burden. He wasn't a watchdog for conservatives; he was a seething shill for the conglomerate that employed him, a man paid to get ratings, come what may.

Harper found Leamer's wit dull as a spoon's edge, his doctrines vile as tainted veal. But she was able to accept it for what it was—sick entertainment for the disenfranchised; until she got to his chapter on animal rights, an eight-page screed that barely stopped short of recommending public bludgeoning of anything deemed bun-worthy. "Animals," he quoted Nietzsche, "were God's second mistake." Then added his own punch line, "so let's see if we can help The Almighty tidy up."

Harper's blood curdled. She leaped off the love seat and began busying herself with cleaning up, getting clothes in the wash, anything to channel her fury into something positive. This man, so pathetic in his adolescent tirades, had gotten to her too. She felt the pin prick in the voodoo doll; the spoon's edge serrated enough to cut.

One hot bath and most of a Mahler concerto later, Harper's feathers were nearly back in place. She had even formulated the skeleton of a plan. But before she could wrestle with the logistics of it, the phone rang. It was Larry, derailing her with his weak, optimistic small talk. That he was hedging, biding his time until he could ask her out, was excruciatingly obvious. He finally donned his lothario mask.

"So, I've ... uh ... I've got two tickets to see Dwight Yoakam Sunday night. Would you like to, you know ... go?"

Truth be known, Harper was sick to death of country music and the spell it cast over the Lone Star state. All the halter-tops and beer guts wandering around the city, bolos on browned necks, Stetsons hiding receding pates. Yet, it was a fact of life in Texas, and one she'd learned to tolerate. And then there was Larry. Her answer was a falsely enthusiastic 'yes'.

Suddenly, Larry couldn't get off the phone soon enough, his mission fulfilled. Harper gave him nary a second thought, and returned to her own charge: unraveling Dutch Leamer.

The next morning, Harper was up and out the door around 7:15. She was headed for Java Juice, but not to clock in. She cruised in for a 'to-go' purchase, The Java Juice Pick-Up—a cardboard box, awkwardly shaped like a truck, which housed a mixture of sweet pastries and soft bagels. That, along with an insulated box of piping coffee, and Harper was back out the door.

She jetted over to KRTX, tied on her Java Juice apron, and carried her bounty to the reception area. The lobby, a dank beige and green box, smelled of snuffed out cigarettes and carpet cleaner. The girl at the reception desk looked like she had been raised in such a room, gaunt and limpid, hair the consistency of tinsel.

"Help you?" she asked, her inquiry rolling out like a belch.

"Yes, I'm from Java Juice. Someone from 'The Dutch Leamer Show' put their business card in our fish bowl and, well, they won this week's drawing for free breakfast for the office."

"Who was it, sugar? I'll page 'em for you."

Harper was shrewd enough to have lifted a name from the acknowledgements in Leamer's book—his producer, Matt Cochran.

"Sugar, he's doing the show right now," said the receptionist. "Can I just take those?"

"I know this is a lot to ask," said Harper, "but can I stick around? I'm a big fan. I'd love to meet Dutch."

"Oh, hon, we have to schedule visitors ahead of time, clear them with Mr. Cochran. It's policy."

"Oh," said Harper, looking crestfallen, a freshly cut rose, crushed underfoot.

The receptionist studied Harper. She seemed harmless enough. "Tell you what. Wait here. I'll see what I can do."

Ten minutes later, Dutch Leamer was off the air, settling into his office with a cup of coffee that could've eaten through jail bars. Harper, following behind the receptionist, was already a welcome sight to Leamer, who smelled her Sumatra in the air before she rounded the corner.

"Dutch," said the lady, "you and Matt hit pay dirt. Won free breakfast from this lady. I didn't get your name . . ."

"Oh. Harper." Her answer directed to Leamer. "So . . . nice to meet you." She studied him: no horns, no pointy tail.

"You too. How'd we get so lucky? Matt, these folks bucking for a sponsorship?"

Matt Cochran, untucked and unkempt, crept in behind Harper and began digging through the box of treats. "I dunno. Free food, though."

"Somebody dropped Mr. Cochran's card in our fish bowl at work. Nothing more," said Harper.

The receptionist was long gone, and Matt disappeared as quickly has he had breezed in, leaving Harper alone with Dutch. Dutch moved his cup of office-brewed coffee aside—"fresh from La Brea," he joked, and then he poured some of the tempting nectar Harper had provided. "My God, little lady, this is more like it!"

"Glad you like it," she said, studying Dutch's office for clues. She scanned his bookshelf, running over with periodicals and reference books. In the corner, second shelf, she saw a ray of light: Kinky Friedman's *Elvis, Jesus, and Coca-Cola*, saddled beside *God Bless John Wayne*. The iconoclastic

Freidman's writing was hailed by Clinton and Bush alike. His take-no-prisoners wit and Texas roots likely drew Leamer to him. To Harper, it was his work with Utopia Animal Rescue Ranch in neighboring Medina. Kinky was her connecting rod.

"*Elvis, Jesus, and Coca-Cola*!" Harper exclaimed.

"You like Kinky?"

She knew of him more than knew his work, so she'd have to tread lightly. "You bet!"

"He's a good fella. Met him a couple of times out at The Imus Ranch."

"My ex-boyfriend ran off with my copy. I don't suppose I could borrow yours, just for a week or so?" His generosity would insure a second meeting.

"It's autographed, hon. Never leaves the office."

"Oh . . . of course."

"Now, have you got any of his CD's?" Dutch asked. Harper shook her head.

"'*Pearls in the Snow*'," said Leamer, opening the bottom drawer of his desk. "Lyle Lovett, Marty Stuart, Willie . . . bunch a' folks singing Kinky's songs. Of course, The Texas Jewboys are on it too."

What a horrible name, thought Harper; and Christ, more country music? She took the CD from Dutch's plump hand.

"Enjoy it, just be sure to bring it back by here in a couple of weeks," he said.

"Not a problem," Harper assured. "I appreciate it, Dutch!" She turned away, confident of two things: the groundwork had been laid, and she had another trip to make to the bookstore. Harper looked back as she rounded the corner and Dutch was still eyeing her. This is what she had hoped, but the warm blush run up the back of her neck; that was unexpected.

She was curled up on the love seat throughout much of the weekend, reading the two Friedman volumes, mysteries both. So buried in her research was she that when the doorbell rang on Sunday evening—6 o'clock sharp—it startled her. A gaze through the peephole gave her a fisheye view of Larry, trying desperately to ease a cowlick back into line with its meager neighbors.

"Shit," muttered Harper, dressed more like a teen at a slumber party than a girl on the verge of a night of honky-tonking. She raced to the bedroom and threw on a robe. She apologized for not being ready. A work deadline, she claimed, ate up her afternoon. Larry seemed willing to buy the myth, though Harper was sickened by how good she was getting at lying.

The concert was a blur, Harper as distant from Larry and the music as their seats were from the stage. Larry sensed this, and commented as he drove her home. Harper assured him she was just tired. And she was. Her wheels, so often in pristine motion, seemed to be spinning in the mud these last few days. She had opened the door for two energy-sucking high maintenance projects. Yet, she couldn't relent. Larry was an egg, too fragile to drop; and Dutch, he was Everest, to be conquered just because he was there.

Harper dismissed Larry's clumsy advances—an attempt to come up for a drink, and a reach in the front seat that felt like a sophomore trying his first moves after the sock hop. Tired, she said. Headache. Migraine, maybe. Larry dropped her off and drove away, turning up the stereo to keep from having to think about it too much. His first attempt to sweep his new girl off her feet, and he rated it a "D+". He took refuge in his Dwight Yoakam CD on the ride home: guitars, Cadillacs, and hillbilly music—the only things that kept him hanging on.

Less than a week later, Harper was back at the radio station, returning "Pearls in the Snow" and requesting another audience with Dutch. This time, she came not in her matronly apron, but in full Texas housewife regalia: spaghetti strap halter-top, contoured jeans, and backless sandals that clacked joyously with every step. Dutch noticed. Harper thanked him for his compliment. So far, this man, in their two brief meetings, had exhibited none of the piggish attributes so prevalent in his work. He was, if she didn't know better, a Southern gentleman. His duality was assuring— it meant the thick layer of skin that he wore on the air was daily peeled away to reveal insecurity ripe for change.

The CD exchanged hands, Harper keeping hers extended long enough for Dutch to notice that it bore no wedding ring. "You like it?" he asked.

"Oh, yeah. Loved it," she answered. "Well, thanks again. I guess I better get out of your way."

"You ever seen a radio station before? I mean, you want a quick tour of the place?"

"Sure."

He introduced Harper around. She feigned great interest in the control room, the production suites, even the sales cubicles. They made their way around until they were by the entrance. "Listen, I appreciate the tour. I better let you get back to work," said Harper. She shook his hand and pushed open the large glass door, hovering, hoping.

"Hey, wait!" said Leamer. "You . . . uh. You wanna grab some coffee?"

And now, the chess game. Risk a pawn, snare a king. "Now? I'm kind of late for . . ."

"Or another time. Just . . . maybe sometime."

"Sometime, yeah . . . I'd like that."

"Tomorrow? Meet you here, after the show?"

"Better yet . . . why not dinner? My place. I'm a helluva cook. Really. I'd be thrilled to cook for you."

Leamer checked his Palm Pilot, and found that Friday was his next free night. She accepted, jotted down her address, and promised him a meal fit for a king. Checkmate.

Driving home, Harper pondered the enigma that was Dutch Leamer: so infuriating and obtuse in his rants, on air and in print; in person, however, disarmingly pleasant. Which one was the act? Why couldn't she tell?

Friday night, Leamer wheeled into her driveway in his cherry red convertible, a Freudian complex with reinforced radials. In one arm, a half-dozen yellow roses; in the other, a 1999 La Mondotte Bordeaux, imported from France.

His knock was a steady, confident rap, his greeting almost a bow. Harper let him in, and then let out a tiny gasp when she read the label on the wine. She was a quasi-connoisseur, and this was a fine vintage—a month's rent, at least. Dutch popped and poured, while Harper took dinner out of the oven.

The air sweetened with the promise of spinach and ricotta conchiglie, swimming in a fresh passata sauce. Nutmeg and pine nuts danced atop the shells. A buttery sheen glistened off a sculpted loaf of garlic bread. The wine was in good company. James Taylor's latest rose from the speakers, and all was well in their tiny world.

Harper was enjoying the game, knowing that they both were concealing identities, she with her vegetarian agenda, and he with, well, she wasn't sure. This was an exhilarating change, though, as most of the men she'd welcomed into her home the last two years were as obtuse as granite. Good guys, guys who she found fondness for, but they lacked complexity to be sure. Dutch had a mystique though, be he a devil in disguise or an angel dressed in black.

As a second round of Bordeaux trickled into their glasses, and forkfuls of pasta warmed their bellies, a truck slowed to a crawl outside Harper's window; inching its way along the cul-de-sac, its driver straining to get a better glimpse of the convertible in the driveway, to hear through the downstairs window. Then, after two passes, the truck sped off with the screech of abandoned rubber.

Dutch looked over toward the window. "Oh . . . teenagers," said Harper. "There're a couple of boys down the block who think they're James Dean."

The truck skidding out of the subdivision was no Spider, though, and the driver no causeless rebel. It was Larry, stopping by to surprise Harper with ice cream and a stuffed plush Eeyore doll. He tried to assuage himself—maybe it was a friend, or a neighbor popping by for a chat. But Harper's window was open, and Larry heard laughter. He smelled the commingling of sauces and herbs. In his mind, it had all the distant markings of a rendezvous.

Larry finally pulled over by a mini-mart. He hopped out of the truck, hurled the two cups of Moose Tracks ice cream in the general direction of a Dipsy Dumpster, and Eeyore went tumbling after. He stormed toward the doors of the mini-mart, ready to invest in something that would turn his green-eyed envy bloodshot red; but before Larry reached the welcome mat, his hand slipped in his pocket. He felt the chip. He carried it with him everywhere, and it—a solitary blue poker chip—weighed in his pants like an anchor, grounding him when days got rough, or nights got lonely. The chip proved to him that he could get by without the crutch. But tonight was the toughest test in months.

"Get away from the opportunity to drink," he remembered his sponsor told him. "Put something between you and the booze." He waddled back to his truck, and wedged himself behind the wheel. Almost as quickly as he'd sped in, he turned out of the station and was on the road back to Harper's. Maybe he could watch from a distance, and get to the bottom of this. Otherwise, there would be no closure tonight.

Larry parked a half block away from Harper's house, up the hill from the cul-de-sac, next to a house with no cars and no lights, a perfect place to set up camp. An overweight man in a multi-patterned shirt and leather boots, Larry was no black ninja creeping through the night on cat's paws. Still, he managed to skulk close to Harper's open window and settle himself behind the shrubs that outlined her walkway. Already, he wished he hadn't come back.

The smell of coffee lingered in the air, and a warm sweetness of sugar and fruit, perhaps a pie. Robert Duvall's voice on the television registered clear with Larry, as did the overzealous giggles of Harper. Larry couldn't see them, but pictured some Texas stud pinning her to the sofa, covering her tender neck in thousands of moist kisses. Truthfully, Harper had played her foot fetish card again, and was getting her soles raked by Dutch while she dangled her naked feet over the arm of the love seat; flirtatious, yes, but hardly the felonious act of passion that Larry had managed to construct.

Maybe it was seeing Dutch behave like a good and decent man, maybe it's that she had become weary of playing cat and mouse with all the men she dated these past two years, or maybe it's just that Dutch, for all his on-air foibles, wasn't Larry. But the directive of her initial blueprint was starting to smudge, and she was tumbling into pure adolescent infatuation.

But Larry was well beyond a boyish crush. Cowardice kept him at bay, but he longed to crash through her window, sending shards spewing in their direction. He wanted someone else to know hurt like he did. Larry was relieved to see Harper stand up, blouse still on, hair in place. Then Dutch followed her to the kitchen, and Larry got his first glimpse of his rival. Dutch was an imposing figure; girthed, yes, but solid too. He lacked Larry's pouch and love handles. Larry's hand ran along his own soft underbelly as he stared.

Harper turned toward the window, sashaying toward the table with a fragrant peach cobbler. The smell of it, the sight of the two of them sitting, eating so intimately, sipping from their matching coffee mugs, was too much for Larry. He crept out of the bushes, back to his truck, and was gone.

One hour later, Dutch was thanking Harper for a 'lovely evening' with a good night kiss on the cheek. Larry was six miles away in his apartment, watching Bruce Lee on TNT, and drinking deeply from a bottle of just purchased gin. He sat in the dark, the sound of fists on faces and feet striking flesh punctuated by his own listless breathing. He felt himself leaning into the kicks and punches. He was tired of being the flesh. He longed to be the fist. Tonight, though, bogged under the heel of a Tanqueray bottle, he was nothing more than a wet washcloth, draped over an upholstered soap dish of a sofa. He heaved, exhaled, and faded into a night of stone hard sleep.

Of the three, only Dutch was at work on time the next morning. Harper forgot to set her alarm, having fallen asleep sometime after two, with Kinky Friedman's tome sliding from her limp fingers; and Larry awoke to the shrill of his store manager's phone call, checking to see if he was sick or dead. In four years, Larry had never even been late for a shift, much less missed one. Larry's teeth worked to remove the coat of fur that he felt draped over his tongue, and he told his manager he was 'sick as a dog', not far from the truth, having fallen face-first off the wagon. His manager gave him respite, and Larry lay on the sofa, his face a throbbing wound, his limbs four strands of overcooked fettuccine. But if there had been a drop left in that jade bottle, he'd have sucked it from the farthest crevice. No regrets.

Harper wasn't feeling so complacent about her situation. Upon waking, forty-five minutes late for her shift, she called in, showered, and threw on her uniform the way a child might accessorize a scarecrow—as long as the attire and the anatomy matched up, it would do. She navigated the consumption of an eggless muffin, bottled water, and her multi-vitamin from behind the wheel of the car, then managed to guide her feet into shoes and socks while alternating them on the pedals. Then, for the last two miles, she settled in and found Dutch's show on the radio. His toady sidekick, Pecos Bill, was babbling on about some promotion: " . . . so come on down next week—we'll be serving buffalo wings and all-beef hot dogs."

Then Dutch. "You know, I think this is a first, an on-air promotion for the grand opening of a slaughterhouse. That's not something just anyone has the cajones to do, my friends."

"Not even in Texas," said Pecos Bill.

"Yeah, not since Oprah tagged our hometown meat industry as the devil's right hand. Folks, look, it's simple, we're at the top of the food chain. We get to decide who lives, who dies, and who's for dinner. Animals don't have souls . . . they're like, uh . . ."

" . . . Democrats," came the punch line from Pecos.

"Yeah . . . hey, maybe we'll put Hillary on a meat hook, huh? Like that guy in 'Goodfellas'!"

Harper winced, a sickness slowly rising in her stomach. She cut off the radio with a quick jab of her index finger. Dutch, so tender and decorous just hours ago, had once again resumed the pretense of unredeemable swine. Worse yet, Harper's inability to distinguish mask from man gnawed at her throughout her shift. She had brought this hailstorm of confusion upon herself, and she was willing to shoulder the consequences, but she couldn't keep doing this dance much longer. Harper needed to get out before she found herself inextricably bound. She obviously was capable of adjusting her blinders to suit her whims, and that realization was fatal.

Harper returned home after the lunch rush, intent on giving focus to a client's new brochure, a local gym hoping to churn out a monthly newsletter of weight loss updates, supplement offers, and such. Instead, she arrived to find her belongings strewn all over the den, as if the house had given birth to a gulf storm. Nothing seemed to be missing, but no room had gone untouched: her clothes, her computer disks, her toiletries, all lying in a sacrificial mound in the middle of the floor. Property stew.

She called the police, and filed a report with a surly beat cop who looked as if he'd rather have been reading the obituaries than dealing with her. "No missing items?" he asked in a bark.

"Not that I can tell. But this is still a crime, right?"

"Standard B&E, vandalism," he said. "Likely came in through that open window over there." He pointed to the window facing the street. "You might as well have put a neon sign out for him."

"It's a quiet neighborhood. Are you saying this is my fault?"

He sighed, the indignant huff of a man who'd had to withstand the constant hum of idiocy in his ears since the break of dawn. "No. I'm saying you make it easy for someone to break in, they're gonna finger you over the person with the alarm set and the windows locked. Anything else to report?"

"No," said Harper, aware she was talking to a chasmal void.

"We'll call if we get any leads. You call us if you find anything that might be helpful."

As the officer left, Harper thought about those cop shows where detectives dust for prints, and wear high-tech goggles to find hair follicles embedded in upholstery. This was not one of those shows. And so, the clean up began.

While she was swiping toothpaste off her CDs, the phone rang. Long lost Larry was on the other end, asking if he could drop by. She told him about the break-in, and that this wasn't a good time. He offered to help, pleaded really. Harper said 'sure', and he was on his way.

Larry had managed to keep the ramifications of a hangover at bay by purchasing a bottle of Chivas and taking it to half-mast by lunchtime. He was anxious to get close to Harper again, pry and prod, seeing if she might break. He also wanted to see what she thought about this seemingly random break-in, and make sure he hadn't left any evidence of his presence behind. He was, after all, not yet in full control of his senses when he climbed through that front window, his big ass dangling like a denim-clad orb for the whole frocking subdivision to see.

Harper was a sight, still in her work clothes, knees rug burned from kneeling on the floor for so long, face streaked with mascara and eye liner, tears still rolling in and out like the tide. Larry liked how weak she was. It was the first time he'd felt superior to her. He liked helping her put the room back together, seeing her little world being reconstructed, each item's value and meaning coming into full light.

Of course, it was only a matter of time before Harper connected the stench in the room with Larry. He was an unshaven mess, alcohol emanating from his pores. Given her track record since awakening, she opted to make nothing of it. It wasn't like Larry was going to be around much longer anyway. She had to make a clean break of both of these men, for obvious reasons. So what if he was a drunk? No one was what he seemed, anyway. Carnival barkers and shell games.

Larry picked up one of the Kinky Friedman books. "What is this?"

"Oh, a friend of mine recommended that. It's a mystery—very funny. You should read it."

Larry was searching for subtext. *Who was the friend? Why should he read it? Did she not think he was smart enough to be her boyfriend?* But he was no more equipped to drill her on these questions than he was to share his honorable adoration on their first couple of dates. Larry put the book down, and snatched up the DVD case for the Duvall movie that, in his mind, she had been showing to every stud in town; foreplay cinema. "You haven't returned this yet?"

"Oh . . . no," said Harper, a slight blush coming over her.

"You better get it back. Those late fees rack up like credit card debt . . . unless you're hanging on to it for your next hot date." His indictment had teeth, the bravest he'd been their whole short relationship.

"No . . . once was enough. It was good. I'll take it back tomorrow."

Harper wasn't coming clean, that was evident. *Once is enough.* She'd just proven herself a liar on the basest level. Larry couldn't look at her. "Listen, I gotta get out of here. I gotta cover a shift later this afternoon."

"Sure, Larry. Thanks for coming and helping me. I couldn't have done it without you."

His response, a low 'ha-rumph', registered with Harper, but too late for her to question it. He was out the door, slamming it with a weighty thud. She wrote the whole abrupt episode off to the stench of liquor leaking through his yellow teeth.

Two hours later, the last of her belongings were back in their rightful spots. She sank into the love seat and rubbed her knees, now red with swelling. She thought about parochial school, and how she always had to drop to her knees for communion. The thought was somehow reassuring. She'd hated the whole formal scene—the nuns, the endless masses, those fucking candles. But, right now, it felt safe. It was a time when her dad still called her 'honey-bun' and her dreams still stretched out in front of her. After having her home violated, her belongings raped by some rubber-gloved stranger, she appreciated the tug of something that ensconced her snugly in the untouchable past. She remembered the phrase 'blood of the Lamb' and how, despite all its powerful ramifications of redemption, it nauseated her. A pure creature drained of its life force to satisfy some superstitious hoodoo. Yet, it was a complete offering; the sacrifice of innocence to remove the human stain of treachery from the soul, from this earth. She'd never bought into it—Jesus, hell, the vicious drug trip that was the Book of Revelation—but that image, 'the blood of the Lamb'. Why was that rolling around her head again after all these years?

It stayed on the periphery of her mind all night, and in her dreams as well. It was only the next morning when she dared to tune in to the volatile Mr. Leamer that her heavenly static found its antenna. Perhaps she could purify herself and Dutch in one well-plotted act. He, so antagonistic in his disdain for animals—at least ones not shrink-wrapped for grilling—required an awakening of Buddha-like proportions. She, having walked the steps of a healer of men/savior of animals for over two years, had found herself ensnared by her own good intentions, and needed to retire from the ranks of subversive eco-agent. She had to show Dutch the blood of the innocent, up close; get him inside the slaughterhouse, closed in with the rotting flesh, the huddled herds, crippled and moaning for death to come to alleviate their anguish; the sick mechanics of it all. He had to see what he was promoting: an animal holocaust. Even if he had no capacity for empathy, the conditions alone would send him racing into the bean fields.

And Larry? Well, Larry would fade into the sunset soon enough. He was already acting aloof, dismissive. She certainly felt she'd overestimated his vulnerability, so there'd likely be no broken heart to scrape off the sidewalk—just a couple of unreturned phone calls and he'd step back. Then she could claim a new life and get out from the nagging dark that had been hovering over her since she stared at Dutch's duplicity, and saw smatterings of herself.

There would be a picnic, on the rim of the slaughterhouse's property. It would be a 'favorite old spot. They'd feed each other strawberries dipped in chocolate, drink wine from plastic chalices, and tell stories about the picnics of their childhood. Then, they'd clasp hands to take an innocent walk, something to help the food settle. That's when they'd stumble upon the sounds, the smells, and that's when she'd feign an air of mischief to get him up-close to his animal brethren. It'd have to be a Sunday, a day the workers would not be around. Not this Sunday, but the next, she thought. That'd give the facility time to get up and running, and her time to do her homework on the matter. She'd spend some time on the Internet, boning up on the ebb and flow of the murderous chain. She'd even go to Dutch's abhorrent radio simulcast at the 'grand opening' tomorrow, not as a protester, but as a supporter—someone there to celebrate the carnage, the birthing of the Bubba burgers.

She called Dutch at work and got him on the second ring. She offered up her picnic date, and he gleefully accepted. Then she mentioned she'd like to come by the remote at the slaughterhouse, A&G's Processing Plant, an ambiguous charade of a name, to be sure. Dutch told her that the remote would be down the road a mile or so at the town square. They weren't allowed to hold the remote on the property of the slaughterhouse, and besides, they say the stench is atrocious. This was even better, she thought. Now, the slaughterhouse property would be unfamiliar to Dutch, her trap all the easier to set.

It was a lot to bet on, to be sure, but Harper was devoted to doing her homework. She read a half-dozen Internet articles about slaughterhouses, getting a sense of how the animals are housed and stored. She had seen the random animal rights promotional pics before, but she had to immerse herself now if she was going to go to the wall with this mission.

She read about the four stations on the killing floor, where animals are herded into the killing stall, slaughtered and butchered. She saw graphic photos online of cows' hooves, udders, and milk sacs being removed, as well as the spilling of feces and urine that wasn't drained by the initial gutting. She read in horror about how they are slit, and peeled, lifted by hooks, and sawed in half. Then, finally, in a step that seemed almost humane to Harper, they are sprayed, weighed, and cooled, before being taken to deep freeze.

And that was just the cattle. The additional reports on the de-beaking process of chicks, and the gassing of pigs, who are then strung up by their feet, slashed at the throat, and left to bleed out, hopefully before they regain consciousness, left Harper with no appetite for so much as a crisp Roma apple, much less the company of anyone who still enjoyed a good cheeseburger. But, it also strengthened her resolve. Now more than ever, the domino effect of Dutch Leamer's enlightenment was essential.

Harper arrived at the remote about an hour after it began. The town square was humming with shoppers and strollers. There were plenty of folks on hand for the radio promotion as well. Few really cared about the meat plant going up a mile or so away; this was just a chance to meet their hero, their cavalier crusader for all things politically incorrect.

Dutch was in the middle of a prize giveaway: a KRTX t-shirt with Dutch's caricature on the front to the first person who could bust open a cow-shaped piñata filled with beer. A husky local won the shirt, knocking the papier-mâché cow and its sudsy contents off the cable it was dangling on and right at Harper, some 15 feet away. The piñata landed with a juicy thud, spraying Harper's meticulously coordinated western attire with lukewarm beer. She shrieked, leaping away from the stream, and catching Dutch's eye in the process. He was embarrassed. He had been thinking about how to make a lasting, sweeping impression on Harper today. This was not the best of starts. Dutch broke away from the remote to apologize to Harper, offering to buy her a new pair of jeans and sandals. No, she insisted. "I just hate having to smell like beer the rest of the afternoon is all."

As Dutch knelt down to towel off Harper's pant leg, a pocket of fans gathered for a closer view. A little farther back, another pair of eyes locked onto the odd tableau. It was Larry. He had followed Harper to the remote, lagging about a block behind her all the way there, obscured in a Rangers cap, sunglasses, and the half-hearted beard he had grown since the last time Harper saw him.

The way Dutch was toweling her off was too familiar for Larry—not the panicked stumbling of an embarrassed stranger, but the methodic stroke of someone who felt at home in her space, brushing her calves, hovering around her bare ankles. Then, he recognized Dutch as the man whom he'd gotten glimpses of in her house the week before.

Again, Larry chose flight, scuttling back to his car, parked behind the local hardware store two blocks back. A wave of panic rose through his core as he moved through the crowd, as if he were suffocating, each brush against passing flesh robbing him of a sliver of his life's last breath, each stranger's glance an indictment. He was sixteen again, running through the school parking lot, after watching his high school crush walk into the homecoming dance on the arm of some wide receiver from the senior class.

Larry gunned his engine, and peeled down the road, a red streak of unrequited love.

Meantime, Dutch slipped back to his KRTX table to continue hawking the station and rallying the troops, but with Harper in his midst, he seemed more tame, civil even. His edge was dulled by his desire to retain the white gloves of chivalry. Harper sensed his discomfort, the nudge of trying to shock at odds with the pull of hoping to please. For now, she'd let him off the hook, allowing him to get back to his on-air swagger. She'd made her appearance, shown her support. She could leave Dutch now, knowing that the plans were in motion for their picnic. She mouthed a 'good bye' to him from a few yards away, gave a 'call me' gesture, and walked back to her car.

Harper's duties not yet done, she drove to the road behind A&G's Processing Plant, and plotted out the picnic. The slaughterhouse sat in a ravine, backing up against a rolling meadow—a perfect spot for a romantic picnic. Their after-dinner walk would take them to the property line, where they'd hop a rather unimpressive looking fence, and peek inside. If there were security, Dutch's credentials as a local celebrity would get them a hall pass, she thought.

Harper spent the rest of the week backpedaling with doubt. Her plan, she realized, had holes—big ones, in fact. What if they couldn't find a way into the actual killing floor? What if, in fact, they did and Dutch found the display of carcasses and hostages merely unsettling, rather than life altering? These thoughts kept her up nights, sipping hot tea and watching old sit-coms to distract her anxious brain. Outside her window, almost nightly, was Larry, driving by slowly, deliberately, like a Crip scoping who was on his turf before green-lighting a drive-by.

Larry took respite in that Harper seemed to be alone. Maybe she'd broken it off with her radio buddy. He flat out refused to call her. Let her dangle, he thought, with a reed of hope that the reason she was up at 1:30 in the morning was because his absence haunted her in some quiet way.

At this point, Larry had all but devoted himself to keeping tabs on Harper. He'd asked to cut his shifts back to weekdays only—no nights or weekends. "I'm taking night classes, and need the weekend to study," he told his boss. His tenure there got him a few weeks of slack, and he was using the time to monitor Harper's comings and goings with an eerie precision.

On Sunday morning, he parked in the driveway of a nearby house boasting a 'for rent' sign. He had a thermos of bourbon, a dozen doughnut holes, the morning paper, and a pair of binoculars. A little after 1pm, Dutch whirled by in his convertible and slid into Harper's driveway. Harper practically skipped down the drive to meet him, bare shoulders shining in the sunlight, a picnic basket bouncing in her left hand. Larry ducked down in his seat, and waited for them to pass.

Larry stayed back, keeping up with their turns, which lead off the main roads and into a rural area that he feared might not allow him to maintain his distance. But before the pair could exceed his grasp, Dutch pulled over on the shoulder, just a hundred feet or so from the mouth of the meadow. Larry was able to park at the top of a hill, obscured from their view. Then, grabbing a duffel bag from under the front seat, he wandered down on foot, watching them through a patch of trees as they picked out their lunching spot.

Larry curled up behind a stony slab, straining to hear their conversation, peering to view the ritual. Dutch's voice, a low announcer's sibilance, carried well, and Larry picked up more than one of his flirtations. Though he couldn't hear Harper's volleys, the tableau they struck told the story of a couple all too happy to be alone in God's country.

As the chocolate dip clung to the last of the strawberries, and the plastic wine goblets emptied a second time, Dutch made his way from one end of the blanket to the other, squaring himself behind Harper, and caressing her shoulders. His breath made the hairs on her neck stand on end, and his gentle lips traced her nape so softly she could barely feel them. The wine, the sun, and the touch of this contradiction of a man might've swept her away, might've taken her off her choreographed course, if Larry hadn't gone into his now predictable flight pattern. Upon seeing Dutch's advances, and Harper's willing reception of them, he took off like a wounded coyote. Running further up the hill, the pounding of his heavy boots caught Harper's attention. She leapt to her feet, looking up the knoll, seeing only the rustling of tree limbs as Larry disappeared over the hilltop. "What was that?"

"I dunno," said Dutch. "Dog maybe? A stray. No big deal."

"Hell of a dog, if it was," she said.

"Well, it ran that way, and we're here, so . . ." he said, coaxing her back down.

But the mood was broken, and Harper was now a bundle of raw nerves. She knew she had to go ahead and get Dutch to the slaughterhouse, or she'd find herself abandoning her plan for the sake of an impassioned roll in the meadow. "Let's take a walk," she said.

"What? Are you kidding? We were . . . we were kind of in the middle of something here."

"I know . . . it was nice. I just wanna, you know, build up to it. Let's walk, let the food settle a bit. We'll come back."

Dutch still opposed the idea, but by now, Harper was strapping her sandals back on and tossing food scraps back in the basket. "Sure . . . why not," he said, hoping this was extended foreplay rather than protracted rejection.

Harper took Dutch's hand and they walked through the meadow and down toward A&G's. Larry, meanwhile, had spotted the slaughterhouse upon reaching the other side of the rise. He, too, headed toward the property, seeking his next vantage point. "What's this? A mill?" asked Dutch.

"No, I think this is that new . . ."

"Sweet Jesus! What the hell is that?" asked Dutch, his nostrils filling with a reaper's stench.

"It's the new slaughterhouse, Dutch. The one you were plugging last weekend . . ." Harper, too, covered her nose with her forearm, trying to keep the reek from invading her senses.

"Let's go back. This is awful," he said.

"I wanna see inside," said Harper.

"What? Are you kidding? Why?"

"Aren't you curious?"

"No. Not in the slightest." He said. "Dead animals. Lots of dead animals is all."

"Yeah, but . . ." Harper had hoped for more fortitude from her tough talking faux beau. She broke away. "I'm going in!" she said, like a teen threatening to skinny dip on a dare.

"Harper! Stop!"

Harper raced to the gated area and scaled the fence, sundress and all. Dutch chased behind her, still begging her to stop. The smell was matched now by the sounds: the rapid, frantic moos of distressed cattle—dozens of them, piled up in a holding pen too tightly to budge, and the relentless rooting of pigs, pressing against the walls, as if freedom could be willed by mere struggle and cries.

Larry, on the other hand, had no problem with the odor of carcass. It was in his job description, after all. He was already on the other side of the corrugated metal structure that housed the killing floor, and found himself not ten feet away from one hundred head of cattle, all pressed together in a holding stall along the side of the building, trapped there for the weekend until their death sentence could be carried on when the Monday whistle blew.

The pin was loaded beyond capacity; a hundred cattle where eighty could stand, and perhaps as few as fifty could exist with any notion of comfort. Larry's eyes bulged with fear, and then, to his surprise, pity. He gazed into the eyes of the cows facing him by the edge of the pen, and they seemed to be looking to him with some glint of hope. One smallish Jersey cow was stuck, her head wedged in the fencing of the pen. She, in particular, appeared to be begging for a measure of mercy.

Larry found himself drawn to her. He walked to the fence, and tried to free her, yanking at the lattice, helping her crane her wounded neck a little in either direction, but to no avail. She was stuck, and there she'd have to stay, suffering until the blade came down some nineteen hours later. Larry knew this was no way to live out your last day. Her death was inevitable, but her misery was not. Larry reached into his shoulder bag and pulled out a butcher knife. He'd brought it along in case he ran into trouble, in case he needed to scare his own prey by waving it around. Who was he kidding? He brought it for a showdown. It had gotten to that point. But, when his urge was strongest to leap from the trees and plunge the blade into Dutch's back, just to watch his thick fingers slide down

Harper's silky shoulders in sweet release, he'd chosen to run instead. In the end, he always ran.

Now, though, there was this animal. This beast that would likely end up shrink wrapped in his own meat department by week's end; all of them, lowing for clemency, and one little gal in particular, longing to be freed from her growing hurt. Larry lacked the brains or impulses to find a way to set them all loose, though that's what he'd have loved to do. Instead, he gave this one sweet cow her ticket out of the indignity that was the rest of her life. He swung the blade back, underhand, and drove it through her throat. The cry was demonic, a freight train echoing through the canyon. The rest of the cows panicked. Larry hadn't stopped to think about this. He was only focused on that one little one's pain. The rest of the world—Harper, Dutch, the law—were all shut out from his factory. But now, the one hundred plus were pressing, struggling with a newfound intensity, screaming like abandoned babies. Larry dropped the knife and ran, sensing that, rather than bringing peace, he'd just stirred up a tsunami.

His path took him back up the hill. Harper, still playing cat and mouse with Dutch, turned the corner, trying to lead Dutch toward the commotion. She spotted Larry scaling his way up the knoll. Then, she saw the butchered cow, the knife on the ground, and the screaming herd. She hadn't had time to piece it all together when the cattle's terror reached its climax. The gate, locked tight but hinged by a minimum wage contractor, gave way. The cattle sensed a hint of freedom, a freedom that resided just beyond where Harper and Dutch stood, frozen by fear.

The cows made their escape in a pounding, horrified stampede. Larry could only stand and watch. Animal instinct. Hooves, bone, and dust. Then, as quickly as it had started, it was over. The cattle staggered along the distant hillside, searching for the sweetest patches of grass to replenish their famished bellies. Larry saw the bodies in the dirt, then looked down at his hands, stained with the crimson of his sacrificial lamb. The blood, he thought, would never come off.

17

THE MUTINEER
(for Hunter S. Thompson)

H e was the only volunteer from a legion of men, all resigned to a scoundrel's life at sea. Most had nothing else to offer: heartless, mindless, and too restless for the land. The others were mere boys who took one drink too many in a seaside tavern and woke up miles from land; hoodwinked into a life of plundering. "Take up a station or take three steps overboard," was the swearing-in ceremony for lads who'd fallen for the bait.

But The Mutineer wore a different swath. He signed on willingly, ready to wade out in shark-infested waters, to take up arms against any corsair who tried to loot what was by all rights yours and mine. He'd face Jack Ketch himself to see to it.

He filled his lights with pipe and his belly with the rarest of rum, stolen from the kingdoms he'd pillaged. Slicing the mainbrace with those who'd listen to his tales of the cresting of waves and the deaths of fine men who sailed out to sea, their deadlights set on new horizons, only to find their boats springing leaks, their bodies lacerated by barnacles.

He stood high up in the crow's nest, promising us he'd warn us of danger, of rebels on the horizon bent on robbing us of our spirits and our souls. He kept watch for four or five days at a time, fueled only by hardtack, a clap of thunder in his blackjack, and veins coursing with indignation.

In '68, he sailed with a scurvy band who initiated him with a keelhaul, dangling him from a rope two inches thick, flailing from port to starboard until he was bloodied and half-drowned. Marooned with nothing but a cutlass and a half-empty bottle of gin, he built his own craft from the sparse timber scattered on the shore—Lono's scraps—and christened his new home with the bottle, licking the last drops of nectar from jagged glass as gin and blood mingled with the tide.

Sailing alone suited him. No man's ship could be entrusted to a fleet of draftees and warmongers. A mutineer himself, he knew not to trust anyone with that same spark in their eye. *Yon Cassius has a lean and hungry look . . . such men are dangerous.*

In '71, he wandered into deep waters, and kept a faithful journal of his quest for that most elusive of treasures. In '72, The Mutineer single-handedly brought down Blackbeard, a rapscallion running roughshod over a people still too stunned by their king's murder, their nation's upheaval, the war their sons had gone off to fight, to know better. The Mutineer prodded him to the edge of the plank and let him time his own final, fatal step.

From then on, his legend on the seas was cemented. Even the bravest of buccaneers steered far from The Mutineer's vessel. He could poison your grog from a mile away. Put a hole in your boat with an assemblage of words, staccato-streams of bullets that sought heat, and rarely missed.

He shared the sea with Captain Melville and The Old Man. Part man, part shark, never sleeping, always moving forward. No quarter. Rust never sleeps. It will creep in on you, leeching on and feeding like a remora if you aren't keeping her at thirty knots or more. He sailed in waters too choppy for us landlubbers. We could only read about his adventures in letters sent home on the legs of crooked sea bats, carrier pigeons of the damned.

And so, he sailed; top speed until he ran out of ocean. Dante's port ahead. A pirate looks at seventy, and blinks. His eyes failing, one bum leg replaced by a slab of polished wood. He couldn't even taste the salt anymore.

Word came from the mainland that Blackbeard, long since dead, had children, twice as twisted and evil as their patriarch. They'd kill you just for speaking their name in vain; invade innocent countries to exact revenge for someone else's crimes. Hang a man from the gibbets if he dared to question their craft's route. They were illegitimate privateers, diseased with a strain of yellow jack that consumed their very conscience. Scurvy, vile addle pates—a ship's fill of hornswagglers and interlopers, promoted from pirates to king's men—and there were too many to count. The Mutineer was tired. For the first time, he doubted his aim.

So he spread himself over the mouth of a cannon and lit the fuse. Man overboard. A hell bound hail shot cast toward heaven. His ashes hurled over five hundred miles of a sea so blue it would make you squint. He had sailed the sea. There was nothing left to prove, and so, he became a part of it.

But, his ship sails on, circling the earth, waiting for someone to take the wheel. There is no edge, so said Magellan. But The Mutineer knew better. The edge was all there ever was.

18

BEAUTIFUL DESPAIR

She was lost in a book, utterly adrift between the pages of someone's secret life. I came in, changed into pajamas. She lowered the book a half-inch, just enough for me to see those reading glasses she wears that never fail to beguile me. Something about the way they tilt on her face, giving her cheekbones sweet dimension. They make her look as smart as she is.

"How was your night?" The book sinks another two inches. I see her lips. I wish for the energy to sit down by her, kiss them, work the book from her grip. But it's not there; five years ago, maybe. Today it's understood, everything's an effort.

"I don't think I can keep teaching these classes," I tell her.

"Why's that?"

"There's no reward in watching people take the work so lightly."

"It's a community program, hon. You knew what you were getting into."

"Still, if we hadn't needed Christmas money..."

"But we did. Three more Saturdays and you're done. Then, we can take the kids to get a tree, sit by the fireplace. You can listen to your jazz and drink Pinot until you pass out." She pedaled her feet under the comforter, excited at the mere mention of a peaceful holiday at home.

"You don't even like jazz."

"I didn't say I'd be in the room too." Her smirk disappeared behind the dust jacket of the book, a picture of a pair of female feet, holding a daisy between her toes. *Chick lit*, I thought. *I won't be getting her attention again.*

I went into the kitchen and found a bag of chips on the counter, the good ones that they add powdered lime to. I ate straight from the bag as I went through the mail. Under the catalogs and bills was a package from Aspen, Colorado. I had joined a trading tree on the internet, swapping copies of my bootleg CDs and concert videos with other like-minded addicts. For a VHS dub of Tom Waits' "Big Time", a surreal horror film disguised as a concert, I received a DVD of Chet Baker, Live 1988. That was the year he fell to his death. There's a note enclosed: "Not sure about much on this one. Sound is good, picture is grainy. Don't know sidemen, setlist, or locale. Hope it lives up to expectations. Keep trading. Best, Sam."

I opened a bottle of Pinot Noir. The good wine, reserved for holidays, celebrations, guests; the wine from *Sideways*, she calls it. Costa de Oro, 2003. I turned out all the lights in the den and put the DVD in the player. Me. Chet. Alone together.

The video opened with a close-up of a face, worn and leathery, each wrinkle hard earned. Chet was 59. He could've been a hundred and nine. Front teeth gone in a deal gone bad, skin sapped by heroin, life drained from his eyes by years of looking straight into the sun. Chet licked his lips for what seemed an eternity, an old jazz man's warm up tosses. His eyes were fixed on a world somewhere other than here. I was transfixed before a note sounded. He counted off in a whisper and drew the horn to his mouth. The first note was pure, an angelic exaltation, the next, a beatific cry for help. The camera pulled back to reveal Chet sitting in a hard chair, too worn to walk, a skeleton in borrowed skin. All the muscles leaned toward the lungs, giving what they had.

Chet played a couple of songs, a wounded sparrow still certain enough of his song to make the notes soar. It was hard to believe that something pure could come through a vessel so poisoned. Now and then, a note trembled, but it never sank. Then, he leaned toward the microphone and sang, "My funny valentine . . . sweet comic valentine." The words were so frail I thought they might crumble as they slipped from that dry ruddy cavern of a mouth. My bones ached at beauty's last breath. The Pinot would not see another day.

I was on my third glass when Chet started in on "Let's Get Lost". The invitation was superfluous, I was already there. Then, she drifted in. "Aren't you coming to bed?"

"I'll be along."

"What are you watching? You get a new tape?"

"Concert, yeah." I sipped while she squinted at the television. I leaned in, willing that she'd get tangled in the fragility, the thin strings that held this man upright to play. I needed her to.

She snickered, and then laughed. It was a hearty laugh that rang out over Chet's bassist, who had taken a solo. "I hope you didn't spend a lot on this one," she said.

"What?" I felt the blood and wine race to my head.

"Look at him, just sitting there. You're watching a guy *sit* and play the trumpet. For that, you could've just bought the CD! I mean, what's the point?" She was right, and I resented her for it.

"I'll be to bed when this is over." I folded my tongue under my teeth; realizing anger would get me nowhere. She couldn't see it, even with her smart glasses. Where she saw a pale cartoon, I saw a hungry ghost. After so many years, she had come to recognize my curtness for what it hid: a sulking and wounded male id that preferred to seethe rather than negotiate. For a moment both long and melancholy, we glared in silence, a stare-down across a ravine we'd have to accept we'd never cross.

"Good night. Sorry." She kissed me on the forehead while I stared straight ahead, watching Chet heft himself into the opening strains of "They All Laughed". Indeed.

Chet treated me to three more songs, closing with "Everything Happens to Me". The DVD cut off, rolled to a blue screen, and I sat drinking the dregs of the Pinot right from the bottle. I curled up on the sofa and closed my eyes, the TV's blue hue cutting through the darkness. I wondered how two people could be so effortlessly entwined in love's soft rope while one saw beauty in the blooming of a rose, the other in the decaying of that same flower; one enchanted by the spirit of life, the other entranced by its transience.

The dogs began to yelp. A thunderstorm rolled in from the east. Loud, angry thunder rattled the window panes. I got up and watched the lightning cut through the night sky, sheets of it, striking with precision through a sky sewn with gray clouds. I wondered if she saw it from our bedroom window, and if she did, whether she believed it meant something more than rain.

19

THE GHOSTS OF BIRDLAND
(December 2001)

"If jazz ain't about hope and love, what is?"—Branford Marsalis

I t's Christmas Eve, and I'm standing outside Birdland—the original Birdland at Broadway and 52nd. I remind myself that it was torn down decades ago, that I must be in the midst of some Capra-esque fantasy, but there it is, shining like light cascading off a brass sax: Birdland. It's so real I can smell the mingling of Lucky Strikes and Jack Daniels already invading my clothes.

The front door is shackled shut by a rusty chain and padlock. Undeterred, I creep around the corner to a side door, marked "Deliveries Only". Seeing it is narrowly wedged open by a rolled up newspaper, I peek in, surveying a back hallway, scantly lit and seemingly vacant. Still convinced this must be slumber's sweetest mirage, I am compelled to enter—little to lose, and so much to gain.

I inch down the hall, following a growing trail of men's laughter and the exhalation of broken scales, notes abandoned at birth. I find that the source of these sounds is a green room, a backstage lounge area where musicians gather to relax or warm up before a gig. This, however, was no ordinary green room. I peer around the doorframe, fully expecting to spot a cluster of strangers, a nameless ensemble chilling before their opening set. Instead, I find myself amid an assemblage of bygone genius.

Standing not ten feet away from me is Dizzy Gillespie, engaged in a cuttin' contest with Clifford Brown. In a folding chair by the far wall, Thelonious Monk stares off into space, his lips moving gently to the melody he must be creating in his head. Miles Davis has his finest threads on, and is gazing hard at himself in the mirror, a proud black prince admiring his royal garments.

Bud Powell is egging Charlie Mingus on, trying to get the beefy bassist to don a Santa suit for the show. Mingus' riposte is neither jolly nor genteel. In the most remote corner of the room, behind a tray piled high with plates of half-eaten shrimp cocktail and cheeses, is a young Chet Baker. His eyes shine with the brightness of a man free from demons and hungry for another dance with his muse.

Slack jawed, I step into the room, eager to have an audience with these legendary musicians. My presence is immediately felt as I cross the threshold. Before I can utter a solitary accolade, Dexter Gordon calls me out. "There you are . . . knew you'd make it."

"'bout damn time," mutters Miles in his trademark whisper, a slight smile revealing gentle intent.

What are these men talking about, I wonder. A chill runs through my body as I fear the worst: *They think I'm here to sit in!* That I can't play a note, save a few folksy guitar chords, is something I must bring to their attention quickly. But my tongue, now feeling gravity's pull, squares firmly into a knot of nerves. I stand before the giants of jazz, and I am a drooling idiot.

Swooping in to save me from the hallway, every bit as gentlemanly you would expect, is Duke Ellington, who tugs my elbow and leads me down the hall. Little can shock me now, so I surpass the formalities and adulation. "Duke . . . what the hell am I . . ."

He cuts me off, "Bird will explain." He guides me past a second room, where the ladies of the blues—Billie, Ella, Sarah—are comparing shoes and stories of broken hearts. I freeze as we pass their doorway, gawking at their grace. "We'll catch them later, I promise," reassures Duke, who is now pulling me with the eager abandon of a child heading downstairs on Christmas morning.

Duke stops just short of the main room, leaving me in a tiny backstage area, with instructions to 'stay put'. Naturally, I agree, but the sounds of the main hall begin to tug at my ears. *Is that Bill Evans on piano out there?* Before I can peer around the curtain, I feel a presence come up on me. I turn and find myself eye to eye with Charlie Parker. The Yardbird. The reason there is a Birdland, the reason there is so much that is beautiful in jazz. "You're here," he smirks.

I can keep my ebullience in check no longer. "You're Charlie Parker!" I exclaim.

He knows this already, and tells me as much.

"Yes, I am. And you're here to make sure people know about this."

"About what?"

"You saw the green room, right?" he asks.

"Yeah," I smile, awaiting an explanation for these apparitions, these specters of song.

"Well, this is a one-night-only kind of gig. We all came down for it," says Bird, rolling up the sleeve of his button-down tuxedo shirt.

I start to ask what he means, but am distracted as his sleeve makes it above the crease of his elbow. Anyone who knows anything about Charlie Parker knows that his inner arm must look like a tattered road map from punctuated veins and needle tracks, the Devil's fangs that filled his blood with venom. But Bird's arm is as smooth as a newborn's. No marks, no evidence of his poisonous self-destruction.

Bird grins. "I'm clean. Clean as new fallen snow," he swears. "Now, I want you to go have a seat out there." He points through the curtain to the main room. "You gotta get down on paper all the shit that's going down here tonight."

"Why?" I ask.

"'cause nobody would believe it. Probably still won't," he chuckles. "But you can tell 'em you saw it with your own eyes. Paint 'em a picture. Make it feel real. That's what's important. Now, get your ass out there, kid, you're holding up my set." That gets me moving. Nobody, nobody stands between Bird and his music. Whatever my purpose, whatever my calling here is in this fantastic netherworld, I'll find out soon enough. Right now, I'm about to witness the most amazing set in the history of jazz.

I wander into the main room, and squint to avert the glow of stage lights, which focus directly on Bill Evans performing a solo piano version of "Stella by Starlight", accentuated by a playful coda of "Santa Claus is Coming To Town". The house is packed, but I can only make out the shapes of shoulders and heads, the starkness denying me clarity of faces. I grab the only seat I can find, a one-top by a column in the corner; secluded, but with an enviable view. Perched from my high seat, my Bird's nest if you will, I am able to see the stage as if I was seated upon it.

A shy Evans finishes his number and gives the audience a kind, meager wave as he exits. Seconds later Bird ambles onstage and speaks. "It's

Christmas Eve, friends. I know this whole scene is still new to you folks, but you're here tonight because the Big Man said some spirits needed lifting, that some souls needed refilling. We're gonna take care of all that for you the best way we know how."

I'm puzzled, but before I can process his message, the stage is filled with an ensemble of performers only the most fertile of imaginations could conjure. Bird on alto sax, Dexter on tenor sax, Mingus on bass, Bud and Monk side by side at the piano, Miles, Diz, Chet, and Clifford on trumpets, and the sure-handed professor, Art Blakey on drums. It is a metaphysical menagerie, a jam session only God Himself could've pulled off.

Miles counts them off in a whisper. On four, they burst into Monk's "Round Midnight" with the unbridled fury of feral steeds. They pass choruses back and forth, fingers like dry lightning, eyes stony steel. Yet, amid this rampage of sound, there is joy; perhaps more joy than these men of jazz were ever known for revealing onstage in their day. Miles is playing to the crowd, Bird and Diz are sharing musical jokes in their choruses, truly the other half of each other's heartbeat. And Mingus, grouchy old Charles Mingus, has acquiesced and is slapping his mammoth bass with a Santa hat perched atop his wiry mane.

"Round Midnight" fades into "Confirmation", followed by the light blue fire of "So What", and the chiseled beauty of "Straight, No Chaser". "Autumn Leaves" bleeds into a bluesy "Winter Wonderland". Bird shares licks with Diz and Dexter on "White Christmas" before Dexter's warm tone embraces "The Christmas Song". Mingus takes us to church with "Better Git It In Yo' Soul", and Chet wraps his gossamer wings around "Everything Happens to Me". Then more surprises unfold.

Billie, Sarah, and Ella share the stage; a triumvirate of harmonies, unified by gin soaked throats that have tasted love's sweetened honey and heartache. Then, as Sarah takes a turn on "Body and Soul", Coleman Hawkins ambles onstage to take a sax solo. Chills dance on spines as Ella belts "Good Morning Blues". Then, in a moment that aches with private history, Lester Young appears by Billie's side and, laying down his long-carried torch, kindly holds her hand as she sings "My Man".

The set lasts some four hours, a blur of genius hurled upon a bittersweet canvas, each note hanging in the air just long enough to leave its nectar. With midnight only minutes away, Bird says he has saved the best for last. Everyone in the house, jazz aficionados and new converts alike, gasps with the joy of recognition, as a familiar, worn face shines through the backstage curtain. It is Pops. Louis Armstrong.

The crowd rises as one, and holds its collective breath. He says nothing, merely smiling that ever-present grin, and counts off. As the familiar notes begin, I am jolted by the irony of his psalm. It is "What a Wonderful World", a song that in recent times has seemed sadly unbefitting. We are, after all, a people who have found ourselves suddenly bound by fear and uncertainty. The lyrics hearken back to an innocence we did not recognize belonged to us. How could anyone now hear this song and not absolutely implode from emotion? Will a single eye be dry?

Pops sings it with the grace of a poet, and as his gravelly foghorn fills the room with the final chorus, the house lights slowly rise. Darkness lifts, and I see, for the first time, my fellow patrons. These are faces filled with light, with the calm sense of a peace I've never known. These are the souls of the departed, our fallen at rest. And they are home.

As the mighty Satchmo holds his final note for a gentle eternity, the audience breaks me from my stare with fulminating applause for the men and women who have shared their musical mercy this night.

Then, as quickly as the song ends, the patrons are gone. The house, only moments before alive with warm spirits, is empty. The musicians clamor back to the green room, but as I make my way to follow, I am stopped at the backstage curtain.

"Sorry . . . you can't go back there," says Bird.

"But, I want to talk to them, find out what they have to say!"

"You just heard what they have to say, now go tell it," says Bird, his face harder than before.

"Yes, yes . . . of course, I just . . ." I clamor to ask one more question before being sent away.

"What is it? You know who we are, and you know who these people were here tonight. Those they left behind need to know you saw their faces . . . their shining, peaceful faces."

I turn, committed to the notion that I've been given a gift this night, and must piece the puzzle together from here. But there is still one question burning in my throat, one query that should be meaningless given the scope of this evening's wonders. Still, I have to ask.

"Bird," I holler, as he is closing the curtain. "There's one thing I don't get. It's just . . . um . . . why isn't Trane here?"

"Good, kid. Very good. I guess there is one more thing you should know." Bird hollers to the musicians waiting in the back. "You guys wait up. I'll be back."

"Come with me, kid," Bird smiles as he tilts his head indicating passage via the chained front door. Then, he walks through the door as if he were mere smoke. I stand, staring at the solid steel barrier for a moment, then, assessing the events of the evening thus far, take a leap of faith that will either result in gaseous travel through a ghostly byway, or a broken nose.

My faith rewards itself, and I find myself on the darkened corner of 52nd and Broadway, the Father of Be-bop by my side.

"Grab my coattail, kid, and don't let go," directs Bird. With that, we take flight, putting to rest the origins of his nickname. That I am riding Charlie Parker's coattails, too, strikes me as funny. So many have. But as New York shrinks beneath us on our ascent, I am too humbled to joke.

Moments later, after a fleeting ride over Union Square and the Village, Bird's and my feet come to rest on the snowy sidewalk of Lower Manhattan's financial district. The streets bustle, not with last minute shoppers, but with rescue workers, still vigilantly clearing away the rubble of ruins that shook the mighty city, and all of us, just three months earlier.

The snowfall is gentle, and rather than impeding their progress, it seems to inspire, each of the flakes kindly hugging the tired shoulders of workers as they dance down from heaven.

"Man, it's almost Christmas morning. What keeps these people going?" I ask.

Bird grins as wide as I have ever seen a man smile. He points across the street, nodding affirmation. There, under the serene glow of a single streetlight, wrapped in the merest of coats, is the gentle giant of jazz: John Coltrane. Trane breathes into his saxophone, releasing a rhapsody so sweet, the air around us seems to tingle with energy . . . with assurance. With a love supreme.

Men and women in blue uniforms walk within a few feet of the mighty master, seemingly oblivious to his presence. Some practically brush against him, their arms loaded down with debris. He is impermeable.

"Do they . . . know he's there?" I ask.

"Yes," assures Bird.

"But they seem to be wa . . ."

"I didn't say they could see him. I said they know he's there."

"So, while you guys were delivering the love, Trane was out here . . ."

Bird finishes my thought, "with the hope."

As the clock strikes midnight, we turn and watch Coltrane lifting the burdens off the street's sorrowful shoulders, sending the opening strains of "My Favorite Things" into the Manhattan night.

I'd love to tell you that I shook John's hand. I did not. Or that he took a break from weaving his healing tapestry to chat with the likes of me. He did not. What happened next was anti-climatic. I awaken, curled tightly in the embrace of a down comforter, my wife's and son's fingers unconsciously draped down my arm as they slept. I untangle my bare feet from the confines of layered wool blankets, slide them into the familiar warmth of worn brown slippers, and crawl to the kitchen for a pre-dawn dose of coffee. I ask myself, "Was it really just a dream?"

No. This was no dream. This was real. I was there. I heard the groove and swing of that glorious night, and I saw those who have moved on. I tasted the bittersweet nightclub air and the cold mix of snow and ashes on the street. I watched mighty legends, whose offstage dances with demons rivaled their own legacies as musical giants, become their own better angels in a single act of grace.

I saw love. I heard hope. Both are as alive as the warm grooves that permeate the air every time music is voiced. In a world riddled with uncertainty and fear, we struggle against unseen gusts as we round each corner. But still, those notes play, and when we hear them, we find strength, assurance, and just enough peace to wrap our fingers around for another day.

I feel my chest warm, only to realize I haven't even begun to drink my coffee. The kitchen window leaks in a glint of sunlight, and I lift it gently to welcome dawn's chill. When I do, I am greeted by the sound of a solitary bird. He's playing a song this morning.

It's a song of hope.

Works Cited

Cash, Johnny. *Unchained*. Liner notes from CD. American Recordings. 1994.

Hemingway, Ernest. *The Snows of Kilimanjaro and Other Stories*. New York: HarperCollins. 1977 edition.

ACKNOWLEDGMENTS

Cover photography by Wendy Palmer.

Thanks to Wendy, Grady, and Maggie for a life unimagined.

Thanks to Tiffany Yates and Steve Coulter for willingly being my "B.S. barometers".

Thanks to Jordan Zevon for giving his blessing to "The Mutineer".

Thanks for the fuel . . .

Bruce Springsteen, John Coltrane, Tom Waits, Miles Davis, Emmylou Harris, Lou Reed, Charles Mingus, Chet Baker, Kris Kristofferson, Rodney Crowell, Branford Marsalis, Wynton Marsalis, Thelonious Monk, Dwight Yoakam, Indigo Girls, Elvis Costello, Warren Zevon, Johnny Cash, Kevin Lawson, U2, Charlie Parker, Robert Johnson, Steve Earle, Lyle Lovett, John Hiatt, Townes Van Zandt, Sugarland, Robbie Robertson, Sting, Lucinda Williams, Gwen Hughes, Bruce Hornsby, Bonnie Raitt, John Prine.